D0843846

HOW to SAVE the UNIVERSE AGAIN

Rob Payne

PUFFIN
CANADA

PUFFIN CANADA

Published by the Penguin Group

Penguin Group (Canada), 90 Eglinton Avenue East, Suite 700, Toronto, Ontario, Canada
M4P 2Y3 (a division of Pearson Canada Inc.)

Penguin Group (USA) Inc., 375 Hudson Street, New York, New York 10014, U.S.A.
Penguin Books Ltd, 80 Strand, London WC2R 0RL, England
Penguin Ireland, 25 St Stephen's Green, Dublin 2, Ireland (a division of Penguin Books Ltd)
Penguin Group (Australia), 250 Camberwell Road, Camberwell, Victoria 3124, Australia
(a division of Pearson Australia Group Pty Ltd)
Penguin Books India Pvt Ltd, 11 Community Centre, Panchsheel Park, New Delhi – 110 017, India
Penguin Group (NZ), 67 Apollo Drive, Rosedale, North Shore 0632, Auckland, New Zealand
(a division of Pearson New Zealand Ltd)
Penguin Books (South Africa) (Pty) Ltd, 24 Sturdee Avenue, Rosebank, Johannesburg 2196,
South Africa

Penguin Books Ltd, Registered Offices: 80 Strand, London WC2R 0RL, England

First published 2007

1 2 3 4 5 6 7 8 9 10 (WEB)

Copyright © Rob Payne, 2007

All rights reserved. Without limiting the rights under copyright reserved above,
no part of this publication may be reproduced, stored in or introduced into
a retrieval system, or transmitted in any form or by any means (electronic, mechanical,
photocopying, recording or otherwise), without the prior written permission
of both the copyright owner and the above publisher of this book.

*Publisher's note: This book is a work of fiction. Names, characters, places and incidents
either are the product of the author's imagination or are used fictitiously, and any
resemblance to actual persons living or dead, events, or locales is entirely coincidental.*

Manufactured in Canada.

ISBN-13: 978-0-14-331242-0
ISBN-10: 0-14-331242-1

Library and Archives Canada Cataloguing in Publication data available upon request.

Visit the Penguin Group (Canada) website at **www.penguin.ca**

Special and corporate bulk purchase rates available; please see
www.penguin.ca/corporatesales or call 1-800-810-3104, ext. 477 or 474

HOW to SAVE the UNIVERSE AGAIN

CHAPTER 1

I COULDN'T BELIEVE I was back behind the counter of Burger Hut, the world's greasiest fast-food restaurant. Three weeks earlier I'd returned from a bizarre journey through an alternative universe, having slipped through a hole in the space–time continuum. Along with a motley crew of other non-dimensionals I'd escaped DIMCO, a diabolical government agency determined to rid us from Earth 5. I looked down at my humiliating orange-striped uniform shirt and adjusted the stupid paper hat on my head. A month ago I was making world-altering decisions and foiling inter-dimensional criminals. Now I was your average seventeen-year-old geek bagging junk food in Toronto. Life was too strange.

A few feet away at the second cash, Amanda, the hottest girl I'd ever known, examined her nail polish. She sighed and moved several strands of blond hair from her perfect face, which was full and buoyant and complemented by butterfly-inducing dimples. Her lips were what fashion magazines would call "bee-stung" and were so glossy you'd swear they were coated in honey. We'd worked together for about six months, and to the best of my recollection she'd never said more than ten words to me. Unless of course you count "I need a double burger combo and mega-size the fries," which I don't. There's just no romantic ring to it.

She caught me staring. I pretended to wipe dust from my cash register, which seemed stupid even to me. There was so much grease in the air that dust didn't stand a chance of floating anywhere. Apparently Amanda was feeling as bored as I was, because she suddenly broke her long-standing tradition of being too cool to associate with any guy our age.

"So, John," she began. "I thought you were going to England this summer."

"Uh, I did," I mumbled.

"You're back kind of soon, aren't you?"

"Um, yeah. I just went for the weekend."

She looked at me as if I'd just said I ate cockroaches as a hobby. My trip had lasted close to two weeks on Earth 5, but thanks to the strange laws of inter-dimensional travel I'd returned only a day after leaving home. The universe was a tricky place. We lapsed back into silence and I thought about my summer. I wasn't supposed to be back in this dump. I'd been fired just after exams thanks to my co-worker Kevin Flarch's *scientific pondering*. It's a long story, but our former manager, Gavin, happened to appear during Kevin's now-infamous *mucus experiment*. A few days after Gavin fired us he quit due to stress. The only reason we got our jobs back was that the owner, Mr. Moriarty, never found out that his chicken nuggets were being served up with a helping of phlegm.

"Travel is totally my thing," Amanda said, twirling hair around her finger. "I'll probably go to Europe soon. My family is French."

"Really?"

"Yeah. My great-great-great-great grandfather or someone was from a city called Nice. It's, like, where pâté and French bread come from. My family eats a lot of smelly cheese and is totally proud of our heritage."

I wanted to say something funny and insightful, but the only hilarious noise that came out of my mouth was a dull drone, like a sick porpoise at Marine World. I made a few lip movements like I was going to speak, but no words came out.

"Do you like soccer?" she asked.

"Yeah, kind of ..."

"You must have watched soccer over there, eh?" Amanda continued. "I saw a travel show a while ago. English people love soccer and Winston Churchill and the Beatles and fish and chips in newspaper. Weird."

There were a million things I could tell her about England on Earth 5: how so many of the buildings were old, but regal and different from anything in Toronto; or how the mustard is so hot that it blows your head off; or how a person should never, ever stay in any building claiming to be a *student hotel*. But I didn't think it was wise to divulge details of my secret life experience. Instead, I scraped hardened ketchup off the countertop with my thumb and nodded stupidly. Luckily, a guy in a plaid jacket and greasy baseball cap approached Amanda's cash, ending the conversation.

I tried to collect my thoughts. I'd been on an unbelievable adventure, but standing here in my unfashionable, semi-flammable polyester uniform, it seemed unreal. My memories were getting blurry already. Occasionally I'd catch myself wondering if it had even happened. After all, people didn't normally cross dimensions into other worlds. And yet I knew I was sane, simply because my house was now filled with visitors, some of whom belonged in this dimension and some who didn't. Our British pilot, Rex, and the alternative-universe version of my father, Nate2, were currently stuck on our plane of existence until my father could find a way to get them home. The only working porthole between dimensions had been blocked shortly after my father sent non-dimensionals Julia and Simon the accountant back. Apparently there were other passages to Earth 5, but their locations and stability were hard to calculate. My father, a quantum physicist, had been working on the problem non-stop ever since my return.

Our arrival party had also included people from this dimension: Gus, a slacker Australian, and Delores, a Texan Goth with a mild temper, along with an assortment of other teenagers, including Ellen, Jen, and Andrew, who'd since returned to Sweden, New Zealand, and Australia, respectively, to recuperate from their near-death adventures. Gus had decided to hang out in Canada for a while, saying he was in no rush to get back to the daily grind of being an unemployed student in Brisbane. Delores remained for a less appealing reason. She was suffering from a strange bout of what my father referred to as *Post D-Zone Stress Disorder*. She spent most of her days in our spare bedroom reading music magazines and watching afternoon repeats of *Degrassi Junior High*.

I focused back on the present as an old couple came shuffling through the glass doors of Burger Hut. They were at least seventy, completely wrinkled and kind of stooped. The man had a cane and an old-fashioned fedora, the kind worn by Indiana Jones, and the woman wore pale blue pants with an elastic waistband and thick white shoes. They approached my register, squinting hard at the menu board.

"Get combo number two," the man said. "And a drink for yourself. We'll split it."

He turned and shuffled toward a table, moving like his legs were made out of wood. They bowed outward as though he'd spent years straddling a barrel. The woman continued to stare at the board, not stepping up to order. I looked to Amanda, who shrugged. Just as the man was about to sit down, he turned and slowly made his way back to his wife's side, shuffling about a mile an hour. I'd seen earthworms move faster.

"You're getting a hamburger, right?" he said.

"Yes," the woman answered.

"That's what I thought. Get what you want on it. I'll take things off."

He turned to go, then stopped. "And ask them to cut it."

The woman looked at me and smiled.

"Combo number two?" I asked.

"I'll be a second," she said curtly.

At least my recent adventure had resolved my doubts about my future studies. I sure as heck wasn't going to work at Burger Hut for the rest of my life. I'd seen the randomness of the universe and realized that science helped keep civilization from going completely nuts. Physics kept trains moving and prevented bridges from collapsing. It also helped prevent government agencies in other dimensions from stealing vital resources. Our journey had ended with us managing to temporarily defeat DIMCO—that stood for Department of International Modernization and Constructive Order—and their plan to snatch ozone and polar ice from our planet.

The old woman continued to stare at the board, one finger pressed against her lip, as if waiting for prices to drop or a fabulous secret burger to be added to the menu. The old man went halfway to a table and then came back yet again.

"They have ketchup on the table," he said. "So don't get any. Are you getting french fries? You know what those onion rings do to my stomach. I didn't see knives and forks. Make sure the boy cuts the burger."

If the man came back one more time I was going to have to leap over the counter and choke him to death, or at least forcibly drag him to his table to wait for his meal. Trust me, customer service isn't nearly as easy as it appears. The woman looked down from the board, reached into her purse for money, and then smiled pleasantly at me as though she'd just walked in.

"I'll have combo number two, with french-fried potatoes and a hot chocolate."

"Would you like the burger cut?" I asked.

"That would be lovely, thank you."

Surprise, surprise …

CHAPTER 2

As I WALKED HOME from work I was still thinking about life's change-ability. My old life seemed a million miles away. I knew I should go inside and be nice, since our guests were friends who could be zapped into oblivion at any moment, but I was growing steadily sick of their lingering presence in my house. Three weeks doesn't usually seem like a long time, but our home wasn't palatial enough for seven people.

I couldn't get mad, I told myself. Everyone was trying, kind of.... Delores certainly wasn't to blame. She looked dreadfully pale and still slept half the day. Nate2 and Rex probably could have been doing more to be good house guests, but they were desperately bored. Rex spent his days reading and working out—running on our downstairs treadmill and bouncing for hours on the outdoor trampoline. He was already in fantastic shape, with lean, hard muscles—the kind I never managed to get despite hours of bicep curls and hours of tennis. Coupled with his brown, spiky hair, general good looks, and Hugh Grant–like accent, it was enough to make a guy sick. Nate2 tried to make himself useful, but his idea of cleaning up the place was wiping *most* of the mayonnaise that had fallen from his tuna sandwich onto the carpet.

As I searched for my key, my mom opened the front door.

"You're home early," I said, following her into the living room.

She forced a smile. "I've scaled back my workload to try to cope with this place. My government study paper on pigeon lice isn't due for two months and I noticed your father pulling out small tufts of hair when he was searching for a clean coffee mug the other day."

"So you'll be around the asylum more," I mused.

"I go where I'm needed most."

As if on cue, Nate2 emerged from around the corner wearing a 1970s paisley smoking jacket recently found in a trunk full of old clothes in the attic. As my dad's exact double, Nate2 was large and generally freakish, with size-fifteen feet, a crazy-coloured long goatee, and shaggy black hair. Like my dad, he could be described as *larger than life,* because he was impossible to ignore. He hummed operettas at an improbably high volume, took impossibly long showers, urinated loudly in the middle of the night, walked down stairs like he was blowing up the floor-boards, dropped drinking glasses on a regular basis, and talked to characters on TV while you were trying desperately to listen. Of course, his most annoying trait was his hopeless infatuation with my mother.

His chest was moving nervously, in short, rapid heaves. He glanced at my mom and then dropped his gaze. "Reading again," he blurted. "How nice."

"Mmm-hmm," my mom replied, pretending to be engrossed in a magazine.

He sat down awkwardly in a chaise lounge. As was his habit, he wasn't wearing anything underneath the robe. He and my dad shared the theory that the most hygienic way to get water off after a shower was to *air-dry*. They also both believed that a man could never wear too much Old Spice aftershave.

"You certainly are bookish," he continued. "In a good way. Reading is tremendously alluring." He winced at his own comment and turned a light shade of cotton candy. "In a purely mental way. Not in an attraction sense."

"Thanks," my mom mumbled. "Once again, I'm glad you approve of my hobbies."

"Have I mentioned your reading before?"

"Yes. About six times."

Nate2 stopped picking his toe and uncrossed his long, hairy legs. "You have a fine eye for details, Helen. But then, you've got many nice qualities: you're intelligent, incredibly kind to awkward men, and have calves—" He caught himself again and turned a shade closer to stop-sign red.

"Calves are good to have," I said.

"Yes," Nate2 murmured, laughing nervously. "Difficult to walk without them. And your mother's are very nice. Strong, like a Clydesdale's."

Nate2 had always claimed to be intensely nervous around women, and I can honestly say he wasn't exaggerating. As he twiddled the silky belt I noticed with alarm that his robe was beginning to open slightly, exposing a thatch of black chest hair and even more leg. I motioned for him to close up. He mimicked my wave, his eyebrows arching in puzzlement. I mimed the action of tying a cloth belt.

"Are you cold?" Nate2 asked.

My mother began to lower her magazine. I coughed loudly to distract her.

"I have a sore throat," I said. "Probably because of the air conditioning at work. We should all put on *extra clothes* to stay warm."

"It's the middle of a heat wave," Nate2 said. "I'm broiling like a roasting hen."

Mom turned toward him and made to speak, probably to mention that today's high had only been twenty-five, but the words didn't make it past her lips. She blinked several times at Nate2's half-exposed body and buried her face in her magazine again.

"We're having a BBQ tonight," she squeaked, getting up. "I should go chop something."

"Oh lovely," Nate2 said. "Grilled meat will be good for my diet. Our recent turmoil has put me in the mood to trim down. I've been working out on a strange contraption called an Ab-Flex in the basement. Don't suppose you need a hand with the onions?"

"I'll be fine, thank you."

Nate2 twirled his robe belt absently. "All this hostess business must have you worn out. Can't be easy going through life as a *domestic goddess.*"

To my horror, my mother actually laughed at this pathetic line, exactly the same way she did when my dad made similar remarks. Thankfully she disappeared around the corner toward the kitchen before the situation could get creepier. I turned on Nate2.

"What are you doing?" I asked.

He took a deep breath, as though he'd just broken the ocean's surface after several long minutes under water. "There's a slight chance I might be having a stroke. Feel my pulse. I've lost all sensation in my legs and my entire left side appears to be paralyzed."

"Please do up your robe."

He looked down and squawked in terror, fastening quickly. He put a hand on his chest. "Could be a massive coronary. I feel a definite tingling sensation. I might need to see a doctor."

"You'll need an ambulance if you don't stop hitting on my mom."

"I was just being polite." He slapped his left arm a few times, searching for feeling, then stopped and leaned forward normally. "But if I were flirting, how would you say I was doing?"

I didn't have the heart to say *terribly*. I didn't mind if he got to know my mom's likes and dislikes so that he could find the version of her in his own dimension, but I couldn't handle him showing genuine feelings. Though I supposed it was only natural, since she was the woman of my father's dreams. My head began to throb. I left Nate2 to ponder his life and ran into Gus in the hall. He was leaning his gangly body against the wall and scratching his fuzzy hair.

"What are you doing?" I asked.

He motioned toward Delores's closed bedroom door. "I'm bored out of my skull and have been trying to think of new ways to gently torment our Visigoth comrade-in-arms. Delores always seems so much livelier when she's in a rage. I miss her feisty spirit."

"Maybe you should just leave her alone to recuperate."

Gus shook his head. "D is the kind of woman who needs to be aggravated, just like most of my ex-girlfriends. They like the teasing, even if they tell you to drop dead and then pretend not to be at home when you can clearly see them hiding behind the curtains."

I supposed Delores could use some company. I only hoped that Gus wouldn't push her too far. We knocked gently and jumped back as something solid hit the door—likely a kicking foot. I had the feeling this wasn't Gus's first incursion of the afternoon. He nudged me to speak.

"It's John," I said.

A series of rustling noises were followed by the knob turning and the door cracking open a half inch. Even without her black makeup, Delores's features—pupils, eyelashes, and the faint circles under her green eyes—all appeared dark and menacing. On the wall I could see the map of Texas that my father had bought for her to make her feel closer to home. No doubt as soon as she was strong enough she'd be on a plane back to the States and out of my life completely.

"What?" she snapped.

"We thought you might be lonely," I mumbled.

"Do I look lonely?"

"You look rosy," Gus said, pushing in front of me. "Like you should be wearing lavender. You'll make some man a lovely homemaker one day. He might even be a farmer. I could see you milking cows."

"Gus," Delores said coolly in her slow Texan drawl. "What do you think you'd say if I pulled your tongue out with my bare hands? Do you think you'd be able to sass me with something witty?"

"No," Gus replied. "I'd probably make a series of wet, indecipherable screams and then pass out. You can lose a surprising amount of blood through your tongue."

"Lord give me patience," Delores murmured. "If I had my druthers …"

I'd gotten used to Delores's accent and could now perfectly understand almost everything she said, but I still had trouble when she fell into Texas slang. That was like an entirely different language only locals might know. I had no idea what a druther was or what she might do with one.

"But all flirting aside," Gus continued. "Why don't you come to the local shops with us? I'll buy you an ice cream or some fishhooks to pierce your eyebrows. You can get back to being more Gothic. I miss the old you."

Delores's jaw made a slow circling motion, prompting an image of a shark moving in for a kill. I wanted to say something to break up the tension and make everyone happy, but the flirting remark had me distracted. Did Gus actually like Delores? And why had he compared her to his ex-girlfriends? Was everyone falling in love with each other in this stupid house? I cleared my throat.

"Why don't you come for a walk," I said. "The sun's nice."

"Bad move," Gus whispered. "Her kind can't go out in direct light."

"I'd love to," Delores said to me, ignoring Gus, but suddenly sounding weary. "But I'm tired as an old mule and gotta rest up. Doctor's orders. Besides, last time I tried walking I made it only halfway down the driveway. I'm hoping these new pills your dad got me will put the joys of spring back in me."

"I get allergies in the spring," Gus said.

"Good," Delores muttered.

Without waiting for a reply, she closed the door. I felt the air leave my chest. I used to be cool with Delores and able to communicate, but since we got stuck in the house we were more like strangers. She'd kissed me on the plane to Toronto, and yet I could only figure that she regretted it, because she didn't seem that eager to be around me. Clearly I was about as debonair with women as Nate2.

"Ah well," Gus said. "Women are a mystery. Fancy an ice cream, mate?"

"We're eating soon," I pointed out.

Gus looked at his watch. "I have to eat constantly to keep my metabolic rate high; otherwise I ... well, nothing happens. I suppose I'm just a glutton."

He disappeared down the front steps, leaving me to wonder how someone who ate such a vast amount of food stayed lean and gangly. I looked down at my skinny arms and small frame and conceded that I wasn't exactly stacked with muscle either.

CHAPTER 3

THE PLANETARIUM was a round brick structure that looked like a wood-fired pizza oven with a large telescope poking out. Our chubby white cat, Skittles, was lingering outside the low-slung door looking anxious to get in. My father opened the door slightly and plunged his woolly head out. He desperately needed a haircut and a beard trim. He looked unkempt at the best of times, but now his home-dyed, beet-red hair was exploding off his skull like a thousand springs jumping in all directions. He was always changing his look—he said it helped him think—but things had gotten ridiculous. His goatee had three colours: orange, green, and a disturbing natural black around the chin. I'd never seen his real hair colour before. It was a bad sign.

"Are you alone?" he asked.

"Thankfully yes. I can't cope."

His eyes shifted back and forth across the yard, then he reversed and let me in. Skittles decided a group meeting was in order and tried to nudge in near our feet, but my father directed her back out by turning her enormous body in the opposite direction and giving her an affectionate pat.

"Hate to lock her out, but she won't leave me alone. She nearly knocked coffee onto the wave sensor motherboard, which would have fried my circuitry. She's far too fat for such a small room."

Skittles wasn't used to my father being so frantically busy. As we glanced out the window she turned her back on us and began to lick her fur aggressively. I guess we were all feeling the strain of our current circumstances. Dad spent almost all his time in the planetarium now, trying to find a way to get Nate2 and Rex home. He had a small hotplate for soup, a popcorn maker, and a kettle, and only occasionally made it into the house for a meal. He'd definitely lost some weight.

"Oh, Skittles," he muttered, looking out. "Keep your pecker up."

My dad had emigrated from England when he was twenty, but still managed to keep certain traits and embarrassing expressions from his native land. Pecker actually meant chin.

"How are things going?" I asked.

He snorted. "Finding a stable, open porthole is proving extremely difficult. I'm not really equipped for precision mapping. Anton Kavordnic is the only man to ever locate proper seams in the space–time continuum, but he's stopped collecting his e-mail."

Anton Kavordnic was the father of inter-dimensional theory—the man who'd discovered how to move between planes of space and time—and was also a highly regarded piano player and a not-so-well-respected pulp novelist. Unfortunately, no one ever seemed able to find him.

"Is Mr. Kavordnic all right?" I asked.

My dad bit his lip. "He's too smart to be captured by those bureaucrats at DIMCO."

I informed him of the BBQ. He nodded, looking around the cluttered room with an expression of guilt. Once my father got going on a project he was pretty hard to distract, but my mom had a definite knack for pulling him away when he needed a break. She was the only person he really listened to in life. I looked over his maps, diagrams, and mountains of calculations. One of the computers appeared to be smoking.

"Spilled a bit of soup into the monitor unit," my dad said. "Tomato. I think a crouton might still be lodged in the fan."

"She wants to have dinner at 6:30."

"But what *is* 6:30, John?"

"An hour after 5:30. You should probably change your shirt. You've got mustard on your sleeve."

He glanced down at a yellow blotch, then leaned back in his chair and stared at the brick roof. "What an apt metaphor," he began. "Humans perceive time as a straight line—past, present, and future—but it's not. Time is a big swirling mess, like a giant celestial mustard stain. We know so little about the cosmos."

"I think we're having sausages."

He put his arms behind his head. "The edges of which are rounded, much like space and time are curved, similar to the Earth's circumference. And if you follow a curve far enough you get a circle."

I'd like to say his ramblings surprised or confused me, but he'd pretty much done this sort of thing all my life. The only way to snap him out of his train of thought was to prod him to the end as quickly as possible.

"So the space–time continuum is round, like a globe?" I asked dutifully.

"Essentially," he replied, cupping his hands in open air. "But unlike the Earth, nothing stays still, so you can't map it easily. The continuum hates a lack of motion, absolutely detests it, which makes nailing down reliable points of reference, such as the north and south poles, nearly impossible."

"Still no luck with the portholes," I said.

He tossed his pencil onto the desk. "Nope. And until I get reliable readings I can't risk sending Rex and Nate back in case they clip a porthole edge or hit a distortion wave and get instantaneously disintegrated."

I turned to go, realizing why I so rarely had heart-to-heart talks with my dad any more. They were simply too depressing. "Well, at least we have sausages. I'll tell Mom you're going to fire up the BBQ at six. Thankfully Rex and Nate don't have to worry about distortion waves while they're here."

My father yanked on his goatee several times, as if he was trying to start a lawnmower. I'd seen the manoeuvre before and felt a twinge of dread. Distortion waves are randomly occurring atmospheric pulses that affect people who aren't in their own dimension. These waves combine with a person's thoughts at the moment of impact and create a third realm of existence—a reality distortion—where the world around you becomes as real as your own life, only filled with freakish and often dangerous things. Not long ago, in the other universe, we'd had to overcome a homicidal nun, killer hair, and a sadistic game show host. The only way to end these reality distortions had been to confront and overcome the thing your mind had created. I had overcome the killer hair by bashing it apart with a blender. The other two hadn't been nearly as easy to escape.

"Your force field around the house is still blocking distortion waves, isn't it?" I asked.

My dad nodded. "Yes. But I can't keep Rex and Nate2 protected forever. I'm getting some troublesome spikes on the spectrogram. The longer they stay in this dimension, the more energy masses against them. Once the waves break through, they'll fade quickly and disappear entirely. This is why I should be working instead of having BBQs."

"Maybe you need a break to clear your mind," I croaked.

"A good meal might help me think." He tasted a bit of the dried mustard he'd scraped off his sleeve with his fingernail. "Dijon. Must have been from my corned beef sandwich yesterday. Okay, tell your mother six. Maybe a few hours away from these figures will recharge my mind and help me see what I'm clearly missing."

CHAPTER 4

OVER THE FOLLOWING DAYS things didn't improve. Despite his dinner spent socializing with us, my dad continued to struggle with the porthole issue. He stayed up nights, slept for an hour here and there, and began to mumble to himself in his dishevelled clothes.

I kept the news of increasing wave energy to myself and, my dad's instructions to the contrary, encouraged Gus to get Nate2 out of the house as much as possible, figuring he'd be less of a distraction. I agreed to meet up with them at a dim sum restaurant in Chinatown one afternoon after work. I didn't have much trouble finding them. Although the room was the size of a football field and jammed full of people dining on dumplings, fried noodles, and steamed buns, their table by far surpassed the usual ratio of dishes-to-visible-tablecloth. Every square inch of surface space was covered by a plate, bamboo dish, or bowl of sauce, in some cases all three. As I slid into a chair Gus hoisted a plate my way.

"Try these custard tarts," he said. "They're fantastic—nice and gooey—just the way I like my sweets. I've had four already and can't eat another bite."

"Told you not to eat that ninth Singapore dumpling," Nate2 remarked.

"Couldn't help it. My eyes were bigger than my stomach."

Nate2 waved a chopstick. "I actually knew a man with that very affliction. I think they called it *ocular sclerosis*. He used to hang

17

around the high street in giant glasses feeding pigeons scraps of sausage meat that he'd buy wholesale with his government cheques. He always ordered far too much."

Gus pushed the last bite of his custard tart away and slid back in his chair with a sour expression. Nate2 was wearing thick, dark sunglasses and rubbing one hand over his stomach in a counter-clockwise direction. Leaning against the table next to him was the long white walking stick rigged up as protection. My father's freshly patented wave inhibitor outfit made Nate2 look as though he were blind, but at least he wasn't suffering perverse realities away from the house's force field. Not yet … From the mess of his plate, however, he'd probably be suffering some strange indigestion-fuelled dreams later in the night.

"Have whatever you want," Gus said to me. "I think we're stuffed."

"You know," Nate2 began, "in Roman times, at this sort of feast, people would eat until they were full and then wander off to the *vomitorium*. That was a special hallway where they could throw up after overindulging. They would expunge and return to eat another six or seven courses. Those parties used to last for weeks on end."

"Suppose there wasn't much else to do back then," Gus said. "TV couldn't have been up to much."

Nate2 motioned toward a dish containing several lumps of a gelatinous white meatlike substance. "Try the abalone," he suggested.

"What is it?"

"Some sort of aquatic creature."

"Is it good?" I asked, poking a chopstick at the rubbery lump.

"Goodness, no," Nate2 replied. "It's horrendous—tastes like stagnant seawater. But it was the most expensive item on the menu and I'd hate to see it go to waste. I didn't like that, or the shark stew, or the bun filled with pork liver, or the pale yellow creature in the shell that crawled off the table."

"I didn't like the chicken feet," Gus added. "They were definitely undercooked."

"I do prefer them with the claws removed," Nate2 conceded.

He pointed to a plate of gnarly legs. Apparently they'd ordered everything on the menu and hadn't even had the common courtesy to wait for me to arrive from work. I took advantage of the copious amounts of now-cooling food and filled my plate. I figured we'd be wise to get a doggie bag so as not to waste anything, and wondered if we'd have to get a taxi or even a flatbed truck to get it home.

"Who's paying for all this?" I asked.

Gus winked and flipped out his wallet full of British currency. "I've been itching to use some of this airport dosh."

On our way home from the other dimension we'd been temporarily suspended in a reality distortion, and Gus had used the opportunity to collect bags of cash—over sixty thousand British pounds.

I hesitated. "My dad said not to spend that money."

"A few quid won't hurt. What's the worst that can happen?"

As I finished eating Gus waved his hand to a waitress pushing a cart full of dishes. She explained that the kitchen had no more food and asked us to pay at the cash register by the door. As we rose and wandered past a large glass aquarium full of lobsters the entire restaurant stopped talking and began to clap, amazed that my friends could even stand after eating the entire kitchen. Gus and Nate2 waved and bowed proudly, but I could only cover my face in embarrassment. They were tourists in Toronto. I had to live here. Besides, we weren't supposed to draw attention to ourselves, and this was just the kind of freakish behaviour that makes people want to stare.

At the counter, a shrivelled old woman calculated the bill and shoved a yellowing piece of paper toward Gus. I'd never seen one meal come to $700, at least not with only three people in a place with plastic tablecloths. Gus nodded and gratefully accepted a handful of free mints the woman was pushing toward him.

"Hope you take British money," Gus said. "Hong Kong used to be a colony, so I suppose things are still kosher. I must say I admire your ceramic cat. Don't suppose you'd like to barter?"

"Lucky cat not for sale," the woman said. She frowned at the wad of red fifty-pound notes on the counter, held up a finger for us to wait, and then shuffled toward a door near the kitchen. She went in and we waited, my instinctive sense of dread growing. I wondered why Gus couldn't at least try to be cautious. He winked as Nate2 took the opportunity to tap his white cane against the aquarium full of lobsters.

"What are you doing?" I hissed.

"I think that animal on the left just gave me a rude gesture with his claw."

"Stop tapping the glass. You're supposed to be blind. You shouldn't even know that's a lobster tank."

Nate2 lowered his cane. "If anyone asks, I'll tell them I thought it was a television and was looking for the volume control. Don't worry. I'm very clandestine." He chuckled. "Goodness knows women haven't noticed me for years. Except for one in Kings Cross Station last November who thought I was Napoleon Bonaparte. She wouldn't let me go until I convinced her I had to go battle the Holy Roman Empire." His gaze faded off wistfully. "I really should have got her number."

"You lead a fascinating life," I muttered.

"It certainly has its interesting moments," Nate2 said. "Seven of them at last count."

A man's head poked around the corner of the office and turned our way. He looked us up and down, scowled, and disappeared from view. I hoped the delay was due only to the restaurant's unwillingness to accept foreign currency. If that was the case I could call my dad and have him pay with his credit card. I doubted he'd love that. My parents were already financing everyone's meals, water, and electricity. The man from the office came striding out holding up the bills. The old woman trailed cautiously behind him, her head tilted and her eyes narrow.

"Do you have other money?" the man asked.

"We can go to a bank and get those converted into Canadian dollars," I said. "My friends are tourists, and not particularly bright. They'll stay here while I go. It's not a problem."

"Bank not want these," the man said, tossing them across the counter. "What you trying to do? These not even good fakes! Yes, they have good security feature—perfect thread, watermark, quality paper—but the fat man with the perm on the back is all wrong! I look up real bill on the Internet and he not winking!"

Nate2 picked up a bill and held it to his face. "That's Sir John Houblon," he exclaimed. "The Bank of England's first governor. Of course he's winking. The treasury drew him like that because he invented the Whoopee Cushion. Of course, Antoine Laurent Lavoisier claimed to be the true inventor, but the French guillotined him during the revolution, so some of the details are sketchy. The Gallic race is very sensitive about flatulence. They'll let their dogs defecate all over the sidewalks, but break wind in a packed café and they treat you like a social outcast."

The restaurant manager cocked an eye. "What you talking about, giant man?"

Nate2 fidgeted with his cane handle. "I had a short, very unsuccessful trip to Paris seventeen years, two months, and three days ago. Looking back, I can see that my troubles began when P&O Ferries announced a special on their beans-on-toast breakfast."

The Chinese man stood staring at Nate2 like he was from another dimension, which of course he was. Now I knew why my father had for so long resisted letting him go out.

Nate2 handed the note back to the woman. "Looks perfectly fine to me," he said.

The restaurant manager pointed. "Wait a minute! You are not blind!"

Nate2 blushed. "I never made the claim. Just because a man wanders around with opaque glasses and a white cane does not mean he's impaired. You shouldn't assume. It's terribly impolite. And besides, you don't see a dog anywhere, do you?"

"I'm calling police."

"No wait!" I said. "Let me contact my dad. He can sort out this mess. He's got loads of money and doesn't mind giving *big* tips."

Gus was waving his hands to interrupt, so I stepped sideways to block him out of the conversation. Unfortunately, he was a full head taller than me, so my efforts were futile. He extended a long arm over my head and handed the man what I immediately recognized as a credit card we'd been given in the alternative dimension for emergencies. The odds of it working in our universe were slim to none. The manager looked suitably skeptical.

"You kidding me?" he said.

"I'm very serious," Gus replied. "Phone it in to the credit card company. And if there's any problem, I'll trot down to my Mercedes-Benz and get my other wallet, the big one that's chock full of *Australian* money. Everyone in the world takes that ..."

"It's even better than American money," I muttered.

The manager squinted at us, but true to form, Gus played the part cool, at least until he leaned against the front cash, slid, and nearly toppled the miniature cat statue. The man waved to a very large, very burly cook who came stumping out of the kitchen, his legs crashing down like two concrete arches come to life. Needless to say, the cook didn't smile back when Nate2 waved and greeted him heartily, and instead planted himself with his arms crossed in front of the glass exit doors. I could see Spadina Avenue down a short flight of stairs.

"There's always a moral decision to be made in these cases," Nate2 said quietly from the side of his mouth. "We've done our best to pay with legal tender, and I don't see frantic pleading working, so we have no other option."

"What are you saying?" I snapped.

He leaned closer. "I'm not in the mood to tell the police why I have no passport or proper identification. I've already been arrested once this month, and quite honestly, I can't face another cell with a communal toilet. I have a very shy bladder. We'll mail them a cheque later."

Before I could say another word he whirled and slammed the end of his cane against the aquarium glass, shouting "Freedom for all!" Unfortunately, his thin, whippy walking stick did little more than make a sharp slapping sound, frightening several near-comatose lobsters. As the cook reared back to slug Gus, who'd clearly been caught off guard by the outburst, I grabbed Nate2's cane and aimed for the man's shins. I'm not usually violent, but I was saving Gus some dental work. The stick connected with bone and splintered spectacularly as the cook howled. As I turned toward the exit I caught sight of a computer chip that had dislodged from the cane and was now spinning under a nearby table, but I didn't have time to retrieve what was probably a very sophisticated, high-tech piece of equipment. We raced down the stairs, took the glass doors at full speed, and careened into the street.

CHAPTER 5

THERE HAD BEEN A TIME, not long ago, when I wouldn't have known what to do when my life was under threat. Now I was always thinking ahead, planning for the next great foul-up. As we hit the sidewalk Gus lost his footing on a stray lychee and slid under a cart of spring onions, banging his head solidly on a box of bok choy. A shout of anger went up from a restaurant above and seconds later its doorway was filled with moving bodies and livid faces.

I hadn't been the one to order every possible dish on the menu with no practical means of paying, but here I was tossing vegetables at an irate Chinese manager, an old woman, and a hobbling chef who looked to be on the verge of tears. I managed to wing the manager with a hunk of ginger as he stuck his head out. Nate2 helped Gus from under the cart and I jammed a few husks of corn through the door handles as a temporary obstruction.

We raced past rusty buckets full of discount shoes, ceramic plates, and chopsticks; past food stalls and a corner shop selling ceramic busts of Elvis, Buddha, cats, dogs, and assorted saints. The sidewalks were jammed with people and vendors, so we had to weave, jump, and push our way forward. We dashed across streetcar tracks and down a back street past one of the six million construction sites in the city, and ran on for several minutes before finally coming to rest on the University of Toronto campus.

"Well," Gus wheezed, collapsing onto a set of steps. "Nothing works off the calories from a meal like some light jogging. Did anyone pick up my lungs a couple blocks back?"

"Serves you right," I gasped.

"They lost a very large tip."

I clenched my fists. "The money was no good. And besides, my dad told you not to spend it."

"I have issues with authority," Gus replied. "I have nothing against your dad. I just don't like anyone placing restrictions on my freedom. I'm like a bird who can't be caged."

I glanced toward Nate2, who was on all fours trying to catch his breath. He was the colour of a maraschino cherry and his bulging eyes made him look like a very surprised tuna. A fat, mangy squirrel trotted over and stood on its hind legs near Nate2's left ear. Nate2 let out a weak yelp.

"It's a squirrel," I said. "Get over it."

"It's a mutant. Look at its fur."

Clearly the animal had seen better days—its coat was patchy in places and one ear was missing—but I supposed city life was hard on squirrels. All the construction couldn't have been good for their nerves. The braying jackhammers certainly weren't doing much for me. The squirrel sniffed the air and then made a short scurry closer. Nate2 squeaked and backed away slowly, as if the animal were a rattlesnake, but that only seemed to anger it, because it bounded forward again and nipped at Nate2's ankle as he turned to rise.

"I didn't think squirrels bit," Gus said.

"They will if they're rabid," I replied coyly.

Nate2 let out another screech, bolted away, and jumped onto a bench. The squirrel followed him, leisurely bouncing behind. I pulled out my wallet and wondered if I could empty my bank account at an ATM and go back to the restaurant before the cops arrived. I'd had enough run-ins with authorities lately and didn't need extra trouble.

"We'll pay them back later," Gus said, as if reading my mind. "The restaurant won't report a dine-and-dash. People skip out on bills all the time. It's a sign of the times really."

"We just stiffed the place $700."

"Yeah, but ..." He paused. "You used to be more fun when we were being hunted in that other dimension. A settled life doesn't do much for your personality."

"I'm thinking about our safety."

"I'm thinking about having a chocolate bar. I need something sweet to cleanse my palate."

Clearly I needed Delores to keep Gus in check. She was better than me at making him take responsibility for his actions. When we'd caught our collective breath we hurried through streets that any other time of the year would have been teeming with students. But with the high humidity and school vacation in full swing, the place was mostly empty. As we crossed the green expanse of Queen's Park, Nate2 made a gurgling noise, then grabbed his stomach and doubled over.

"Told you not to eat that thousand-year-old egg," Gus said. "Of course the sea cucumber didn't taste quite right, either."

We trotted over to help Nate2 get upright. When I took his elbow I felt a sudden ripple course through my body, like I was being lifted off my feet, then my stomach cramped with a familiar sensation. Of course! He'd lost his cane, the vital second part of his distortion inhibitor, and he'd put the sunglasses in his pocket during the escape. This was obviously a wave pulsing through our dimension, and by latching onto him, Gus and I were being pulled into his reality distortion. I wanted to tell him to think positive thoughts, but the wave's undertow knocked me off my feet and the next thing I knew Gus was standing over me looking ill.

"Here we go again," he said.

Nate2 meanwhile was brushing grass off his elbows, looking completely indifferent. Gus and I were both tense, looking around slowly and trying to see what in the park might have changed. Nate2 fell in beside us and scanned.

"Nice enough park," he murmured. "Bit small, and the eight lanes of traffic don't do much to provide an illusion of country-side. Still, I suppose office workers need a place to relax and eat their cheese sandwiches."

"That was a reality distortion," I said. "It may have seemed milder than usual, but you can bet money we're in a screwed-up world created by our thoughts right now. Tell me you weren't thinking about radioactive squirrels."

Nate2 flinched and looked down at his foot. "Do you think that rodent was radioactive?"

"No, but—"

"Where would it have been exposed to nuclear waste?"

"It was just an example of a thought we don't want to deal with."

Nate2 continued on, not listening. "Because I think its tiny teeth might have broken the skin on my ankle. It certainly ruined these socks, which are the only ones I have in this city. And look, that little glorified rat scuffed my loafer after I paid that nice gentleman in the subway station two dollars to buff them just this morning!"

"What were you thinking about?" Gus interrupted, grabbing Nate2's shirt and shaking him violently. "I'd love to hear more about your feet, but the kid who could have been your son had you been born in this dimension has a point. We're in a reality distortion. Your thoughts are about to become real and we're going to need a plan to overcome them so that we can get back to real life."

Nate2 glanced around as if suddenly aware, then made a skeptical face and exhaled deeply. "Everything looks fine to me."

Apparently he really did think his cramps had been from semi-rotten eggs and strange aquatic food. Gus put his face in his hands and wandered away. The woodland and its population all seemed normal—no chipmunks were glowing neon and the strolling tourists weren't conspiring against us—but we'd fallen into a misguided feeling of security before. Things always got weird the second you relaxed. Nate2 gestured at a large bronze statue of King Edward VII that overlooked the park.

"But just for the record," he began. "At the time of my cramps, I was considering this fascinating piece of public art. I've never had much time for statues, but seeing this one made me long for my rain-drenched homeland."

"You've been away from England for less than a month," I pointed out.

"True. But you must remember I've never been anywhere in my life. This is an emotional upheaval." He contemplated the towering metal horse-and-rider figure solemnly. "Amazing. You wouldn't think four pigeons could all sit on King Edward's head at once."

As much as I wanted to let my central nervous system calm down and release a soothing cocktail of chemicals into my bloodstream, I couldn't help but be disturbed by the low vibrating sound emanating around us. Gus appeared beside me.

"Tell me that's a construction site," he murmured.

When I didn't reply, his shoulders slumped wearily and his forehead dropped so far toward his chest that I couldn't see his face. We turned and stared up at the enormous bronze statue that was clearly beginning to pulse. The hard tendons of the horse's leg flexed and strained to rise from the concrete base as the late king's eyes opened and he began to crane his thick metal neck around the area.

"No chance that's a fascinating interactive display?" Nate2 said, swallowing hard. "Perhaps a marketing stunt to promote tourism or an upcoming television documentary?"

As we made to grab him, the first leg of the statue burst from the base with a resounding crash, spewing chunks of concrete and metal through the air like shrapnel. The metal horse turned its snout and snorted aggressively. For all the talk of the king being the father of the Empire, Edward VII wasn't looking too parental. Unless of course you believe the old saying *Spare the rod, spoil the child*. He pointed his riding stick our way and in a deep metallic voice grumbled words we couldn't understand.

"Oh great," Gus muttered. "More running."

We took off across the park along with a hundred other afternoon revellers. Everyone was screaming and racing wildly, dropping picnic baskets and backpacks in their panic to flee. We'd gone less than a hundred metres when Gus slowed to a virtual crawl, his legs lifting and moving forward as if they were stuck in mud or deep water. He grabbed a thigh and tried to speed up his pace.

"Come on!" I shouted.

Behind us, the horse had freed three legs and was teetering unsteadily, trying to jump free. A family of tourists stood nearby with a camcorder, taking turns getting in the vacation video. They were waving pleasantly at the camera, pointing to the statue and making peace signs. Gus had now come to a complete stop and was unable to raise his foot.

"I've never been keen on exercise," he began. "All that running made me think my muscles were made of sand. Just once I'd like a distortion wave to catch a positive thought. My neural net can't be this consistently negative."

As the statue stomped a small Toyota, Nate2 seemed to finally firmly accept that this wasn't a harmless prank. He took a deep breath and straightened his posture, as if getting ready to go into battle. He motioned for me to grab Gus under the arm and we hoisted him up, hobbling awkwardly toward the downtown core. Gus might have been thin, but he was long-limbed and awkward to carry. Whenever I'd get a good hold, his weight would shift and he'd begin to slip. It was like trying to carry a bag of potatoes while wearing boxing gloves. A tearing noise ripped through the air behind us, and seconds later an entire tree crashed to our left. Not only was the horse muscular, Edward himself had obviously been to the gym.

"And he was my favourite king!" Nate2 yelled. "When I get home I'm selling all my ceremonial plates. And I'm writing a letter. I've always been a staunch monarchist, but perhaps the republican movement has a point. I can't abide this!"

"Don't worry," Gus moaned. "The first couple distortions in a new dimension are always hardest on the brain. You'll get used to being mental soon enough."

"People have been telling me that for years!"

I looked back to see half the trees uprooted and the benches smashed to splinters. The horse and rider were whirling around ferociously, lashing out at anything in their way, as if they had no other purpose but total destruction. My eyes met those of the king. He pointed in our direction again, and the horse went into a full gallop. Clearly we were now his prime targets.

In desperation, I looked around and spotted a knapsack that had been abandoned in someone's hurry to get away. Next to it was a pair of new pink inline skates with Velcro clasps.

"I have an idea," I said.

With the earthquake assault of steel hooves on ground echoing from behind, we slipped the skates onto Gus's stinky feet, tossed his runners into the knapsack, and wheeled him crazily through traffic.

"I've never been on skates before!" he yelped.

"Just hold still."

"I can't seem to do anything else."

We raced down a wide road and then plunged into a narrow passageway between two buildings as another tree trunk flew through the air and slammed into a nearby building. I turned to see a steel fist lash at a brick wall, gouging a hole that exposed an office. A man sat stunned at his desk as the statue knocked over a power line and kicked a corner mailbox into the grille of a delivery van. As we flew down the passageway I turned to see the king approaching the opening with furious speed. Then, without warning, I stumbled into Gus and Nate2, who'd stopped dead in front of me, and fell to the ground. When I opened my eyes, out of breath and winded from the impact, I recognized the source of our trouble immediately. I was all for security, but this was a really, really bad place for someone to have put up a ten-foot-high chain link gate.

Together, the three of us turned to face the snorting beast that was blocking our path back to the street. There were no doors or windows in the passageway and no visible way to get to the roof. Four eyes were bearing down on us, the king rapping his riding crop against his leg with a deep, steely pinging sound. As he hovered above us at the entrance to the narrow lane he seemed to be waiting for a cue—or perhaps just prolonging our terror.

"Think we can talk our way out of this one?" I said.

"Does that statue even have ears?" Nate2 replied.

"Wheel me closer to the gate's lock," Gus grunted. "And hand me that piece of wire. At least my fingers still work."

"Not for long."

With a screech, the horse reared on four legs and plunged forward toward our prone bodies. Hooves echoed like thunderclaps, metal drums, and a hundred car accidents all at once. I'd never hated public art so much in all my life.

CHAPTER 6

THEY SAY that before you die your life passes before your eyes. I guess my time wasn't up yet, because my brain went totally blank as the ten-ton statue came pounding down. Not only had my brain given up its memory duties, it completely abandoned control over motor skills as well. My body was locked in place like a … well, like a statue. The only saving grace was that it maintained control over my bladder so that I didn't pee my pants. Nice to have some pride.

Nate2 showed his mettle by removing the sunglasses from his pocket and throwing them at the charging beast. He threw poorly and they clattered across the ground and under some stray litter.

The statue came at us like an ocean liner sliding into the sea, looming above, heaving and crashing in an explosion of dust and debris against the buildings on both sides. Bricks sailed toward us and metal and stone collided. I backed into the high chain-link gate ready for a swift, merciful death … and was surprised when it gave way and I stumbled back into a parking lot. Above me, a smiling Gus stood holding the padlock in one hand as Nate2 rolled him into the paved lot, then turned and hauled me away from a descending hoof.

Police, fire trucks, and ambulances were pulling up around the area, followed closely by news vans, and the sky was practically black with helicopters. I had a sneaking suspicion that the incident would be hard to explain. Behind us the king attempted to come after us again, but appeared to have become jammed in the slim passageway. The horse strained, but its head was stuck in an insurance firm boardroom and its tail had been trapped in debris from a partially collapsed wall. Edward slumped in his saddle and stewed bitterly.

"Once again, the royal family is a disappointment," Nate2 said.

Gus tossed the lock my way with an awkward flip of his wrist. "HB-50 series, known for having a faulty third tumbler. They recalled them in Australia, but I guess you Canadians aren't as safety conscious. Sixteen seconds is my new record."

"Amazing what you can do with a homicidal steel equine staring you down," Nate2 remarked.

"I had no idea you could pick locks," I said.

"Childhood hobby," Gus murmured. "For a time I thought about being a magician—the Aussie Harry Houdini. I got discouraged, though. My uncle said I didn't have the discipline and would be better suited to a life of crime. Still, it's a good skill to have."

"Well, uh, thanks … we owe you."

"Ah, mate," Gus said. "No worries. You can buy me some of these roller shoes as payback. I like the idea of gliding around with little to no effort. It's what I've striven for all my life."

We stopped speaking as several cops crept toward us with their guns out. I thought they were being a bit aggressive, given that we obviously hadn't been *directly* responsible for the neighbourhood's destruction. Then a thought struck me. We still hadn't encountered my part of the distortion reality, and needed to before we'd return to our natural existence. I had a bad feeling.

"I doubt bullets will be much good against that beast," Nate2 said to the cops. "If anything you'll get a nasty ricochet and take your eye out. It's difficult ordering doughnuts when you can't see the honey glazed properly."

He chuckled lightly, but the cop's expression didn't change. Instead he cocked the hammer of his pistol. Nate2's laughter trailed off as he cleared his throat and adjusted his dust-smeared collar. "I watch a lot of police shows on television," he said. "I know how the constabulary on this continent like their sweet comestibles. Of course that could be a malicious stereotype. Were you a fan of *NYPD Blue*?"

The police were fanning out around us, forming a circle. I looked around to see who might be in charge, but they all wore identical uniforms and badges. A shiver of panic flew up my spine and I wondered if maybe this was DIMCO's anti-terror squad infiltrating our distortion. If they could break across the continuum, they might have found a way to get inside our mind-altered universe. This thought was short-lived, however, as a female cop grabbed me from behind, yanked me away from the other two, and handed me a revolver. The gun was cold and heavy in my hand and my first instinct was to drop it.

"Go ahead," she said.

"We can go?" Nate2 asked cheerfully.

"Not until it's done," the woman replied.

My skin was cold despite the temperature. I hadn't meant the thought literally. I'd just been upset about how they'd skipped the bill and gone against my father's instructions about the money. I didn't honestly want to— The cop pushed me forward roughly. Gus and Nate2 looked on curiously.

"They really annoyed you," the cop continued. "You wanted to kill them. You clearly had that idea in your mind, and quite frankly I don't blame you. Don't worry; we'll report their deaths as accidental. Now do it."

The only way to get out of a reality distortion is to overcome the situation created by your thoughts. It's like fear. To move beyond, you have to diminish the intensity of whatever's haunting you. With a cold revolver in my hand and instructions to shoot my friends, I didn't see many viable options. Without overcoming the last part of this reality we'd be stuck here forever.

"Kill them," the female cop repeated.

"I can't. I didn't mean the thought literally."

"What are you, a chicken?"

The other cops all snickered and laughed. I felt like I was in gym class. I handed back the gun, which she took with a smile before lashing me hard across the temple. Blood spurted from my face onto the concrete, pooling for a second before seeping into a dark splotch in the dust. I put a hand over what felt like a gash of several inches and tried not to crumple to my knees as a pounding swirl flooded my vision and hot waves pulsated as though all the nerve endings in my body were a fiery elastic band that had been violently snapped. Colours flashed before my eyes in a burning rainbow like gasoline spreading through water, and for a second I thought everything might drop to black. Blood ran wet down the side of my face as I stood back up and squinted at the female cop.

"Can we go?" I asked.

She hit me again. "That was for your friend's doughnut comment."

"I meant it in a nice manner," Nate2 said.

She fired a warning shot near his foot and looked back at me. "I know you want to pump a few rounds into these losers. They've caused you nothing but trouble and no one's going to miss them. You're tired of having them in your house and want them gone. What if we say it was self-defence?"

"No."

Her glare did not waver. "If you're not going to shoot them, we'll take you all back to the station and torture you slowly."

"Isn't that against regulations?" Nate2 asked.

The cop shrugged. I looked down the alleyway and actually hoped the statue would jerk itself free and stomp out this exchange. But the horse seemed to have settled down considerably and King Edward VII was calmly cleaning his teeth with the end of his riding crop. As I watched, his arm stopped moving and the statue appeared to re-solidify. The horse's heaving torso became rigid and all signs of life disappeared. Then I noticed that everyone around me was frozen too, even Nate2 and Gus. I walked out of the circle, examining the cops' stiff bodies. I pushed one gently and he toppled sideways without even putting out a hand to break his fall. Time appeared to have stopped.

"Anything you'd like to tell me?"

I whirled around to see my father standing at the corner, red-faced and panting to regain his breath. He put one hand on a car and coughed. The last time he'd appeared out of nowhere I'd been in a youth hostel in Scotland looking for a midnight snack.

"I didn't do it," I said.

"Mmm … I knew letting them out of the house was a bad idea." He motioned toward Nate2. "He's got some stellar qualities—most notably being dead handsome—but there are certain traits a person has to purge from his personality after the age of thirty."

"He's had a more difficult life than you," I said.

"You think being me is easy?"

"And it wasn't really his fault. Gus started the trouble."

My dad walked into the alleyway, looking up at the horse and rider suspended in the building frame. Then he picked up Nate2's sunglasses and came back to stand beside me. I noticed that he had Nate2's broken cane and the computer chip that had slid under the table at the Chinese restaurant. He exhaled, wiggling his fingers in front of his pursed lips as if his mouth were a music instrument of some kind. He always did this when he was deep in thought. He used to scratch his head with his fingernails, but the dandruff residue bugged my mom too much and she broke him of the habit.

"Can you get us out of here?" I asked.

He grimaced. "Theoretically, yes. But there's a slight problem."

"You don't know how to make time start up again?"

"Oh, it's still going out there somewhere," he replied, waving vaguely toward the horizon. "No one can stop time. Like I've said, if there's one thing the universe absolutely hates, it's a lack of movement. Every particle always has to be going somewhere, like half-crazed commuters on the subway at rush hour. Goodness I hate coming home at that time of day. Never mind getting a seat, you're lucky if you're not jammed up against the doors while someone reads a broadsheet newspaper inches from your nose. I'm a big supporter of public transportation—it's good for the environment—but really, this city needs another north-south subway line."

"Dad?"

"Yes?"

"Can you get us out of here?"

His eyes flitted back to the scene. "Oh right … What I did was lift your distorted reality and drop it rather unceremoniously back into our world. I didn't like the size of the blip anomaly on Nate2's chart. I've kept him hooked up with electrodes to monitor his frequency just in case anything out of the ordinary occurred, like for instance a run-in with a giant metal horse."

"What are you saying?"

My dad looked around at the devastation. "You don't have to worry about the fuzz, but I can't undo the damage King Edward did to these buildings. Once we wheel Gus and Nate2 out of here and kick-start this fragment of reality, these people aren't going to remember how they got here or why there's a very large statue jammed between two small businesses. But this will have really happened in our world."

"I guess we'll be able to watch it on the six o'clock news."

He didn't seem to find my remark in any way amusing.

CHAPTER 7

THAT NIGHT, even the BBC in England had picked up the remarkably perplexing story of the statue that had moved a full city block and become wedged in a passageway. Everyone from the Canadian prime minister to magician David Copperfield could be found on TV musing about how vandals might have relocated the ten-ton work without leaving a single clue. As to be expected, the Internet was rife with speculation that aliens had used a transporter beam, which was about as close as anyone came to the truth.

The more news outlets flashed footage, the more my father groaned. You'd think Nate2 and Gus would have been suitably embarrassed about the whole incident, but Gus maintained his claims of innocence and Nate2 simply mumbled an excuse about having post-traumatic memory loss.

As I made my way upstairs for the night, Delores stepped out from her room. She had slightly more colour in her cheeks, and looked better than usual. I was amazed at how young she looked when she didn't have makeup on and wasn't snarling at Gus. I also knew how much she hated anyone pointing out the fact.

"Hey," she said. "Heard you had an interesting day."

"Yeah, same old, same old. You're lucky you weren't around for the adventure. Though I have to say I could have used your help. It was the first reality distortion without you for a long while."

We talked for a bit, and I filled her in on events and made subtle inquiries as to her condition. She agreed that Gus had been reckless with the U.K. money and suggested that the next time he got out of line I should whack him. I mentioned that wasn't really my style. As we sat, two thoughts ran through my mind: we were talking like old times, without the recent self-consciousness, and if she was getting better she'd likely fly home and away from me soon. Life seemed to be a constant balancing act of positives and negatives.

As HUMILIATING as dishing hamburgers and french fries to rude customers at Burger Hut could be, the next day I was happier than ever to get away from the situation at home for my night shift. The statue debacle had put everyone on edge. We were definitely reaching our breaking point. As I left for work I overheard a conversation my parents were having in the driveway as they cleaned up spilled garbage from the lawn. This was the third time in a week that an animal had gotten into the trash. We figured it was probably a family of raccoons scavenging for scraps. I stopped to eavesdrop to get a clearer sense of how they felt about the statue debacle.

"He's started writing haikus," my mother was saying.

She read from a crumpled paper in her hands:

Cool
Cat am I
Weird enough for you?
Your body
Wow

"And good ones at that," my father intoned. "I never knew he had so much talent. I wonder if I could do that."

"I'm having a hard time coping with a second you, not to mention the rest of them."

"Nate and I are not the same person, Helen. We've had vastly different lives and personalities. And he bites his spoon when he eats soup. Have you noticed that? Think of him as my twin brother."

"Yeah, you guys are really different. He happens to hum the same songs, like the same foods, and have *several* of the same bad habits as my husband. I caught him painting his toenails with my polish this morning."

"Disgusting."

"*You* did the same thing the first year we were married."

My father stood up holding a bacon grease–stained serviette. "I never."

"You most certainly did. Trust me. It's not something a woman forgets. You said you were curious and loved the smell."

My father frowned. "I must say I'm not completely happy about all the attention he pays my wife. And sometimes I think she secretly likes it, despite her protests."

"Occasionally it *is* cute."

My father stopped scraping rancid mashed potato off the sidewalk and looked at her with a perplexed expression. Obviously he'd been fishing and had caught exactly the wrong answer. I felt a weird twinge of nausea, like weedy salt water had suddenly been pumped into my throat. If my mother had fallen for my father with his shtick, there couldn't be much to prevent her from being attracted to Nate2's bizarre flirting. After all, they did look the same, were similarly odd, and both flattered her to an inch of death. We definitely had to resolve the house-guest logjam ASAP.

"He's even more unashamedly forward than you were," my mother continued.

"Once again, that's because Nate and I are not an identical match. Yes, we have a similar genetic makeup and ancestry, and many of our childhood experiences are the same, but we're totally different people." He paused and then mumbled defensively, "And he's flabbier than I am despite working out on the Ab-Flex."

"He says he's lost an inch off his waist already."

"I'd say he's put on five pounds. He lacks focus and discipline."

My mother's mouth dropped open in shock. "So did you when we met. You weren't lazy, but you certainly weren't ambitious. I believe you came to university to study beer and women."

"Got an A on the last subject."

"And as for Rex," my mom continued, ignoring his comment, "he's got to stop with the 6:00 A.M. workouts on the trampoline or I'm booking him a hotel."

My dad shrugged. "We can't kick him out. It wouldn't just be out onto the street, it would be onto a very fragile plane of existence. He and Nate are vulnerable. They need us. I promise they won't be here much longer."

My mother dropped a wad of tinfoil into the green garbage bag. "I never said we should kick them out. I'm simply letting you know that I'm stressed. Find someone else with spare rooms."

"I've tried, but the circle of contacts I trust is small. Everything will work out."

My father made to plant a kiss on her cheek, but my mother was bending to pick up mouldy rice and didn't see him. She swore loudly. I slunk away feeling more depressed than ever.

When I arrived at the Hut the new manager, Ryan, was standing at the counter. He clicked a stopwatch and scribbled on a clipboard. I was five minutes early, so I wouldn't be issued a *demerit* today. This was Ryan's own system of improving the staff's efficiency. His uniform was perfectly pressed and his manager's badge gleamed. He was in his early twenties but had been with the company forever. He saluted me crisply, nearly knocking off his paper hat.

"Congratulations, John Fitzgerald. Because of your punctuality and consistently good work ethic we've decided to move you to Temporary Kitchen Swing Man tonight. You'll be helping Kevin Flarch. He'll train you on the fry station."

"I used to work there all the time," I replied. "I don't really need train—"

"It's an extra ten cents an hour, but you won't get overtime until sixty hours a week. And you'll have to have a hairnet on 24-7. This reminds me of my first promotion with Burger Hut. I was younger than you—only fifteen—the youngest Junior Burger Sculptor in company history. I was marked for great things, as you are, but you have to fulfill that potential."

Somehow, I didn't see being the youngest grill guy as a big accomplishment, especially since the chain had only six outlets and half of those had opened in the last eighteen months. Ryan banged off a salute again and handed me a scraper.

"I'll inspect this weapon at random—when you least expect it—so keep it clean and ready for action at all times. Tonight's a bit slow, so I thought you might de-grease the grills. Let's get serious and aim for hundred percent gristle-free ranges."

I walked around the corner to the kitchen where Flarch was wisely pretending to be engrossed in continually flipping the same chicken patty. As Ryan strode proudly to the office, Flarch dumped the overcooked burger into a bin and burst into mocking laughter. He dipped his hand into a vat of brine, pulled out a handful of pickles, and shovelled them into his mouth.

"Back in the greasy foxhole, eh?" he said through bits of mashed green.

"Is that what Ryan's calling the kitchen?" I asked.

"Yup. Says it'll promote a feeling of brotherhood. Apparently he whacked his melon on the windshield of his car in an accident when he was in high school and did some major damage to his brain. He went into a coma, and when he woke up he was really good at math but had lost his sense of taste."

"Makes sense that he'd be selling Burger Hut food," I said. "How did you find this out?"

"I did some digging and kicked up gossip from the last Hut where he worked. I just walked into the outlet on College and asked the guy behind the cash. They hate him big time. I'm sure we'll come to feel the same way soon. Do me a favour and smear grease on his jacket in the employees' room. I've been putting small stains on it for a week and want to see how long before he snaps."

Suddenly, working on cash in awkward silence with Amanda seemed a wonderful option. I'd forgotten how bad Flarch was for both my sanity and job security. Despite the rambling drunks, people with horrid B.O., and old folks who snapped about the two-ketchup packet per customer rule, at least out front I wasn't likely to get caught in a manager-baiting scheme.

An order appeared on the computer for seven regular burgers. I wondered if this was for one person, a couple friends, or a family. I'd once seen a guy eat five burgers and a large fries in one sitting. It was a quiet Tuesday night and he looked like he might have been a linebacker—at least six-foot-five and muscled under his bulk. I'd stood by the milkshake machine and in strange fascination watched him take bite after bite.

As I was executing operation "grill the buns" by feeding them through the conveyor belt toaster, Amanda came around the corner looking confused. She stood right next to me and stammered, which was a nice change. Usually I was the one fidgeting with my fingers and making little sense.

"Um, John … did your dad get in an accident?" she asked.

My mind flashed hot with images of his planetarium catching fire. That cramped space full of equipment was an accident waiting to happen. Maybe Skittles had wormed her way in and knocked papers onto the hotplate. Or perhaps DIMCO had sent an assassin or a SWAT team to prevent him from combating their tactics for planetary domination.

"What do you mean?" I asked.

"Well, he's outside in glasses with a white cane and he looks way miserable. Did he, like, go totally blind or is he just being weird?"

My heart rate dropped back into neutral.

In the dining area Nate2 was hunched in the corner sucking absently on the straw of a fountain drink. Outside, the parking lot was dark, barely illuminated by the streetlights and our anemic orange neon sign. The strange hue of the jumbo Burger Hut letters cast an eerie light, making people's faces appear ultra pale and hollowed out. Nate2 didn't need the added effect. He looked miserable enough as it was.

"Ah, John," he said. "You're a sight for sore eyes."

"You just saw me a couple hours ago," I replied.

He took off the glasses and rubbed. "No, I mean that literally. My eyes are killing me. I think I'm having an allergic reaction to that enormous feline of yours. Skat, Scootles …"

"Skittles."

"There's a lot of dander in the air, and it's impossible to keep the little bugger from rubbing against my clothing. It's an attention-starved animal, isn't it?"

"She likes affection and has some issues."

He nodded slowly. "Don't we all. I really think you should cut its feeding schedule. The poor lardball can't even reach its hind legs to lick properly. It keeps rolling every time it stretches."

"My dad is generous with the snacks."

His eyes were rimmed with red and puffy black bags hung beneath them. He leaned his elbows on the table and picked at a serviette. We sat in silence and watched a car race by full of university-aged girls screaming wildly. Nate2 continued to suction up soda until Amanda slid over and placed his tray of burgers on the plastic-coated table. She forced a grimaced smile and mumbled that she hoped he'd be feeling better soon. Nate2 offered me a tinfoil mound.

"No thanks," I said. "It's amazing how sick you get of Hut burgers when you're flipping them all day. I ate a couple dozen during my first two weeks and haven't been able to take a bite since."

Nate2 didn't seem particularly interested in food either. He unwrapped a burger, squished the bun, then pursed his lips and dropped it back onto the silver foil. He made to suction up more drink, but the cup was empty.

"Why'd you order so much food?" I asked.

"Oh, I'm planning to take these to your homestead. It would be rude not to. After all, your father showed great leniency in letting me out of my cage tonight. He said I could leave the property as long as I was supervised."

He motioned around the nearly empty restaurant. Apparently I was babysitting. I couldn't imagine what it was like for a grown man who'd lived (quite miserably and utterly alone) by himself for years to have to follow orders.

"How'd you get here?" I asked.

"Got a lift."

"Did my dad drive you?"

"No, I hitchhiked. Your father was supposed to drive me, but he disappeared into his planetarium and forgot. It was only a few blocks. As merciless as this world is, some people do still stop for blind people stumbling down the street at night. I had the good fortune to trip over a hedgerow at the precise moment a very nice gentleman in a black Buick was creeping by going under thirty."

I laughed. Nate2 seemed haphazard, disorganized, and generally eccentric, but I suspected this was sometimes a bluff to keep people off guard. He stared into the street for a few more minutes, licking his lips from time to time and making quiet noises like he was getting up the gumption to say something. Finally he looked at me directly.

"Do you think people can be bribed with a few hamburgers?" he said. "Or will this be yet another way for me to annoy the household? Honestly, John, how am I doing? I've been trying to be a good guest. I've made tea in the morning, have been happy in my small room, and haven't once commented on the over-abundance of air fresheners spread throughout the house, even though they've completely stuffed up my sinuses. The only thing I can smell any more is wildflowers. I had a dream last night that I was being chased through a forest by a twelve-foot-tall hibiscus."

"You're doing fine," I said. "Everyone is stressed. If people are acting aloof, it's nothing personal. And the house *is* small."

He pushed the burger around absently. "Mmm, I suppose. Still, I don't know if you've noticed, but I do occasionally rub people the wrong way. I'm very much a victim of improperly channelled enthusiasm. I suppose that's why I've kept to myself for so long and had a somewhat spotty record with the ladies despite being dead handsome."

His natural exuberance had been replaced with slouching shoulders, a drooping expression, and an overall listlessness. And he didn't seem at all impressed with the burger, taking the patty out and holding it up to the light. He wasn't the first customer to wonder about our food.

"Things will get better," I said. "Seven people are too many for our house, even with the planetarium. I'm just glad it's not winter, when we'd be stuck inside 90 percent of the time. Of course, you could do more dishes."

"You have a machine."

"Yes, but it has to be stacked and turned on and emptied."

He looked up quizzically. "I thought it did all that automatically."

I noticed that Ryan had emerged from his perfectly ordered office and was talking to Amanda and looking our way. He was always keen to dock people per minute of time spent not working. I told Nate2 I had to get back to work and he nodded.

"I fear I've lived alone too long," he said, getting up. "But I won't complain. Experience has taught me that it's better to keep a diary of grievances against the world and stew silently in anguish. Don't let me depress you. I just needed to unload my burden, and since you're young and generally idealistic I didn't think you'd mind."

"No problem."

"I hope I can sneak back into the house without encountering your neighbours. They're quite interested in our situation too, you know. That gentleman who gave me a lift couldn't stop asking questions about the planetarium and what your father was working on."

I stopped and turned slowly. "What did you tell him?"

"Well …" He fumbled with the burgers, knocking one onto the floor. "It does make for an exciting tale, all this inter-dimensional business."

"You didn't!"

CHAPTER 8

THAT NIGHT, Nate2 didn't make it home. I told everyone about the mysterious stranger who'd driven him to Burger Hut, which didn't seem to surprise my dad as much as I'd expected. He bit his lip apprehensively and muttered about how he should have been more careful. Apparently irregular blips had been appearing on the inter-dimensional scanner since the King Edward VII incident.

"I'd hoped they were anomalies," he said. "But the last time the garbage cans were spilled I had a sneaking suspicion we were being watched. The cuts in those bags were too straight and fine. Raccoons usually leave a jagged, chewed impression on the plastic."

Gus raised his hand tentatively. "I'm sorry, but what's a raccoon?"

"It's an animal composed almost entirely of teeth and claws. There's some grey and black fur, but that's decoration. They're scavengers who carry diseases and occasionally attack humans."

"So they make good pets."

I cleared my throat to interrupt and told my parents every detail of Nate2's showing up at the Hut. My dad twiddled his fingers in front of his mouth and paced from the kitchen to the front window.

"I can locate him from his transmitter, as long as he keeps wearing his glasses, but it'll take some time. Of course, I could find him faster if he took off the glasses and fell victim to a distortion wave, but I'd like to avoid any more destruction in the metropolitan area. I think we have to act on the assumption that DIMCO is behind his disappearance. Tomorrow we move to a safe house."

Rex grunted in the corner. He suggested that we move immediately, but my father explained that his contact couldn't take us sooner. And besides, we needed to pack up all the important equipment in the planetarium and gather our things. My dad looked at the clock on the wall.

"I hope we can get Skittles into the cat hotel tomorrow morning," he murmured.

"Fitzgerald, we've got bigger issues," Rex snapped. "We should get your useless garbage from that brick outhouse and move out immediately. I don't want to be around when DIMCO surrounds this place."

My dad forced a tense smile. "I doubt they're organized enough in this dimension to pull off a sting operation. We'll stay here, remain calm, and leave in a haphazard way in the morning. At this point, our greatest fear is fear itself."

"And vaporization," Gus murmured.

"As long as we stay calm—"

Rex guffawed. "I'm with the hippie. Pardon my French, but calm, my bottom. Fear itself isn't likely to crash through the windows, take us hostage, and expose me to distortion waves."

Gus made to speak, but I cut him off.

"What about the rest of us?" I asked.

"They'll probably use you for experiments," Rex replied.

Gus began to say something, but my dad interjected.

"Let's not exaggerate," he said.

"I wouldn't put it past these people," Rex said. "Remember, I've had a direct relationship with the organization. They work according to their own set of rules."

Gus put up one finger. We all waited expectantly.

"I'm not a hippie," he said finally. "I'm an old soul. I can't remember what else I was going to say."

My dad held his forehead in his hands and mumbled quietly to himself. Delores was sitting silently in misery. She noticed me staring and scowled at my pity. At least her spirit was intact.

"Okay," my mom said, clapping her hands together. "Tomorrow morning at six, we sneak out and meet our contact. Everyone pack one bag—no more."

Gus got up. "I came back to this dimension with a T-shirt, some foul-smelling jocks, and a pair of jeans. My backpack got incinerated when I went through the first porthole. Taking too many bags isn't a problem."

MY DAD and Rex worked through the night to dismantle the equipment in the planetarium. The rest of us were up at five, shovelling whatever we could into suitcases and two enormous trunks brought down from the attic. My mother filled half of one entirely with mementoes and the family photo albums, as if we were never coming back. I headed out to the planetarium to help load the van and walked in on Dad and Rex leaning over the computer monitor having a hushed conversation. I could tell they weren't thrilled that I'd arrived, but then Rex shrugged and offered the swivel chair.

"No," my dad said. "I don't want the kids involved."

"Fitz, your son and his friends navigated their way through my dimension without getting captured or killed. They overcame Ridpath, DIMCO, and a half-dozen distortion waves that would have broken the average person. I think John's earned the right to know what's happening."

My dad hesitated, then nodded slowly and motioned toward the screen.

"This link was sent via e-mail," he said. "It's from a press conference that was held late last night downtown at the Royal Oxford Hotel. Nice place. We stayed there on a wedding anniversary once—our tenth, I believe. You'd have to ask your mother to be sure. I borrowed some room-service silverware as a keepsake, but she insisted it wasn't romantic."

"Can we focus?" Rex grunted.

"Mmm, right," my father replied. "It appears that DIMCO is infiltrating this dimension at a more aggressive rate."

He played the video file. The Royal Oxford was a very old, very ritzy hotel downtown near the train station. Oddly enough, Kevin Flarch's mother had been a maid there for years. On the screen, several men in blue suits were huddled around a podium. I recognized the police chief in uniform and our pale, ginger-haired mayor, who was speaking in an animated manner. His high-pitched voice came through the speakers:

"We have received a credible but highly unspecified threat against the City of Toronto. There is evidence, based on new information provided from an outside agency, that the damage done earlier in the week to our downtown core was perpetrated by a rogue element from the scientific community. The technology used to transplant a national heritage statue is highly advanced. We don't know what they want, but we're sure to track them down very soon."

As the mayor continued on about remaining calm but vigilant my dad muted the sound.

"Gee," I muttered. "I wonder what *outside agency* is being so helpful."

"No need to wonder," Rex replied.

He paused the video link and zoomed in on a face in the background. Despite the picture's graininess the thin moustache, dark, beady eyes, and gaunt contours of the face were instantly recognizable. A thousand marbles tumbled like ice from my brain into my stomach, where they bounced up and down a few times before coming to a heavy rest.

"Ridpath's here," I said.

"The one and only," Rex replied. "He crossed through, which means DIMCO has come up with workable coordinates for at least one other large porthole. I'd like to say we'd come up with similar information, but our man on the spot hasn't been as successful."

My father coughed. "No need to be rude. My current calculations give us an 80–20 chance of navigating two separate portholes. In most areas of life this is an acceptable margin of error, but I don't usually give the green light to anything under a 99.96 rate of probable success when it comes to possible human combustion. That's just me."

"Are you sure that's not *this* dimension's version of Ridpath?" I asked.

Rex shook his head. "Augustus Ridpath in this world is a remarkably *unsuccessful* chicken farmer in the American Midwest. He doesn't even have the Internet. Apparently his great-great-grandfather, Reginald Ridpath, flipped a coin in Bromley on a Sunday afternoon a hundred and twenty years ago. In our dimension, heads came up and he stayed in England and his family line produced the current head of DIMCO. In this dimension, the coin showed tails and Reggie booked a ticket on a fishing vessel for New York. The family has been poor and unremarkable ever since." He turned to my father. "The news fellow said the colonel and the other delegates are staying at the Royal Oxford. Know what I'm thinking?"

"That that's typical of politicians in every dimension," my father said. "They talk about fiscal restraint and then hold all their meetings at the most expensive hotels they can find."

Rex shook his head. "No. I was thinking we should pay the good colonel a visit," he said in a low voice. I sensed he was waiting to be challenged.

"You know Ben Wizard's instructions," my father said quietly. Ben Wizard was the alternative dimension's top scientist and the man who'd gotten Delores, Gus, and me home. For all intents and purposes he was the leader of the resistance movement against DIMCO. "We're to keep a low profile no matter what," my dad continued. "And besides, I can't condone violence, even against a man trying to hunt me down. I'll leave the condoning to other people."

We doubled our packing pace and locked up the house within the hour, certain that very soon strangers would be rifling through our private spaces. The last piece of equipment my dad packed was his paper shredder. He dumped two garbage bags full of confetti by the curb and picked up Skittles on the way back. As the final preparations were in motion, I filled Gus and Delores in on the new developments.

"Shouldn't we try to find the big guy before we get out of Dodge?" Delores asked.

"I think this car's a Hyundai," Gus murmured, looking at the trunk.

"I already asked," I said, turning to Delores and blocking Gus out of view. "I was told that our first priority is relocating to a secure place to live. But I'm with you. We should find a way to rescue Nate. Who knows what they're doing to him right now? Rex said that Ridpath is staying at the Royal Oxford. Maybe we should get into his room and look for clues as to where Nate is being held."

We voiced our concerns in unison but my dad just shook his head and told us to be patient. My parents took the van loaded with gear and we followed in the car. But as we approached the highway Rex drifted the wheel toward the shoulder and jammed on the brakes. He moaned softly and rested his head against his window, his body shuddering in a series of spasms as though he was having a small seizure. To my horror, Delores was doing the same thing in the backseat. Gus looked bewildered.

"I'm okay," Rex said, taking off his dark glasses. "These inhibitors don't work as well away from the house's containment field. Either that or the distortion waves are getting a lot more severe."

"You okay, D?" Gus asked.

"Yeah," Delores replied. "I must have got some reflected wave or something."

A police car rolled by slowly, the constable waving to make sure we were all right. Rex smiled and gave a pleasant thumbs-up, swore gently, then put the car in gear and got back on the road. To my surprise, he pulled into a gas station a minute later and opened the door. He handed me a slip of paper.

"This is the address where you're going. The password is *That was quite a rainstorm we had last week. Good for the farmers, I suppose.* You have to say it with a long, contemplative pause in the middle, like you're making an original and meaningful remark. Your parents should get there before you, but if anything bad happens, you want to talk to Beatrice at the nearest doughnut shop."

"Why wouldn't my parents be at the safe house?" I asked.

He looked out across the pumps. "You know the situation, John. I wouldn't be surprised if we were under surveillance right now. I told your dad we should have moved a week ago, but he wouldn't listen. Now look at the mess we're in from all this piddling about."

I felt my cheeks flush hot. I didn't think it was fair to lay the responsibility on my dad. He'd been working exhausting hours trying to find a new porthole, while Rex had done little more than exercise and complain. But I decided that now wasn't the time to argue.

"Where are you going?" I asked.

"I'm not about to sit back and wait for these waves to break through my inhibitor or for your local police to take me into custody. I plan to test our options."

"You're going to fly through one of the portholes," I said.

"I've done it before with less than an 80–20 chance of success. Remember, I was the best fighter pilot DIMCO ever had. I don't think they've come up with a better replacement since I left. I know all the moves and procedures for inter-dimensional flight. I'll be in touch."

Rex ran over to a cabbie filling up his car and they sped off shortly thereafter. Gus offered to drive, but seeing as he didn't have a licence and had already destroyed one car in Skye not long ago, I got behind the wheel. Delores was looking paler than before, though that could have been the wall of white foundation powder she'd insisted on applying before going out in public.

"You really okay?" I asked.

She slipped off her sunglasses to reveal bloodshot eyes. "I've never felt so crappy in my life, and I ain't a woofin'. I don't think this is just inter-dimensional jetlag. I must've picked up a virus in Scotland, probably from that brown peat water. But I'll be fine."

"At least fatigue makes you less volatile," Gus said. "Maybe not all viruses are bad."

Delores leaned forward. "Keep up your jawing and I'll slap you so hard your clothes will be out of style by the time you stop rolling."

"Ah good, mate. You can't be too sick."

I had an idea. I turned the car around and crossed three lanes, heading back toward the city. Gus looked out the window in puzzlement for a few seconds, but then must have realized where we were headed. He pointed to the CN Tower in the distance—the eternal landmark of Toronto—tapped his nose, and mumbled *Ridpath*. There was no way I could stand going to a safe house while Nate2 lingered in custody somewhere. He'd already been arrested once because of us, and this time I didn't think they'd let him off on the simple belief that he was nuts.

I pulled into the Burger Hut parking lot and hopped out with Gus in tow. Ryan was in the freezer doing stock take, so I didn't have a problem slipping into the kitchen without my uniform.

With the breakfast rush a trickle, Flarch was filling time by aimlessly pulling long brown hairs out of his hairnet and melting them over an open burner flame. As they neared the heat the hairs would begin to bend and curl before suddenly igniting and disappearing into invisible residue. The odour was horrid. Flarch yanked another hair from his head.

"This is what burning bodies smell like," he said. "Except a hundred times worse. They burn people on big bonfires in India. That's the way I want to go."

"Great, Flarch," I replied. "I need a favour."

"You want to swap shifts?"

"Um, not exactly. It's a slightly larger ask."

"You want to date my sister?"

"No."

"Yeah, nobody does … she's a psycho. Who's this guy?"

"Gus Surrey," Gus said. "Of the Brisbane Surreys."

Flarch looked confused.

"I'm from Australia," Gus continued. "But don't ask me to throw a couple shrimp on the barbie or I'll have to thrash you."

Flarch stood completely still and blinked. He looked at me blankly.

"He's my … uh, weird cousin from Down Under," I said.

To his credit, Gus bit his tongue. I outlined the situation to Flarch, leaving out the parts about inter-dimensional travel, Nate2's being an alternate version of my father, and DIMCO. So basically I lied and told him Ridpath was trying to blackmail my father over some stolen technology and that we needed to break into a room at the Royal Oxford with his mother's help.

Flarch clucked his tongue. "Your dad does pretty well for a blind guy. Okay, meet me at my place in an hour. I'll tell General Fish Fingers that I'm sick."

AN HOUR AND A HALF LATER we were sitting on the front step of Flarch's dilapidated apartment building, trying to ignore an old lady on the second floor who kept coming out, leaning off her balcony, and hissing the word *thieves*. I expected her to toss a bucket of water down any minute. The steps were crumbling, papers and cardboard boxes were rotting on the uncut lawn, and the window next to us had been covered in what appeared to be yellowing wax paper. We weren't in Beverly Hills and I supposed stereos had walked out of many of these apartments over the years, so in some way her paranoia was justified. And besides, even I'd be wary of two loitering teenage guys and a dozing Goth.

From a block away a low, pounding bass jangled my body as Flarch came into view in his mom's rusty minivan. The vehicle was rocking back and forth and the glass was quivering. Flarch had invested in a top-of-the-line stereo system with speakers that filled most of the van's trunk. He brought the vehicle to a skidding stop, kicking up a plume of gravel dust, then jerked the parking brake on so hard that the front end jammed to the left on an angle. He hopped out of the van, still wearing his hairnet from work.

"And you call *me* your weird cousin," Gus murmured. "I don't know how cool minivans are in Canada, but in Oz those are

known as family vehicles. They're just not suited to the heavy
metal experience."

"This is your best friend?" Delores asked.

"No," I replied. "I just work with him."

"So where *are* all your friends?" Gus asked. "We've been staying
with you for weeks and I've never even heard you on the phone.
You don't look lame."

"Maybe I'm keeping them away for a reason," I said uncom-
fortably. I didn't want to admit that I wasn't the best at making
friends.

Flarch came to a stop in front of us and looked Delores over
appraisingly. He whistled gently, whispered *Not bad,* then wiggled
his key into the front-door lock, waving to the woman upstairs
who'd come out to stare.

"Come on inside," Flarch said. "Foxy ladies first."

Delores look about to spit. The interior of the building smelled
like old ham bones. Flarch led us up a flight of stairs to his family's
apartment. The place was small and unexpectedly neat. The
furniture looked like it had probably been bought in the 1920s,
but there were covers on the shabbier chairs and a good-size TV.
There were also a fair number of hotel lamps, stationery, and
tablecloths stitched with an ornate RO insignia. They looked well
worn, so I supposed they were discarded items from the hotel
that were no longer needed.

"Hey now," Flarch said, jamming his hand flat against Gus's
chest. "Please take your shoes off at the door. When the government starts vacuuming the streets, then you can wear footwear in
the house."

Gus looked down. "They're clean."

"I'm not sure what excuse you just garbled in that weird,
mouth-full-of-mashed-potatoes accent, but get them off. Things
are probably done differently in your country, but you're in

Canada now, and I don't work all day to come home and clean up after the likes of you."

Flarch said this last part in a high-pitched imitation of his mother, and then laughed hysterically. He swaggered toward his room still wearing his high tops. Gus slipped off his shoes and placed them on a small rack in the hall.

"I'm doing this for his mother," he said. "I feel sorry for her already."

We made our way to Flarch's bedroom, which was exactly what I expected. He had posters of basketball players and swimsuit models on the walls, a small single bed, ancient model planes hanging from the ceiling, and clothes everywhere. If the room was carpeted, I couldn't tell. There was even a dirty white tube sock hanging from his curtain rod.

"I think I'll wait in the living room," Delores muttered.

"We can clear some space," Flarch said.

"No, I wouldn't want to be the first female other than your mother in this room. I'll let some other lucky cowgirl break that record."

Flarch unlocked a drawer and pulled out an assortment of electronic devices. He handed me a piece of white plastic the size of a credit card.

"The maids use these to get into the rooms. They open every door in the Royal Oxford. The sensors record the employees' ID encoded on their card, but this one's a blank extra, so they can't track it to anyone."

"What do you mean by *extra*?" I asked.

"From time to time the cleaners bring in relatives to help out. Maybe they want a half-day off to go to the doctor or something and need to finish their quota of rooms quick. There are a few floating, communal e-keys. I was supposed to give it back, but I guess I forgot. I haven't used it in a few months."

"Are you sure it still works?"

"Don't see why it wouldn't. And that's not all I kept from the hotel." He pointed to his bed. "See those pillows? Christina Aguilera stayed in one of the suites. I haven't even washed them. There's eye shadow stains everywhere."

I had a mental image of Flarch sneaking into various celebrities' rooms and rifling through their underwear drawers, but now wasn't the time for moral judgments. I'd never hung out with him outside the Hut and now I knew why.

"Mind if we have this conversation in the lounge room?" Gus asked, motioning toward the clothes-covered floor and waving a hand in front of his face. "I feel like I'm in someone's armpit. I hear there are some excellent anti-fungal sprays on the market in North America."

Flarch looked at Gus for several long seconds in confusion, and then shook his head. Then he explained that we could find Ridpath's room by going to the sub-basement housekeeping area and checking their daily clipboards for guest names. After all, there was no way the front desk would give us the information. The supervisor, Louise, was usually the only one in the office and was often out on errands or harassing the laundry staff. "If you get nailed in the sub-basement and are likely to get totally busted, you can always say you're looking for my mom. She'll cover for you. But trust me, if you're quiet, you should be able to sneak around without a problem. Most of the regular maids hate their jobs, so they won't snitch on you."

Gus thumbed the plastic access card in his hand. "Amazing. No matter how much security a place has, the greatest weakness is always human error." He turned to Flarch. "I like the way you think, Flinch. You might be a geek, but you're sneaky and underhanded, which I admire."

Flarch shot him a finger gun salute. "I have no idea what you just said, Crocodile Hunter, but right back at you."

He bent down and pulled out a cupboard drawer, exposing a secret compartment. He took out what looked like a heavy black flashlight that had coils instead of a bulb. There was a switch on the side. Flarch explained that it was a Taser that his mom had gotten for self-defence off a guy who worked briefly at the post office. Apparently mailmen were the greatest source for personal defence items, including jalapeño sprays, stun guns, and high-frequency sound emitters, all because of their deep-seated fear of dogs.

"Sounds like you guys could use some backup protection," Flarch said. "Of course, we did pay a lot of money for this thing. It's definitely good in a jam. I don't get any trouble from the pit bull upstairs any more."

"I don't know. I'd rather not—"

"It's an excellent idea," Gus interrupted. He pulled out his wallet and dug around for several familiar-looking red bills. "I'd like to be the one in control of the situation for a change. Do you take British currency?"

Flarch might not have understood Gus, but money was the universal language.

CHAPTER 9

THE ROYAL OXFORD was a tough place to sneak into because the service was too good. As soon as Delores, Gus, and I tumbled through the revolving entrance door a bellhop in a dark blue jacket and peaked cap came rushing over to greet us. He was probably only twenty, but had an intensely formal manner, bowing slightly and standing before us with an attentive, chin-up posture. We hesitated momentarily. Usually this was when Delores would come up with a quick lie, but she was obviously out of practice. I figured our faces might stick in his mind if we ran out, so we reluctantly wandered farther into the opulent lobby. Around us were gleaming copper railings, antique leather chairs, and a plush red carpet that our feet sank into like soft grass.

"May I help you?" the bellhop asked.

Gus looked at Delores, realized she had nothing, then turned to the bellhop and began rambling in an Australian accent much thicker than usual. "I reckon!" he shouted. "If you wouldn't mind, mate. Our luggage is in the taxi and our driver seems a bit *aggro*. The travel agent said the Lambert Arms was a *bewdie,* but this is absolutely *fab-o*. Makes the Crown Plaza look like Meekatharra, if you know what I mean. Way out past the black stump. Biggest flies I've ever seen—like golf balls with wings. I'm gob-smacked we get a kip in this place for fifty-nine bucks a night."

The bellhop's smile half-wilted, but he politely pried it up. "Um, this is the Royal Oxford Hotel. The Lambert Arms is several blocks north, near College station, next to a men's entertainment complex."

"Fair dinkum," Gus said. "I should have known. You don't get this kind of deal on Telstra travel points, now do you?"

"Uh, I wouldn't know."

"That's our phone company," Gus continued absently, running a finger along the gleaming copper railing. "Back home in good old Oz. Crikey I miss the red earth and boundless skies of my native homeland. And of course the sausage rolls. Been away almost fifty-two hours now. Don't know how I'm going to make it. Mind if we have a Captain Cook to see how the snobs live?"

The bellhop's mouth hung open stupidly. "I'm sorry, but I have no idea what you're talking about."

"No one here does," I said.

"He's wondering if we can have a look around," Delores said.

"Like Captain Cook," Gus continued. "The explorer who discovered my fine homeland. Well, he discovered the place several thousand years after the Aborigines, but we won't get into that now."

Gus's abnormal intensity appeared to scare the bellhop, who waved his hands and scampered off to greet more sophisticated guests. I could only assume Gus's run-in with Flarch had prompted the strategy. We strolled around like country bumpkins, pointing at vases and chandeliers.

"That's a bit dodgy for this place," Gus said loudly.

"Laying it on a bit thick, aren't you?" Delores murmured.

"Do you see anyone making eye contact?"

He had a point. If anything, the staffers were treating us as an unpleasant odour that would hopefully soon dissipate. I wondered what exactly he'd said in his own vernacular. Gus cooed excitedly that the place had a Jacuzzi.

"I've heard about them things," he said to a nearby clerk. "It's supposed to be like a big bathtub. Mind if we—"

"Sure," the guy replied. "Take a Captain Cook, *quickly,* but you can't use it. The facilities are for paying guests only. Then promise you'll go."

"Absolutely," Gus said. "On my honour. Have a good one, mate."

We crushed into an elevator going up, hopped off on the recreation mezzanine, then slipped into a service elevator by swiping the staff security card Flarch had passed along, which thankfully still worked. We arrived at the sub-basement and poked our heads out cautiously from between the doors.

The contrast was unreal. Gone were the posh carpets and all the other trappings of wealth, replaced by a dimly lit concrete passageway that was stuffy with heat, humidity, and the faint smell of mildew. From the rumble of machines, I figured we were near the laundry area. Above the din a woman's gravelly voice was spewing abuse. We hurried in the opposite direction under smashed light bulbs, passing random piles of plastic-wrapped napkins, tablecloths, and linen. There were stacks of single-serve jams and instant coffee, spare teapots, toothbrushes, and cleaning supplies. It was as if an army was being readied to move out.

Around the next corner, two women in pale blue uniforms came out of a glass-walled room and shuffled away toward a stairwell. We snuck down the hall and peered into what was clearly housekeeping's command central. Filthy desks were covered in invoices and a little tinny radio was playing a talk radio program about downtown traffic congestion. Lines of clipboards were hung on the wall next to a shelf piled with manila time cards. Seeing no one, I slipped into the room and began to rifle through the room information as Gus and Delores kept a lookout at the entrance for Louise. I started from the top level down and was at the fortieth floor when a thick-boned woman with a grey pony-tail and a red, veined face emerged from a door near the far end of the room. She was carrying a large insulated mug of coffee. I froze.

"Who the hell are you?" she barked.

"I'm—"

"New!" Delores interrupted, coming into the office. "Are you Louise?"

"Yeah."

"So who was abusing the laundry staff down the hall?" Gus asked.

Delores subtly stepped backward onto his shoe and ground her thick heel into his foot. Gus winced and yelped, then took a step back into the door frame, tripped over a box of individual peanut butter servings, and toppled into the hallway. I took the opportunity to flip to the thirty-ninth floor and found Col. A. Ridpath.

"We were sent down about some upcoming work," Delores said. "From the front desk."

Louise's eyes narrowed. "The Royal Oxford don't hire internally. We have an agency that provides people. How'd you get down here?"

"Slipped in through the service elevator," Gus said, getting up.

Louise didn't appear surprised. She picked up the phone on her desk and tapped a couple digits. She took a long drink from her coffee, dribbled some down her chin, and wiped her lips with the back of a liver-spotted hand.

"You might want to get the hell out," she said. "I'm calling security."

We raced back the way we'd come. As we passed a cupboard of folded laundry, Delores swiped three uniforms and shoved them into her bag. We stepped into the service elevator and I pressed the button for the thirty-ninth floor. After we passed the fourteenth Delores hit the emergency stop button on the panel. We came to a jerking halt as she reached for her bag.

"I'm not wearing a uniform," Gus said. "So don't even bother pulling those out. I don't care who's looking for us."

"Honestly, Gus, dealing with you is like trying to herd cats. Just the shirt."

"Forget it. If I get shot breaking into Ridpath's room and my body gets splashed across the evening news in that cheap polyester gear, I'll never live it down. It would be my Year 11 ball all over again."

I raised my eyebrow. Gus licked his lips self-consciously.

"Had a minor accident involving contraband beverages, a really annoyed date, and an ostrich. It's better not to ask. My boarding school was in a rural area."

"You're putting it on," Delores said. "We need cover."

"No way. I'll look ridiculous."

"You'd rather let DIMCO torture Nate than look silly?"

Gus squirmed as she stepped closer, pressing him against the mirrored elevator wall, and took the shirt. He was right. The uniforms did look stupid, especially since mine was far too small and stretched painfully across the chest. The buttons were straining against the polyester fabric, threatening to shoot off like plastic sparks at any moment. We decided that, in the interest of stealth and cunning, Gus and I should remain in our street clothes.

Delores made us turn around as she put her outfit on. I wondered where security might begin looking for us. Hopefully the thirty-ninth floor wouldn't be their starting point. Finally Delores let us turn back around. The uniform coupled with the Doc Martens, black hair, sunglasses, and thick, dark makeup made her look as though she was on her way to a Halloween party. Still, she managed to make the skirt look good. I felt a twist in my stomach and wondered why she resisted a softer appearance and insisted on the rabid raccoon look all the time. She had surprisingly nice, toned legs.

"Looking at something?" she barked.

"Your shoes are a bit of a giveaway," I mumbled. "They don't look like they'd be good for scrubbing bathtubs."

"Doc Martens are the best money can buy. And the traction is perfect for slippery surfaces. I'm a progressive maid."

We put the elevator back into service, got out, and hurried down the hall to 3909 where a DO NOT DISTURB sign was hanging from the doorknob. No guards were around, so my body pumped some eager endorphins into my bloodstream. Delores flicked the sign onto the carpet, handed me her sunglasses, and knocked on the door.

"Housekeeping. I'm here to pick up your crap."

We waited for several long, super-still moments, Delores leaning close to the wood. She shook her head to indicate no signs of life, and so I passed her the swipe card. She was just about to move it across the scanner when the door jerked open. Gus and I pressed up against the hallway wall out of view, standing on our tiptoes and trying to melt into the wallpaper. I heard the security chain rattle as a deep voice filled the air.

"Get away from here," it barked. "We don't want to be bothered. Can't you read, chick?"

"Um, no, I can't," Delores replied. "But thank you for asking. I dropped out of school when I was seven to help support my family in San Antonio. Now can I *please* come in and clean your toilet?"

"There was a DO NOT DISTURB sign on the doorknob. Where'd it go?"

"Kids probably took it. They do that sort of thing, being little animals and all … I've got four. Had the twins when I was fifteen. How about I give the room a quick once-over? Reusing dirty towels is a good way to spread disease, especially with the filthy air conditioning system in this hotel."

"The what?"

Delores was casually craning her neck around, no doubt trying to see who else might be in the room. She began to cough, waving her hand back and forth around the crack of the door. She moaned what sounded like *airborne virus,* swooned slightly, and crumpled to the floor, strategically exposing a fair amount of pale thigh. At least, I hoped it was all an act, and not a result of her recent illness and fatigue. The guy in Ridpath's room didn't unlock the door and come out to help. Instead, like a perfect gentleman, he stretched his leg through the crack and kicked her gently several times.

"Wake up and get lost."

The nudging continued as he tried to roll her away from the door with the toe of his shoe. He lacked the leverage though, and finally, with a hard sigh, the door slammed, the chain slid open, and an enormous pair of shoulders descended to pick Delores up. The man's back was like a three-hundred-year-old tortoise dressed in a black blazer. His head was bigger than a basketball.

He got the first Taser blast right in the teeth.

"Kick me with your dirty foot, will you?" Delores shouted.

The man reeled back holding his face as Delores zapped him a few more times in the chest, neck, and private parts. She had a weird smile on the last zap. Then, holding Flarch's Taser with a shaking arm, she followed as Gus and I threw ourselves on the giant and forced him back into the room. It was like hitting a car, but somehow we managed to pull him down. We slammed the door as the sound of curious guests filled the hallway. No doubt they'd phone the desk and get security too. The man made a move to rise to his feet, but Delores gave him an extra long blast of juice and Gus brought a lamp down on his huge skull. He slumped against the mini bar and twitched, unconscious.

"Probably used up the batteries with that trigger-happy display," Gus remarked.

"Big deal," Delores said. "I'm satisfied. You know, this lying business gets a lot easier the more you do it. I was basically honest before all this inter-dimensional stuff started happening, but now I open my mouth and can talk crap with ease."

"I thought you always talked crap," Gus said.

"Hurry up," I urged. "We've got to find a clue about the big guy's location."

I rifled through the desk. Delores was busy wiping dusty shoe prints off her blue smock. Only when she looked up did she pause and smile. We turned to follow her gaze and spotted a large torso duct-taped to an Edwardian chair with a lampshade covering his face. An inch of coloured goatee hung below.

"Nate!"

In our enthusiasm to free him, when we yanked off the tape we accidentally removed most of the hair around his wrists. Luckily the sock taped into his mouth muffled his screams. The parts of his moustache at the corners of his lips also stuck to the adhesive strips, leaving him looking like the moulting radioactive squirrel from Queen's Park. Though temporarily dazed, he was clearly glad to see us. He rubbed his tongue along his sleeve.

"That'll teach me to wear the same socks for three consecutive days without a wash." He held the soggy item in his fingertips, then shrugged and slipped it onto his bare foot. "I don't suppose there are any of those little complimentary breath mints around. Or how about a nice cup of tea?"

Nate2 stiffened as Delores wrapped him in a hug, but grinned politely and patted her gently on the shoulder. I handed him a mint from a small bowl on the dresser, which he popped into his mouth with a thankful smile. He got up slowly, wobbled, and nearly fell over, grabbing at the TV set that was thankfully bolted onto the chesterfield. I supposed he must have been in the chair for about a day.

"I think my muscles have atrophied," he mumbled. "There go my Olympic hopes."

"We've got to get out of here," I began. "There's a safe house—"

"Is there?"

The voice came from behind us, at the door. The tricky thing about electronic scanners is there's no warning sound of a key turning in a lock—and we hadn't thought to reattach the chain. Standing at the entrance were Ridpath and a second beefy security type even larger than the mammoth crumpled on the floor. Once again I was struck by the cat-food odour and by how small and dark Ridpath's eyes were, as well as that cheesy, overly manicured moustache. Really, what possessed a man to have a little caterpillar of hair crawling across his upper lip? You'd have to be mental; which, granted, he sort of was.

They closed the door and took a step forward. Nate2 threw his soggy complimentary mint in their direction, missing by several feet and hitting a porcelain vase instead. Delores pointed the Taser, shielding us as we instinctively moved back toward the window. I wondered if we could crawl out, sidle across the ledge, and find a rooftop stairwell down to street level. Gus must have had the same idea because he was fumbling with the curtain strings. Unfortunately, the Royal Oxford had undergone renovations over its long and storied history, and the windows weren't the type that opened more than six inches. I guessed they didn't want people falling or hurling themselves out.

At first Ridpath laughed at Delores's meagre defence, but as he looked to the guard on the floor his smile disappeared and he narrowed his gaze. If he squinted any more his eyes would be completely closed. As it was, he looked like a rat unused to the light.

"There's no need for violence," he said calmly. "We're very willing to negotiate. Put down the weapon and let's talk about this unfortunate situation. We've all got issues and agendas that can be resolved in peace. Everyone can gain if we're sensible."

"Who are you, Dr. Phil?" Delores said.

Ridpath tilted his head quizzically.

"Never mind," Delores continued. "He might not have made it to your dimension. Count your lucky stars. But don't give me that psychobabble."

"Quite right," Nate2 remarked. "He said the same thing to me before I got in his car, and look where I ended up. As soon as I let down my guard those oafs were beating my legs with a rubber baton. A man's word is supposed to be his bond."

"We thought you were someone else," Ridpath remarked. "If I had known you were so completely useless, you and your wretched-smelling hamburgers could have kept walking."

"They wouldn't happen to still be around, would they?" Nate2 asked, craning his neck. "I'm awfully peckish after being strapped into that chair for a day without food. I've spent the last several hours thinking about a roast lamb dinner, with baby peas and mint sauce."

"Do shut up," Ridpath said calmly. "I wouldn't want to have to jam *two* socks into that enormous gullet next time."

"You're not going to touch him," Delores said. "Step into the bathroom and lock the door or you'll end up like your friend on the floor. He screamed pretty loudly when I got him in the family jewels."

Ridpath giggled in an almost silly way. He looked down at the comatose security guard and nearly doubled over in laughter. Then he took a long, deep inhalation through his flared nostrils and fingered the flowered wallpaper near his left shoulder.

"How excellent," he said. "I always enjoy a David versus Goliath battle, though I do find that in reality the underdog rarely wins. I'd say you used up a lot of power demobilizing Leonard. That Taser can't have a great capacity."

"Leonard?" Gus said. "No wonder that guy went down like a load of bricks. You'd think he'd go by something more menacing, like Vinny or Heinrich or even some ironic nickname like Tiny."

"I see you're wearing socks as well," Ridpath murmured. "I hope for your sake they're laundered. Alfie, subdue the idiotic one, knock out the big clown again, lock the girl in the cupboard, and leave the small Fitzgerald lad to me."

"Alfie," Gus murmured. "That's a better name …"

Delores tried to zap Alfie as he rocked forward, his arms arched like crab claws and his fists like cannon balls. He danced away from the first couple stings, grunting loudly, but the Taser was clearly losing its strength. The third crack of blue electricity caught him on the hand and he barely flinched. Behind me Nate2 began to moan, echoing how I felt. Though Delores was still prodding with her weapon she was stumbling backward, swaying unsteadily before falling at my feet. As Alfie bent to pick up the fallen Taser Delores grabbed my ankle and Gus's pant leg and I felt a sickening drop in my stomach, followed by a spasm of dizziness. But for the first time ever I welcomed a distortion wave. As Gus turned to snag Nate2's beard, a barking Ridpath faded from view and all went black.

CHAPTER 10

I WOKE UP feeling light-headed, and vaguely liked the feeling. For a few seconds I couldn't seem to open my eyes or move my body. I had the sensation of being cocooned in a great warm and slimy place. But it wasn't uncomfortable. If anything, I felt protected and secure. I sat for a few minutes waiting for the wave's lingering effects to pass, slowly coming to the panicked conclusion that I *really* wasn't myself. I felt this way for a few simple reasons, the first being that I no longer had arms and legs. With a frantic start, I wiggled my head around and discovered that I was stuck to some sort of hard casing.

I craned my neck toward a sliver of light, felt a wet pop along the back of my skull, and was instantly blinded. Illumination burned my closed eyelids like firecrackers exploding on my skin. Colours swirled from red to yellow to purple before calming. When my eyes had adjusted I looked down to see dirt and what appeared to be a spinning grey rock just below my chin. I tried to twist but my skin seemed to be locked into place, fused against the cave my head had emerged from. I extended my neck as far as possible—amazed that it seemed so elastic—and peered from side to side. My breath caught and I swallowed hard. Below me was a twirling shell. I pivoted and noticed two dangling flaps of grey that looked suspiciously like antennae.

I couldn't believe it. I had turned into a snail.

Around me sprawled a glorious garden full of enormous

flowers and budding trees and birds. It was a perfect spring day. An orange-and-black-winged butterfly the size of a pterodactyl fluttered by as I tried like hell to figure out what my stupid mind had been thinking when the distortion hit. As if in response, I heard Nate2 speak.

"Hello little rabbit," he said. "Don't suppose you're going to murder me. Have you perhaps seen two blokes and a chambermaid around here anywhere?"

I tilted my long, wet neck to see Nate2 sitting next to a brown rabbit that was sniffing the air intently. The rabbit looked up at Nate2 and then began to beat its leg against the ground in varying intervals. The ground beneath me shook.

"Morse code, eh?" Nate2 said. "Impressive. Aren't you a smart little fluffball? My moniker is Nate Fitzgerald and I'd like to point out straightaway that I've never been one for jugged hare or rabbit stew. Can't stand the stuff. You're much too gamy for me, so I won't be catching, skinning, and roasting you despite my severe hunger. Don't suppose you've got a carrot lying around."

Nate2 made to get up when the rabbit tapped out another message, this time quicker and more forcefully. It continued to tap out its message as several other bunnies emerged from the leaves and bushes of the garden.

"I'm *not* being condescending," Nate2 replied.

The rabbit stopped for a few seconds to nibble on a piece of vegetation and then turned to two of the larger rabbits. He shook his ears. They bowed slightly, hopped into a bush, and re-emerged a second later with a small laptop computer, which they dragged across the grass. The main rabbit turned from the keyboard and kicked the keys in a blur of motion. An electronic voice came from the tinny speakers.

"I am Jib-Jib-ner, Grand Ruler of Rabbits. This name translates into English as Floppy Ears. Personally, I don't care for the name, but you know how parents can be. We have several issues to discuss with humans and are now ready to enter into negotiations."

I couldn't help but marvel at the eccentricity of Nate2's brain. How he went from being held hostage in a hotel room in a dimension not his own to thinking about rabbits with inter-species concerns to work out was beyond me. But then, I'd somehow ended up as a snail, so maybe our subconscious minds were to blame.

Jib-Jib-ner outlined what could constitute a manifesto, including such issues as the incarceration of wild cats, copyright infringement, and land claims for the states of Maine, Massachusetts, and New York, which Jib-Jib-ner insisted had originally been settled by rabbits. Nate2 looked distressed. I tried to shout, hoping to get his attention so that we could get out of this reality distortion, but I only spit up slime. My throat was full of the stuff.

"Really," Nate2 began. "I'm not sure I can be of much help. I'd say you need someone with a law degree, or perhaps a highly articulate veterinarian. Though honestly, I suggest you bunnies save yourself a great deal of bother and maintain your cuddly demeanour. Political power plays degrade us all."

Jib-Jib-ner typed out another remark with extreme vigour.

"No need for rudeness," Nate2 replied.

As the discussions went on, I realized that my only chance at resolving my distortion and getting back to reality was to make contact. Snails generally aren't noticed unless someone wants to poison them in the garden or has accidentally crushed one underfoot.

I made an attempt to move forward and was amazed at how it felt to contract my foot muscle, flex my slime duct, and propel along a pool of my own juices. After several hard pumps I managed to go almost half an inch. I laughed a strange, low-pitched gurgle and realized I was moving at a *snail's pace*.

After five minutes I'd probably moved half a foot into some rather tall grass. I was exhausted. I could feel the ground vibrating steadily, but couldn't get a good look at Nate2. My duct ached and my muscles were cramping. I wanted to contract my long neck and rest in my shell. The situation was hopeless. Even if I did manage to get close to Nate2, I had no way of getting his attention. For the first time a shiver of fear went through my gelatinous body. There was a real possibility that I might never escape this fragment of existence.

Suddenly a great pressure pressed against my shell. I let out a gurgling scream as a giant human hand reached down and picked me up. A massive eye loomed, casting a shadow across my entire body, and then the face moved away and spoke.

"For heaven's sake, tell me that's not really you?" Delores said.

I made a sloppy, exciting shout. When she didn't react, I nodded my long, grey neck to indicate yes. She handed me to Gus, who was laughing crazily. The vibrations felt like an earthquake and I had to fight my instinct not to panic.

"I recognized the markings on your shell," Gus said. "Don't see many snails with a Reebok symbol on their back. And, like I speculated to D, I was pretty sure Ridpath's *small* comment would stick out in your mind."

Aha.

I could see that we were hiding behind a bush and wondered why they hadn't attracted Nate2's attention so that we could get out of here. Then, with dizzying force, Gus turned me around and I was horrified to see hundreds—or maybe thousands—of little furry bunnies of various sizes dancing and hopping around to the beat of thumping back feet. In the middle of this bizarre scene sat Nate2, starkly pale and paralyzed by the swarm of fur. It was as if he'd become surrounded by an angry ocean of hopping fluffy paws. Long ears bounced through the frenzy like sharks' fins.

"Hmm," Delores began. "I don't have much experience with rabbits, but they're not usually this aggressive. He must have really pissed them off. I suppose we should go kick butt, but there's something strangely disturbing about running through a garden beating up fuzzy bunnies."

"Aren't Goths into that sort of thing?" Gus asked.

"You like your teeth?"

"Sorry, I didn't mean to offend you. I just assumed that your people would start off with the makeup and boots, move on to the aggressive attitude, and eventually graduate to robbing senior citizens and painting pentangles on your lounge-room walls. I figured there was a set progression, or maybe badges, like with the Boy Scouts."

"Where do you get your prejudiced ideas?" Delores snapped.

"Ex-girlfriend. Long story. Maybe she wasn't typical."

I let out an extra-long stream of slime, which seemed to get Gus's attention. He handed me back to Delores and wiped his hand down the length of his jeans. I had no idea whether these two had already overcome their parts of the distortion and figured swift action was needed before the situation became even more complicated. Besides, for all we knew, Ridpath could have some way of breaking into our wave. My dad had done it the last time, so the technology had been invented.

"Johnny's got a rather constipated look on his face," Gus said. "I've seen it before when he gets impatient, though he's not usually this grey and ugly. I suppose we should get the tail-booting party started. Person who kicks the least bunnies buys breakfast."

With a burst of rage, we jumped out from behind the bush, began to scream wildly, and ran full-steam toward the crowd—or at least they did. In the confusion, the thumping music stopped and the rabbits panicked. Many froze—pretending to be statues—while others scampered quickly away with their cotton tails bobbing like frantic Ping-Pong balls. I was surprised that we reached Nate2 without a fight. Despite their feints of aggression, when it comes down to the crunch, bunnies, like most herbivores, appeared to be essentially passive creatures. As Gus made to speak, my vision swirled as though I was being pulled down a whirlpool and for a second my whole being seemed to switch off.

I woke up lying on a city sidewalk, back to my normal size, Feeling nauseated, I turned and threw up a stomach full of thick, clear mucus. Then I heaved several more times, the texture and acidic taste coating every taste bud on my tongue. I felt a hand slap gently on my back and finally looked up to see Delores staring down sympathetically.

"If it makes things better," she began, "I feel like you sound."

"Where are we?"

"I have no idea. I'm from America. I've been in bed for three weeks. This is your city."

"But we're out of the garden, right?"

"Just like Adam and Eve."

It took me a few seconds to get my bearings, but the candy shop on the corner finally clued me in. We were near College subway station at the Lambert Arms hotel. I could only guess that our minds had chosen the best option in our thoughts as to where to spit us back into reality. I shivered, hugging my body tightly for warmth. Not only had I spewed slime, but a thin layer was still coating my arms. That was weird. Usually when we broke out of a distortion reality, all parts of that other world disappeared. I patted my back and shoulder and was glad to find the shell gone.

Gus sauntered over, stuffing a sausage loaded with sauerkraut and raw onions into his mouth. "These hot dog carts are fantastic," he said, motioning to a silver stand shaded by a red sun umbrella. "They're an extremely convenient way to slide into

obesity. Of course, what I could really kill for is a meat pie. Maybe
I'll start an Aussie pastry cart when I get back to Brisbane." He
chewed and swallowed hard, then borrowed a pen from Delores
and began to jot down notes on his ketchup-stained napkin. He
made a quick mock sketch of the cart and drew a giant pie with
an arrow next to it.

"How did you two overcome your reality distortions?" I asked.

"I ended up in a pool full of baby electric eels," Gus murmured.
"Luckily the water wasn't deep and the eels were in a good mood.
I suppose my mind was concentrating on the electric Taser when
the wave hit."

Delores was thumbing her belt and looking preoccupied. I ran
a hand through my hair and wasn't at all surprised to find it gooey
and gross. Gus handed me a second napkin, but it didn't soak up
much liquid.

"D here met up with an old flame," Gus said. "She has some
truly suspect taste in men."

"I thought we weren't going to talk about that," she murmured.

"Johnny asked. Besides, you can always take consolation in the
fact that love is blind. Or in your case deaf, dumb, and pretty
much completely paralyzed. What were you thinking dating that
loser?"

"Larry wasn't *that* bad. He was older than me and I was
impressed by his worldliness. He was twenty and I was fourteen.
He had a car. You can't underestimate the importance of personal
transportation in my home state. We have real hot summers."

"Hotter than a goat's butt in a pepper patch?" Gus asked.

Delores looked confused. "You burn your throat on that hot
dog?"

"No," Gus replied. "I'm trying to understand your culture and
language. I even listened to the Dixie Chicks. You should be flattered instead of looking at me like a cowboy farting in church."

"I don't talk like that," she said.

"You do or my horse is a dog in a big fur jacket."

"You're making these sayings up." Delores shook her head and muttered something under her breath. *Honestly* was all I could understand. She turned to me. "I have no idea why Larry popped up in my mind. I had a hard time getting rid of him when we were dating."

"What'd you do?"

"I was just totally reasonable with him. I explained that I was in high school, he was way older, and that we'd never grow together as a couple. I also mentioned that my dad wasn't impressed. But he really came to see my point of view when my cousin Joe visited him with a Louisville Slugger."

"Is that a cocktail?" Gus asked.

"No, it's a baseball bat," Delores replied. "Don't worry. Joe didn't hit him with it. He just sort of intimidated him and broke his headlights."

I smiled weakly and thought perhaps her dark vibe ran through the whole family. Although essentially good-hearted and truly loyal, maybe she wasn't the right person for me to get involved with romantically. Not that I had plans. I felt my cheeks begin to heat up as we glanced at each other in silence.

"Don't suppose you had a Louisville Slugger in your distortion?" I asked.

"No." Delores said. "Larry wasn't a real muscular guy, so Gus just pushed him into the eel pool. We figured he was a figment of my imagination and interstellar energy, so he wouldn't really get hurt. And they were small eels."

Gus made the final notes on his napkin, tucked it into his pocket, and handed Delores her pen. He wiped crumbs from his hands and sat down beside me. The summer humidity seemed greater than usual and my shirt was soaked. People walking by were either looking at me in horror or acting as though I didn't exist. They probably thought I was some street kid freaked out on drugs. A line of thick goop rolled down the side of my cheek. Delores pretended not to notice as I quickly wiped it away.

"You all right, mate?" Gus asked. "You seem to be lubricating."

"It must be residual slime from the distortion. I'll be fine. Where's Nate?"

"Went to the bar on the corner," Gus replied. "Said he needed a scotch and some crisps. I suppose we should be responsible, find him, and make a move away from this place. I had no idea that when the bellhop said the Lancaster Arms was near a *men's entertainment centre* that he meant a seedy strip club."

Delores offered me a hand up, then looked at my moist palm, thought better of it, and went off to retrieve our alternative-dimension friend on her own. Gus made a *tsk* sound as we watched her disappear into a nearby English-style pub.

"I don't think the mucus is doing it for her," he said. "I've been sitting back watching you two skirt around the L-O-V-E issue since you met, and I have to say the lack of progress makes me despair."

"I'm not in love with Delores."

"I didn't say love. But you've definitely got the hots for her. I caught you eyeing that maid uniform. And Johnny, I also know from my vast experience how hard it is for a single guy to make a move on a strong woman. When you haven't dated for a while you feel ugly and geeky and uncomfortable. Let's face it, you feel like a loser."

"Thanks. And by the way, you did say love."

Gus tilted his head philosophically and put his hand on his chin. "Oh right. I spelled it. Regardless, attraction is the way of the world. And a body coated in slime doesn't help those feelings of inadequacy. Dating is so weird. When things are bad you feel like a repulsive, unworthy slug, or snail even. But then when you do get a girlfriend all those worries disappear and you get cocky, way too loud, and begin to think you're really good looking. Take that a step farther and you inevitably screw things up by flirting with her best friend at a birthday party."

"What are you talking about?" I asked.

"Ex-girlfriend. Long story. I'll tell you later. As for D, if you're going to make a move, why don't you pretend this is a reality distortion and she's not real? That way failure doesn't matter."

"That's not bad advice," I mumbled. "Not that I'm interested."

"Yeah, well … In case you do get keen, try not to spew up a bellyful of slime in front of her again. That wasn't pretty."

"I had just metamorphosed from being a snail!"

A couple stepped off the sidewalk and moved past us in a wide, safe arc. I attempted to stand and felt a sharp jab in my thigh. In my pocket were Delores's sunglasses, which she'd handed me in the hotel hall before knocking on Ridpath's door. I noticed that they had a pulsing red light on the inside of one arm. That was strange …

We went into the pub and found Nate2 on a stool, slumped onto the bar guzzling a tumbler full of amber liquid and surrounded by empty chip packages.

"Hey, slow down on that stuff," I said, pointing to his glass. "You're too big to carry out of here if you're drunk."

"It's iced tea," Nate2 replied. "I decided scotch on an empty stomach was a bad idea. Besides, I'm light-headed and confused enough without the help of alcohol. Typically, navigating the aisles of my local grocery store causes me extreme stress, never mind these distortions."

Gus ordered a bourbon, was asked for ID, didn't argue, and settled down with a cola. Though the booths and decor were reminiscent of an English pub, the place was distinctly North

American. Baseball games were playing on several TVs and posters for Canadian brands of beer hung on the walls. Dangerous as our situation was, I was still glad to be in my own country, surrounded by familiar things.

Nate2 followed my glance around the place. "They'd be hard-pressed to stick maple leaves on any more surfaces," he said. "Not to mention the copious beavers. I thought you people were supposed to be a humble race. Every Canadian I've met has mentioned that they're not patriotic, and yet here I am in a national shrine. Explain the rationale of having a boat hung from the rafters."

I looked up at a canoe suspended by wire near a bearskin rug tacked to the wood-panelled wall. I guess we did have quite a few symbols of national pride.

"You've even got a beer named *Canadian*," Nate2 said. "Talk about self-obsession."

"What's your point?" I asked.

Nate2 rubbed his face with both hands and moaned. "My point is that after those rabbits, I have a great urge to go home to my dull and uneventful life. I'm pining to sit and read for the entire day without getting accosted by woodland creatures or public statues. I'd give anything for a miserable grey afternoon, driving rain, and a stiff, bracing English wind."

"What happened to your thirst for great adventure?"

He looked into his iced tea and didn't say a word. I ordered a ginger ale to get the congealed gloop out of my mouth, reached for the glass, and felt it slip through my slick fingers onto the floor. Shards of glass and sugary liquid exploded in all directions and I felt my cheeks grow hot with each turning glance. No matter how many times I wiped, I couldn't get my palm completely dry.

A SHORT TIME LATER we returned to the car and made the long trip to the safe house, none of us saying much. Considering how tired I felt from all the spent adrenalin and stress of transforming, I could only wonder how Delores managed to stay awake given her condition. She was pasty and glassy eyed, but didn't complain once.

We had some trouble finding the safe house, mainly because we were looking for an actual *house*. Instead, the address on the paper Rex had given us corresponded to a beauty salon on the side of a four-lane highway, in the middle of a strip mall in desperate need of a paint job. The parking lot was full of holes and the illuminated signs were missing half their bulbs. Clearly DIMCO had a much bigger budget than the ragtag rebellion we had joined.

"Betty's House of Loveliness," I read out. "This beauty salon appears to … uh, be our safe house."

"At least there's a special on acrylic nails," Gus murmured. "Maybe I'll get a pedicure while I wait for DIMCO to break down the door."

"Don't mock a pedicure," Nate2 replied. "Keeping your toenails in good condition is vitally important. Trench foot killed more men in the First World War than German artillery, you know. And besides, there's nothing more relaxing than a large Eastern European woman scrubbing your cuticles."

The three of us made a spontaneous *eeeeewww* sound and got out of the car before we could hear more. The windows of Betty's place were dimmed with dust, and a flimsy piece of paper on the door announced BACK IN 5 MINUTES—GONE TO TOILET. The shops on either side were empty, their windows covered in crusty adhesive-tape residue and realty signs. I supposed this was a good enough cover, seeing as no one who cared about beauty would come to a place like this. I noted that the only outlet actually doing business was a lonely doughnut shop full of men in plaid jackets. We wandered around the plaza to the back, looking for an entrance.

Sure enough, there was a steel door with the address freshly painted in black. I rang the buzzer and waited, glancing around for any sign of my parents' van. The silence crept into my skin, spreading out like a cold hand that swept along my spine and into my chest. I told myself that they'd probably hidden the van for security purposes. Or maybe this was the wrong place. Rex could have taken the address down wrong, which would be a problem, but not a tragedy. My dad would figure out the mistake.

Nate2 put his large hand on my shoulder and shifted me toward Delores, whose look wasn't comforting. She swallowed and put her arm around me as Nate2 levelled his shoulder against the door. He winced as his body collided with the steel.

Gus tapped him on the other shoulder and reached for the doorknob. "The door opens outward," he said. "And it doesn't appear to be locked. Someone's used a modified hacksaw blade, a torque wrench, and some spray oil to pick the deadbolt. They're left handed. You can tell by the upward-arched marks. Bit sloppy, but I'd say it took them no more than seven seconds."

I bolted past them, not even thinking that the place might be booby-trapped or that DIMCO could be waiting inside. My mind didn't care about logic, only information about my parents. My dad had said that he trusted only a few people in his circle of contacts. I wondered if the situation had made him confide in the wrong one. The hallway opened into a big storage room that had been completely ransacked. Mattresses, lamps, mannequins, and boxes of wires were strewn across the floor among old wigs and acrylic nails that looked like a thousand white plastic cockroaches. A desk in the corner was covered in dust except for the visible outline of a now disappeared computer.

Across the hall was a small, filthy bathroom. The porcelain was grey with dirt and the rancid toilet was overflowing gently, creating a shallow pool of sulphur-smelling water on the cracked tile floor. Gus craned his neck around the door frame.

"Nice," he said. "DIMCO breaks in, ransacks the place, and someone decides to have an enormous poo to clog the toilet before leaving. Can't say they aren't professionals."

"Unless that's not human excrement blocking the loo," Nate2 murmured. "Perhaps someone has tried unsuccessfully to flush a vital piece of evidence. That sign out front advising us that someone had gone to the toilet could be a clue."

Gus swept his hand toward the overflowing mess. "You should probably reach in and see what you find."

"You have thinner arms. You can get up the drain farther."

I left the debate in progress and wandered to the front room. The shop looked like it had once been a working salon, but from the amount of dust on everything I could tell it hadn't been in business in months, if not years. There were a few swipes through the layers of grime, as though hands had been run across the odd shelf and counter, but mostly the place was undisturbed. I wondered what had happened and figured we should probably leave soon in case the shop was being watched or the assailants came back for another look around. I realized that my head and cheeks were throbbing with pain, thanks largely to the fact that I was grinding my teeth together. I'd heard about people having to wear mouth guards to bed for this sort of thing, to prevent them from breaking their teeth or wearing them down to jagged stumps. I took a deep breath, picked up a mannequin head at my feet, then spun around and threw it hard against the concrete wall. Gus shrieked and ducked out of the way. I hadn't heard him come into the room behind me. Skin-coloured plastic exploded everywhere, spinning and sliding across the long hallway.

"You almost took my eye out with a fragment of ear!" he shouted as Delores and Nate2 flew into the room. "I realize you're upset, but there's no need to physically impair me with jagged plastic!"

"They've taken my parents," I replied. "Sorry if I'm upset. I wasn't throwing the mannequin at you. And even if I were, that ricochet didn't come that close."

"Oh my god!" Nate2 said suddenly. "They've taken Helen!"

The rest of us paused as Nate2 chewed his lip and rapidly yanked at his beard. He seemed lost in thought. Panicked scenarios were no doubt racing through his brain. He looked down at me.

"And your father too," he mumbled.

"There's no proof they've been taken," Delores said. "All we know is that this place has been compromised. And we can't even say for sure that DIMCO was the cause. Maybe some kids broke in. Your parents might have shown up, saw that the lock was picked, and gone somewhere else. We shouldn't jump to conclusions."

I supposed she had a point, but the likelihood of this being a coincidence seemed awfully remote. Ever since the King Edward VII incident, DIMCO seemed to know our every move. They'd picked Nate2 up pretty easily, Ridpath had walked in on us at the Royal Oxford Hotel, and now the safe house had been ransacked. If I didn't know better, I'd think there was a spy in the ranks. I fingered the sunglasses in my pocket. Suddenly it all made sense. I turned to Delores.

"Who are you?" I asked.

She looked at me blankly. "I'm sorry, but what the hell are you talking about?"

"When did you switch places with her? Was it on the plane back to this dimension or at our house?"

Gus put a hand on my shoulder. "You're starting to sound a little strung out, Johnny. Why don't we go for a doughnut and get your blood sugar up."

"Didn't you notice in the Royal Oxford?" I stammered. "Delores was swamped by that distortion wave at the same time as Nate. And the sunglasses she's been wearing are equipped with an inhibitor, which is unnecessary for someone from our dimension. And even more oddly, DIMCO seems to know our every move before we make it."

"Your dad gave me those glasses," Delores said, taking a step closer to me. All that black makeup swam together on her face to produce a whirlpool of darkness. I stepped back, suddenly unsure, and waited for her to throw a roundhouse into my jaw. But instead her expression crumbled away and she slumped against the wall with sagging shoulders.

"I should have told you," she murmured.

"That you're a spy and are leading us all to our deaths?" Gus said, surprised. "That would have been helpful."

"John's right," Delores continued. "I'm not who you think."

CHAPTER 11

Apparently nothing in the world was ever what it was supposed to be. I couldn't believe how screwed up my life had become in such a short time: an alternative-dimension version of my father was obsessed with my mother; my parents were missing; I was on the run (again); and now one of my most trusted friends had a confession about her true identity.

"Apparently," Delores began, "this isn't my … uh, universe."

"So who are you?" I asked.

"I'm the same person I've always been. When we were on the run in Scotland everyone assumed I was from this dimension—even me. But I got here and none of my symptoms disappeared. Your father ran some tests and apparently my world is another splinter."

This knocked me speechless.

"Does a version of you exist on this planet?" Gus asked.

Delores shrugged. "I don't know. I suppose it's possible."

Gus walked to the counter and came back with a heavy yellow phonebook. He searched the pages, flipping the thin paper loudly, and then dialled for an American operator. He asked for Texas. Nate2 wandered out of the room.

"Are you sure that's a good idea?" I asked.

"We're not paying for the call," Gus replied. "And I doubt whoever owns this dump is coming back."

"But by contacting the real Delores, aren't we messing with the space–time continuum?"

"I don't see how," Gus continued. "She isn't going to know who I am."

Delores looked less than comfortable with the idea, but she did seem mildly curious about what her double was like. I found Nate2 in the bathroom running a coat hanger up the toilet, trying to hook whatever was causing the blockage.

"It's solid," he said.

"Too much information."

"I have to say, the term *safe house* has turned out to be a misnomer. This establishment is neither a house, nor safe." He jiggled the wire and pulled. "Aha, I think I've ... No."

He wrangled around for another minute, and then took a break, leaning against the sink and frowning into the bowl. In the other room I could hear Gus asking someone if they were into black makeup, depressing music, and short Canadian guys. I wiped my forehead and grunted at the continued presence of slime on my skin. I wondered if the inhibitor on Dolores's sunglasses had messed with the natural resolution of the reality distortion or if my pores really did just need to get the lingering snail juice out. I didn't know what I'd tell the doctor if it didn't stop and I had to go to the hospital.

"You know," Nate2 said, "this reminds me of when I lost my parents."

"I haven't lost my parents," I snapped.

He hesitated slightly. "No, no ... I didn't mean to imply. It's just that the *sense* of loss is ... well, anyway. Like your father, my parents in my universe were tragically killed in a car accident on the way to Brighton when I was seventeen, your age. We went every blessed year from the time of my conception and it was the first summer that I refused to go. I'd put up with extreme carsickness for my entire life and thought I was old enough to stay in London on my own." His gaze shifted to a faraway time and he swallowed awkwardly. "I can still smell the combination of seat leather and sweet-scented vomit. They used to make me take ginger tablets to settle my stomach, but they never worked. I'd yak at least five times each way. Regardless, I came home after an afternoon umpiring local cricket and there was a police constable waiting on the front step with the tragic news. Our house might have been full of furniture, but the barrenness was overwhelming. I'm sure you feel a similar sense of emptiness."

I didn't know what to say. I wasn't used to Nate2 being open and sincere, and even though his experiences mirrored my father's life, I felt like I was trespassing. I knew the story of my grandparents' deaths, but Dad had never actually told me the exact details or how he felt. My mom had told me that the accident was the reason he left the U.K. to come to university in Toronto. As I looked at Nate2, I realized there were some similarities between him and me. Like Nate2, I didn't have many friends. I had acquaintances, some regular tennis opponents, and guys I hung out with in the cafeteria during lunch, but outside school I was kind of a loner. No one seemed to be quite like me. I liked sports, but not football, soccer, or hockey, so I was never a member of a team. And girls had never been a priority, so I didn't hang out with them at the mall or go to parties, like Flarch. I didn't think I was a giant geek; I just didn't know where I belonged.

"Did you think of leaving London?" I asked. "I mean, after the accident."

Nate2 forced a stiff smile. "Oh, no. I had my hamsters at the time and there were very strict regulations on taking animals overseas. Besides, I didn't like cars, so why on earth would I get on a large tubular drum that could plunge out of the sky from fifty thousand feet?"

To the best of my knowledge, my father had never mentioned hamsters. I also suspected that my grandparents in this dimension had invested in better life insurance policies. The two worlds were similar in so many ways, and yet had such small but significant differences. It made me wonder about a person's fate. Clearly we all made choices that affected our paths.

"Do you regret not leaving?" I asked. "When you see how my dad's life turned out?"

Nate2 scoffed, avoided my glance, and went back to tugging the wire. "Though I do envy your father's access to your mother's perfectly sculpted legs and gorgeous cheekbones, I refuse to feel regret, even if it has stalked me mercilessly for my entire life. Besides, your father has problems of his own."

"A good career, a house, and a family?"

I was taken aback when Nate2 turned with a mild glare. "Yes, theoretically everything has been wonderful for him and I should feel cowed by my wasted potential. But in the interest of maintaining a sliver of self-esteem, I might point out that he's gotten us all into a bit of a tight spot. I might be a pale shadow of him, but at least I didn't send you hurtling across dimensions into my world or annoy a large security force that stuffs socks into innocent men's mouths."

"That's not my dad's fault," I said. "Blame DIMCO for violating our world. They're the ones stealing our ozone, taking our technology, and dumping their pollutants into our oceans. My dad is the good guy in all this business."

"Yes, but you would be blissfully unaware of it all, toiling away in your fast-food diner, if your father had been more like me. I might not be the most exciting or successful man, but please don't contrast my life with his. I'm not completely pathetic. After all, single, childless people can contribute to the good of society. I pay my TV licence and most of my taxes. Please don't rub your familial bliss in my face."

Nate2's lips were a frosty shade of white and were pursed so tight they looked like a cat's behind. I hadn't considered that he might feel embarrassed about not having achieved as much as my dad, but considering they were sort of the same person I could see where the emotion might come from. He ran a hand across his goatee and relaxed his facial muscles. His voice was softer and lower in tone.

"I understand that you're scared, John. But don't worry. We'll find your parents and sort this kafuffle out. I'm not about to see you become an orphan. It's not very much fun."

I nodded and went to see what was happening in the other room. I wasn't sure where we could go next, but knew staying any longer was a bad idea. If my parents did know this place had been ransacked and had gone to another location, I needed to find a way to get a message to them. Gus was reclining on a computer chair, his feet up on the dusty desk. Delores looked ill.

"He's flirting with this dimension's version of me," she gagged. "Apparently I like the colour pink and want to go to veterinary school. I don't know what went wrong on this planet, but I hope I get help before it's too late."

"I love turtles too," Gus cooed. "I'll definitely swing by on my way back to Oz. We'll do lunch and go to the zoo."

Delores cringed and looked utterly nauseated. I figured if she had to retch she could; it wouldn't diminish the decor. I tried not to think about the implications of Gus flirting with Delores, even if it was another version of her. Obviously there was some attraction, which was probably why he was always goading me into pursuing her. Not that it mattered, really, because she couldn't exist on our planet and therefore there was no hope for us.

Just outside the door a man in a stained baseball cap, jeans, and a beer T-shirt peered in from the dusty parking lot. For a second I expected him to whistle and armed shock troops to come storming through the door, but instead he picked up a Frisbee and held it above his head as a ginger dog jumped up eagerly, landing two paws on his chest. The man turned, threw the Frisbee, then wandered out of view. I nearly collapsed as I breathed for the first time in ten seconds.

"I feel the same way," Delores said. "We should get out of here."

Gus hung up the phone and tucked an address written on lined paper into his back pocket. "You know why people have dogs?" he said, gesturing at the door. "So that they can get out of the house, have fun, and not look silly with a Frisbee or rubber ball. People's motivations in life are so basic. Like, take DIMCO—they're trying to destroy our world for no better reason than because they can. It's power. They don't care about the environment of Earth 5."

"I agree fully," Nate2 said, coming into the room. "Especially with your first point. After a certain age, people aren't allowed to play. In my case, it was seven. My father didn't believe that people of our station in society should be seen sweating. He said that was for the lower classes and Italians. This was shortly before he lost half the family fortune investing in English-built electric cars."

"They didn't catch on?" Gus said.

"Oddly enough, no. I don't know why. They could reach speeds of close to twenty-five kilometres an hour going downhill with a forceful backwind." He paused and looked down at the item in his large hand. "You all mocked my resolve earlier, but look what I discovered hidden away in that toilet."

He held up some sort of electronic keypad, like an iPod or BlackBerry. Delores took it and examined the screen, which was flickering erratically. I was pretty sure I'd seen the device on my father's desk in the planetarium—it was one of the projects he'd been toying with for the past few weeks—which meant that they'd been here and left in a hurry.

"There was barely any excrement on it at all," Nate2 commented.

Delores dropped the pad instinctively and wiped her hand on Gus's shirt. Nate2 looked perturbed as he picked it up and gave it a shake to realign the screen. The impact had blurred the display.

"I did wash it off," he said.

"I don't care," Delores replied.

"There was hand soap."

"Again, I do not care. I don't handle electronics that come from a toilet."

"Teenagers," Nate2 mumbled.

I peered over his shoulder and examined the information on screen. It looked like a global positioning program feeding a selection of maps on a regular loop. In our region, four red dots were clustered near the highway (obviously us) and another was quickly approaching from the west. I didn't like the look of that at all.

"Uh, guys," I said. "We've talked about it for a while, but now we really do have to make a move. I think we've been discovered."

We wasted at least another minute fighting over the console—grabbing at it, juggling it manically between us—before running out the back door. We raced toward the car, but crashed to a stop at the corner of the building. Two men in blue suits and sunglasses were about to enter the doughnut shop, peering in its windows and clearly searching for someone. I pulled Delores behind a Dumpster as Nate2 and Gus retreated. The men glanced around briefly and then walked into the shop. I couldn't believe how stupid we'd been to hang around the safe house making international calls and fiddling with the toilet.

From nearby an engine ripped the air with a high revving scream of acceleration. In front of our eyes a red Corvette convertible jumped off the highway and spun out on the gravel shoulder. The rear end fishtailed as the back wheels sprayed and smoked and ripped into the parking lot. It was Rex, driving toward us at high speed. I stepped out, waving my arms, but as the grille hurtled straight for me I froze in terror and wondered if he'd be able to brake on the sandy grit before taking me out. Somehow he managed to stop approximately two millimetres from my kneecaps.

"Get in!" he shouted.

Delores, Gus, and I hopped over the low edge of the Corvette into the backseat. Nate2 loped over with his long stride, raised one leg, but couldn't get it over the side. He swayed on his heels and looked about to topple backward. Rex grunted, leaned over, and threw open the door while admonishing Nate2 with several colourful obscenities. For all his cop shows, Nate2 clearly hadn't learned much about the art of a quick getaway. In the doughnut shop the two men in blue were frantically trying to get out the door, which was either jammed or had been mysteriously locked.

"Beatrice is on our side," Rex said, hitting the gas. "She runs that shop and doesn't even mind if you smoke. I like a place that flouts the no-smoking law. Of course, if you do happen to ever go there never eat any of the pastries after ten. They taste disgusting and are chock full of nicotine. Now hold on. These sports cars are very light in the back end and are murder to handle."

We shot past the graded exit and flopped over the grass, just missing a bus shelter. Rex might have been a good pilot, but his driving was atrocious. The Corvette's underbelly scraped over the concrete curb and we hit the highway at full speed, weaving around transports and minivans. Rex slowed at the traffic lights and then crept through four lanes of oncoming traffic, waving politely as cars slammed on their brakes and offered rather lewd hand signals in response.

The wind whipped Nate2's mangy hair straight back into Gus's face. It looked like a dark shaggy mop was attacking him. Far behind us, I noted a black sedan with tinted windows coming on fast.

"I found out about the security breach," Rex said. "I don't know how DIMCO discovered that place, but we've got to be doubly careful from now on. And I'm going to trust the one person I know who's never let me down."

"Why thank you," Gus said. "I'm flattered."

"Not you, hippie."

"Ooh, let me have a go," Nate2 shouted above the wind. "I love these sorts of guessing games. Would the person who's never let you down be the best man from your wedding?"

"No," Rex snapped.

"Tony Blair?"

"Fitzgerald—"

"Cherie Blair? The Archbishop of Canterbury? Sir Bob Geldof?"

With every guess Rex's neck muscles bulged and our speed increased. We were passing cars like fish swimming past reeds. Nate2 was getting very animated, waving his hands to stall the end of the game.

"I'm talking about myself!" Rex finally blurted. "I've got a plane set to take me back to London in my dimension. After that, I've got a few tricks up my sleeve. I'm not going to be a guinea pig for other people's plans any more. I should have left already, but I thought I'd rescue you lot first. As soon as I lose this sedan I'll let you out."

"You're ditching us?" I yelled.

"As soon as possible. I'll take the big lug back, but the rest of you belong here. Go back to Australia and Texas. Get as far away from this situation as you can. It isn't for kids."

"We're not kids," Delores noted.

"Sounds good to me," Gus said. "Drop me off at Terminal 3 and I'll hitch a flight back to Oz."

Delores and I looked at him in surprise.

"You're ditching us too?" I said.

He shrugged. "Think about it, Johnny. There's no reason for me to hang around. I'll just get in the way. If I'm this world's best chance to defeat DIMCO, it's in trouble. I'm in no way responsible or dependable. I've enjoyed the intrigue—makes a nice change from the monotony of Brisbane—but I've decided it's best for the team if I opt out of the adventure."

"DIMCO will never let you go back to your old life, with all you know," Nate2 protested.

"I'll sign a pledge," Gus replied. "On my honour, saying I don't care about other dimensions. I just want to sleep in again and walk the streets like a normal human being."

"Good luck with that," Nate2 said. "More likely you'll return home, fall into a false sense of security, and then be whisked away in the dead of night to a secret location where no one will hear your pitiful screams. But do what you like."

"I just want to go back to my regular life," Gus pleaded.

"Some of us can't go back to regular life," I hissed. The anger was welling up in me like never before, my body tense and coiled. Maybe teams were overrated. In the end even your closest friends could be unreliable.

The sedan was closing the gap. We were racing along a section of highway that acted as a main intersection, with ramps, express routes, and numerous merging lanes. Grumbling transports full of consumer goods, building materials, and chemicals crowded us on all sides.

"You'll never make it to the airport without getting caught," I said. "We're miles away and this traffic is nuts."

Rex yanked the wheel hard, squeezed onto the shoulder, and raced past cars lined up beside a section of road under construction. We came within centimetres of sideswiping a Hyundai, shot through the orange pylons marking a half paved off-ramp, and blazed out in a blast of smoke into a closed strip of highway.

"I'm not going to the airport," Rex said.

"But you said a plane …"

Rex looked behind him, pressed the accelerator even closer to the floor, then flapped a hand back toward the sky—and that's when I saw it. The shadow was swooping over us like a hawk, followed by a white underbelly and finally the ear-shattering whoosh of engines. In front of us work trucks pulled off the road, some crashing into the concrete retaining walls as a mid-sized jet landed on the highway, bouncing and finally reversing its engines to come to a stop. Within a minute we reached its idling body and jumped out of the Corvette. The sedan was still following, flying toward us trailing a cape of dust.

"They're too close," Rex said. "You're all going to have to come."

"Why don't I take the car?" Gus asked.

"This road ends in half a kilometre. You'll never escape."

"So you're just going to leave your vehicle?" Nate2 said.

"We can buy another one," Rex replied. "Our organization has certain assets."

"But you were going to let us stay in that dumpy nail shop?"

"Safety and comfort are two different birds."

Nate2 nodded. "Yes, well, that I can understand, having driven with you. You killed at least two birds with that clutch work of yours. I bet the car doesn't have a transmission left. My stomach feels like a Cuisinart on rapid mix."

We scrambled up the stairs to the plane and were moving before the door had been securely refastened. There were probably only fifty seats inside, and the jet shook more violently than the 747 we'd flown back in from Scotland. As we gained speed and made the sudden lift from the road, a thought occurred to me.

"We're going to be in the wrong dimension again," I groaned.

"Speak for yourself, m'boy," Nate2 said. "Some of us are going home."

CHAPTER 12

I DIDN'T NOTICE that we had a sixth passenger until Rex strode up to the cabin and I retreated to the bathroom near the rear of the plane. In the last row, lying sideways across three seats, was a familiar face. He was instantly recognizable thanks to his small eyes, thin moustache, and the smell of cat food assaulting my nasal cavity. I nearly fell over in shock as the eyes looked up at me with a hateful glare. Ridpath attempted to yell, but his mouth was taped shut like Nate2's had been in the Royal Oxford Hotel (minus the dirty sock). His arms were tied behind his back and he looked thoroughly uncomfortable. I went back, informed the others, and together we made our way to the cabin and knocked. The door opened a crack. Rex peered out.

"Inter-dimensional flight regulations stipulate that you have to be in your seat with your seatbelts securely fastened at all times," he said. "We don't want to get sued in case we hit severe turbulence or get torched by a fighter jet."

"How'd you capture Ridpath?" I asked. "And what did he say about my parents?"

Rex looked confused for a second. "Oh, him. That's not the real Ridpath. He's the version from your world, the chicken farmer. I didn't want to restrain him like that, but he refused to cooperate. I decided brute force was necessary when he spat on my shoes. I have to say, he's an arrogant bloke for being so poor and unremarkable."

"We can't take him to an alternative dimension," Delores said. "That's kidnapping. He hasn't done anything wrong."

Rex looked pained. "Listen, I understand your youthful sense of morality, but we're involved in a rather serious business and he's much too handy a resource to squander. Think of the information and insight we can glean about the colonel by having his double. Besides, although this fellow might not have done anything against us, he's still guilty *genetically*. If Ridpath is evil in my dimension, then you can bet this one is equally as bad. Think of it as pre-emptive security."

"You can't treat them the same," I said. "Look at Nate2 and my dad. They're doubles and they're almost nothing alike."

"Good point," Nate2 murmured. "Your father is much tubbier. I agree with the young people on this one. There is a certain ethical line of action to be respected. I might be bankrupt financially, but that doesn't mean I have to be morally insolvent as well. We should drop Ridpath out the back with a parachute and a note."

Rex smiled tightly and shook his head like an impatient jackhammer. "Yes, yes, thank you for your soft-hearted thoughts. But this isn't a group decision. I kidnapped him. He's mine. Consider your consciences clear." He looked my way. "You do want to see your parents alive again, right?"

My breath caught in my throat, like my lungs had gone off-line. "Of course," I said, barely managing a whisper.

"Excellent!" Rex replied. "Because I have reliable information that they've been smuggled into my dimension and are in obvious danger. With luck I can get them out, but let's stop treating this conflict as a pillow fight."

Both Nate2 and Delores seemed uncomfortable, looking to the floor and avoiding my glance. Delores's cheeks were flushed slightly—the most sustained natural colour I'd seen from them in weeks. As much as kidnapping an innocent man appeared wrong, the implications of letting Ridpath's double go were confusing. If we released him and a time came when he could have helped save my parents I'd never survive the guilt. Of course, if he got killed and his chickens starved because no one was around to feed them I'd be responsible too. We did an ethics unit in social studies, but the easy textbook choices weren't much use to me now, in the real world.

"We won't hurt him," Rex said more diplomatically. "We're just borrowing him from his dull and uninteresting life for a while. Trust me, his wife will be glad for the break. He drinks like a fish and has spent more than one pay packet on the plonk. I can tell you that much."

"Plonk means alcohol," Gus confided. "We say it in Oz, too."

Reluctantly, we accepted the situation and tried not to think about how we might be destroying an innocent man's life. Of greater concern at the moment was breaking through the porthole in the small jet. Rex explained that he and the pilot would be inducing a controlled distortion wave from the cockpit in the next hour and that we'd all have to firmly control our thoughts for it to work. Within the wave, Rex would be repeating coordinates to guide us through a porthole into his dimension. If he became distracted we'd move off course, crash into a second wave, and be annihilated, so we had to think positive, non-disruptive thoughts. Still, even if we did get the route right, there were other dangers, namely that DIMCO would break down our artificial wave and enter our distortion in force. The last time we'd crossed dimensions the Red Baron had riddled our wings with bullets and the back of the plane had filled with water and sand. As we ate our mini bags of pretzels (mandatory on all flights, no matter what), Rex assigned us seats far enough away from one another not to get diverted from our tasks.

"As you know, our current mission is more dangerous than even the last time we crossed dimensions," he went on. "DIMCO have no doubt been working hard to improve their technologies along the boundaries of all suspected portholes. We can't let them know what we're doing, so we're going to make this jaunt ten times more difficult by delaying our artificial distortion until the *very last minute*."

"That's close," Gus said. "Sixty seconds before entry."

Rex scratched his head. "Actually, I was using *last minute* purely as a figure of speech. We'll have twenty-three seconds."

"And you think this is our best chance?" Delores said.

"Fingers crossed, yes. We've never actually done anything this reckless, and let's face it, *loopy,* before. But part of being a pilot is extreme arrogance, so there you go. Better to blow up than die old."

"Is that what they taught you in the air force?" Gus asked.

"Oh goodness no. They taught us that no matter what don't hurt the plane. They're very expensive. The U.K. military is much more budget-conscious than you might believe."

I noticed there wasn't a debate on Rex's reckless course of action, and seeing as we were currently fifty thousand feet above the Atlantic Ocean, the prospects of bailing out seemed slim. He seemed confident enough—enthusiastic even—so I told myself everything would turn out okay. I'd noticed on more than one occasion that Rex never seemed fully energized unless there was the possibility of extreme danger and/or possible death. The first time we met he'd snuck me out of a heavily fortified airport terminal, working as a double agent while directly under Ridpath's command. I wasn't sure if he was the bravest guy I'd ever met or just plain nuts.

Over the next ten minutes Rex took us aside in turn to give us specific thoughts that we were to concentrate on at the moment of distortion. Mine involved imagining the plane's outer registration number as DIM-098. Delores looked like a white sheet as she sat back down in her seat. She hadn't said much since takeoff and hadn't touched her pretzels. It had to be dimensional fade. And when I'd been fading from the other dimension, desperate and humiliating measures had been taken to jumpstart my whacked-out neural net—they channelled atmospheric energy using first a clothes hanger hung on my head, then a radio, a satellite dish, and finally a Discman. Although each solution brought more power, my ego had certainly taken a battering. I took Rex aside and mentioned the idea of rigging up a similar device for Delores—partly for practical reasons and partly for petty revenge—and the whole group gathered around her.

"I don't have my Discman," Gus said. "Someone borrowed it, wore it while exercising, and returned it broken."

Nate2 raised his chin. "I took it apart to realign the electronic eye. I can't help it if the manufacturer used substandard plastic."

Gus turned to me. "He snapped the cover off."

"Shoddy goods," Nate2 said.

"Worked fine until Mr. Fix-It used his expertise," Gus continued.

Nate2 threw up his arms in exasperation. "That machine could not possibly have functioned properly for you. From the second I put in my brand-new Mick Hucknall CD the disk did nothing but skip and cut out."

"You were exercising on a pogo stick," Gus replied, turning on him.

"Yes, but the warranty said the device had *shock guard.*"

Rex was waving his hands to interrupt. Finally, he lifted Gus up around the waist and physically turned him away from Nate2. I noticed that he was breathing hard and that his ears were bright red from increased blood pressure.

"If you two don't shut up," Rex said, "I'll vaporize you myself. We need something to transmit energy waves to Delores's brain to ramp up her power. There must be something around this jet."

We roamed through the plane, opening cargo containers and storage shelves. I found four hundred individual servings of strawberry jam, eight thousand bags of pretzels, and some tonic water that must have exploded during takeoff. What I didn't find was anything that could be of use, probably because planes are designed to prevent electronic transmissions so as not to interfere with on-board navigational systems and radar.

I took the opportunity to use cocktail napkins to wipe off the slime that was still being slowly but constantly secreted from my pores. None of us had ever experienced strange after-effects from reality distortions before, except of course for reduced energy. I hoped this wasn't a new strand of virus infecting my body. I ducked into the mini bathroom and examined myself in the mirror. I definitely looked greyer than usual, and I noted that two extremely painful pimples were rising at symmetrical points on my forehead. I touched one of the red bumps and winced in pain. There was a hard lump under the skin.

"I've got something!" Rex shouted.

He'd returned from the cabin with a cell phone. "You should be able to boost your energy flow by holding it against your skull. You'll have to recharge it quite often, so I suggest you call the operator only when you're feeling especially weak. I'd try to wait until we land if you can. The roaming charges out here will be outrageous and Hank, the pilot, isn't exactly a millionaire."

Delores handed the phone back. "I'd rather fade. They've done studies. Excessive use of a cell phone causes brain tumours in rats."

"Who were the rats phoning in these studies?" Nate2 asked. "Doesn't sound like a particularly reliable study to me—or scientific."

"I think those were the old-style phones," Rex continued. "The kind that were the size of a handbag and required an antenna as big as a billiard cue. Look how small this beauty is. You can practically hide it in your ear."

Delores smiled bitterly. "Or you could stick it up your—"

"How about a compromise!" I interrupted. "What if you buy a portable telephone headset when we get to London? You know, the kind that plugs into your ear and makes you look like you're talking to yourself on the street?"

Delores rolled her eyes. "Excellent! I can look like a lunatic!" Then she looked toward the window, sighed in resignation, and turned the phone over in her hands. She dialled 0 and held the receiver first against her ear and then flat to her forehead, at which point she let out a soft murmur and experienced a faint spasm. She kept her eyes closed as the automated voice on the line told her the time would be 6:55 P.M. in five seconds. As the countdown ended in a beep she slid farther into her chair, ran a hand through her hair, and let out a long, slow sigh of relief. Rex cleared his throat.

"Right. We should be coming up on the porthole in the next half-hour or so. I'll keep you informed by intercom."

And with that, we all slinked back to our seats and left Delores to enjoy her recuperation in peace.

The next thirty minutes were the longest of my life. No one was talking. We were all gnashing nervously about the impending collision with DIMCO, unsure about the future but hopeful that Rex and his pilot were skilled enough to at least get us to London. Thinking otherwise was pointless. He and our mystery pilot must have felt justified in taking the chance; otherwise we could have found a second safe house and waited for outside help. But I was glad for the risk, because I couldn't have sat and waited for someone else to free my parents. There are some things you have to do alone in life, or at least with a few serious-minded and highly competent people. I looked around at Gus cracking his knuckles pensively and Nate2 playing computer solitaire. I wished I knew some. Part of me wanted to chat, just to get my mind off the situation, but I was still sore at Gus for wanting to go back to Brisbane. Still, I figured he'd just been talking, finding a way to vent some frustration.

The intercom came to life.

"Thirty seconds to wave initiation," Rex said. "For your convenience, a countdown will appear on the screen embedded in the headrest in front of you. Please ensure that all seatbelts are secured, your seats are in their upright position, trays are returned to their original place, and all hand luggage is safely stowed in the cabin above you or under the chair in front. If you're religious, I'd also suggest you say a final prayer that we avoid total annihilation. Thank you for flying with us today."

Rex had blabbed through the first twelve seconds of the countdown. Finally all went silent. I attempted to breathe deeply and imagine DIM-098 stamped on the outer fuselage. I pictured us flying safely through the porthole without being detected. The screen hit fifteen.

"Are we supposed to count down from ten out loud?" Nate2 asked. "Like on New Year's Eve?"

"No," Delores hissed. "Shut up and concentrate on your objective."

"Rex didn't give me one. He told me to think of a blank sheet of paper. I don't think the man trusts me."

"SHUT UP!"

"No need to be rude. After all, I'm not the dangerous one. I've got as much to lose as the rest of you. My one, small, minor concern with Rex's hallowed plan is what the chicken farmer in the back will be thinking about."

With three seconds left, I felt an immense wave of *panic*. Ridpath's double was just as capable of influencing our artificial reality as the rest of us. He could imagine the plane crashing or …

Three

Us being intercepted or …

Two

DIM-098

One

The cabin lit up with purple light and we shook violently, the seats swaying and the wings dipping and bending as though they could snap right off in the jet stream. I couldn't tell if we were falling, given that the sky outside my small oval window had no points of reference, but I had the feeling we'd dropped several thousand feet. For a few long seconds my skin seemed to stretch and my face morphed like silly putty. The clouds outside flipped between grey and silver before finally settling into a solid white.

As the vibrations faded and the light came back to normal I was shocked to see that the plane's interior had been redecorated in green velour. My chair was plush and reclined smoothly. There was more space in the aisles, which were now lined with thick shag carpet. In fact, the whole interior looked larger and more luxuriant. Gus was lying flat on his back on a long leather couch, his neck stiff and his eyes flickering around nervously. Tentatively, he slid into a seated position.

"Well, this is better than being attacked by wolverines. Who was in charge of remodelling?"

Delores waved. Despite appearances, we'd all experienced these shifts enough times to know that nothing was ever easy. We moved to the windows and looked out, fully expecting to be surrounded by DIMCO fighter jets or flying monkeys. The outside of the plane had changed as well. It was silver and military in style. I was glad to see that our registration number had imprinted perfectly from my brain onto the fuselage.

"Did you do the outside?" Delores asked Gus.

"I had my doubts," he said. "But I must be more artistic than I thought. I even got the colour right."

He showed us the picture Rex had given him. Nate2 was still holding a blank piece of white paper, looking generally annoyed. He flipped it onto the shag carpet and went back to playing solitaire. Remembering Ridpath, I bolted to the back and found him sitting upright, untied, holding an enormous pitcher of what looked like cheap alcoholic cider. He scowled and shielded the brown glass container from view as if I was going to wrestle him for it. He seemed harmless enough with his thin shoulders, caterpillar moustache, pinprick eyes, and odd body odour. I didn't see any reason to tell Rex that he was free of the duct tape and about to propel himself into a drunken stupor.

"Do you think we slipped by DIMCO?" Delores asked behind me.

"There aren't any planes," I said. "And all our thoughts appear to be accounted for, except the pilot's, but I'm thinking he was concentrating on getting us to the other side safely. I'm assuming we've overcome the wave and are on our way to London."

Tentatively, we gave high fives and made our way to the front. Rex popped out of the cockpit and seemed satisfied, though perhaps unnerved at how easy the crossover had been.

Nate2 pointed to my forehead. "You should get those boils looked at when we get to England. I used to get them as a child, so I suppose it's hereditary. Of course, diet plays a role. I ate a lot of gristle in my youth. If you go to a hospital, a nurse will lance them and get the pus sac out. It's the only way to get them to heal."

I stood, unable to speak, and slowly put my hand to the two lumps on my forehead. My throat was like a swizzle straw. My face burned as Delores casually turned and strolled back to her seat. Even Gus seemed uncomfortable with the situation. He patted me on the back and wandered away.

"Ouch," he mumbled. "First mucus and vomit, then this. She's going to be pining for you now."

Nate2 watched them go. "It's true," he said. "I'm sharing the wisdom of experience with you. I don't want you to leave those hideous red lumps and have them get worse and scar. That's how I got the indentation on my left buttock. I didn't want the school nurse to see me with my trousers down. Of course, that was mainly because she was sixty and there had been rumours. Looking back, I can see they were cruel laughs gained at the expense of an elderly spinster with slight mental problems, but at the time you didn't know. Children are cruel."

"They're not boils," I said.

"Oh, but they are. I can tell by the massive, horrifically swollen surface area of the head and the white around the edges. I used to get them on my face, arms, back, legs.... I never got pimples though, which is the strange thing."

"I don't want to hear your stupid stories!" I snapped. "Now leave me alone!"

I marched down the shag carpet toward the back, avoiding Delores's eyes and keenly aware of how the Phantom of the Opera must have felt. I didn't even want the repulsive Ridpath to look at me, but he did, chuckling softly to himself in mockery. The bumps were aching badly—sharp pain coupled with a spreading throbbing, no doubt because the virus inside them was infecting my entire head. I ducked into the bathroom and leaned close to the mirror, poking around at the inflamed edges. I winced as a solid ball moved around under my thumb. I wondered if this must be an actual *pus sac*. No wonder I could never get a date. With my skin, I'd be thirty before my face was clear enough not to scare young children. There was no way I could go to a hospital in the other dimension without looking totally suspicious, so gathering all my courage, I closed my eyes, placed my thumbs at strategic angles around one of the bumps, and pressed hard to burst it open.

Then I screamed and nearly passed out.

The agony was overwhelming, like getting shot or being clobbered with a spiked mallet. I'd squeezed enough zits in my life but had never felt this kind of pain. I spun dizzily, still unable to open my eyes. I didn't even notice that the scream had been followed by a low moan, which was still leaking out between my pursed lips. I looked into the mirror and saw that the bump was now fire-truck red and that the tip had split slightly to expose a narrow slit of wounded flesh. Gingerly, I touched the bump again, trying to see what was inside. It looked leathery.

"Even I'm disgusted by myself," I moaned.

I waited several long minutes for the swelling to go down—as if no one would notice the festering sore if I let it heal for five minutes. I looked so damn ugly. My good qualities were now completely overshadowed by the two beacons of disgusting *geekdom* on my melon. They might as well have been flashing. I drank a few mouthfuls of water, thinking it might help cleanse my immune system.

Finally I reached for the sliding lock, which is when I fell through the floor.

CHAPTER 13

UNLIKE ALICE, I didn't land comfortably on dry leaves and sticks. I landed on my butt, hard. I rolled around on the white tile floor for several long minutes, finally crawling and wondering what I'd done in my life to deserve this much discomfort. When the pain subsided to a warm and constant ache, I discovered that I was in a perfectly white corridor lined with white doors. I'd seen this sort of setup in books and movies countless times and figured that each door contained some danger that had to be overcome. Or at least that was my thinking until the walls fell over.

As the doors tumbled out of view I became aware that I was in a totally white space about the size of my high school gymnasium. Suddenly basketball nets appeared at either end of the room and bleachers slid out of the walls. A siren wailed as a scoreboard appeared reading DIM-098.

I didn't move and tried not to think, afraid of what might happen next. I looked around, wondering if the others were in this place or were isolated in their own strange worlds.

"Right," I murmured.

An invisible force spun me ninety degrees to the right.

"That's not what I meant ..."

I spun back.

"End," I said.

I meant for the distortion to end, but apparently my brain screwed up the translation, because I flew uncontrollably to the

far end of the room, sliding solidly into the white brick wall. I
hadn't screamed this much since infancy. I rubbed my side and
legs and got unsteadily to my feet, looking for an exit. Someone
or something seemed to be controlling my environment, as if
this were a puppet show and I was the one on strings.

"I don't know who's doing this," I mumbled, "but this is total
crap."

A great wad of bird poo landed on my shoulder, followed by
several globs on my head, and I decided to be far more careful
with my complaints. I walked around slowly, looking for an exit,
but the white bricks were solid everywhere. The ceiling looked
normal and the floor didn't bend or give, even when I jumped up
and down. There wasn't even an air vent or exhaust fan.

"I want out!" I yelled.

"There's only one way out," an eerily familiar voice whispered.

I looked around for Ridpath, but didn't see anyone. Then I
noticed that the air was becoming filled with the sound of
marching feet nearing the outside of the walls. I raced to the far
end of the room but the noise there was even stronger, coming
closer with every passing second.

"I need a door!" I shouted.

A thousand doors appeared on the walls, but as I raced around
I discovered that they were all locked. The marching stopped
suddenly. I didn't move, trying to contain the strained frenzy of
my breathing. My chest ached as my heart pumped blood like a
stereo blasting out low bass. I could practically feel a thousand
bodies standing only a thin barrier away.

"Stay locked," I whispered.

At that second all the knobs turned at once—violently—as if
the army outside had been waiting for me to *open* the doors. I
backed away to the centre of the room as the rattling became
more frantic, afraid that the knobs would be ripped off at any

moment and I'd be swarmed. I tried to think of something small, harmless, and preferably without hands that could manipulate doorknobs. I said the first thing that came to mind.

"Ants!"

The knobs fell silent, but a low scuttling sound could be heard. I looked around at the total white and wondered why I'd become snared in this strange cage. I hadn't felt a wave before this mess began, and clearly my ongoing thoughts were much more involved in this strange realm than in a reality distortion. Maybe it was some sort of residual effect of wave exposure. Maybe we didn't know all the rules about changing dimensions. I wondered again what the others were going through as black lines of ants began to march under the door jambs. I remembered stories of plane crashes in Africa in which people had landed on giant anthills and been eaten alive.

"Bigger ants," I whimpered. "Too big to get under these doors!"

Optimists would be glad that only about thirty ants had gotten into the room by this point. Pessimists would point out that they were now the size of golden retrievers. I imagined a baseball bat, my mind becoming more accustomed to the ways of this fantastic world. It seemed that random thoughts didn't stick, only ideas that were held in my mind's eye long enough to imprint onto my consciousness.

I looked at the bat that had suddenly—miraculously—appeared in my hands. Around me the ants were creeping slowly, their giant antennae quivering like licorice whips and their spindly legs bending like pulsating steel pipes. The ants were spreading out, encircling me like an army. I decided there was no time like the present and ran at the largest one, drawing the bat back and screaming as I brought it down on its midsection, splitting the insect into two parts. The front end collapsed while the back end spun away dripping acidic blood. The surrounding ants scattered momentarily before turning together into a long straight line. I suddenly remembered something else: ants usually attack only if you break their formation.

Too late …

The lead ant rushed toward me, then paused and swayed its bulbous black head back and forth for several long, agonizing seconds, as if attempting to hypnotize me with its movement. Its long, wiry pincers snapped open and shut like giant lobster claws. I held my ground—my body buzzing like electrified jelly. I couldn't think and my shaking hands felt as though they might drop my only weapon at any second. Without warning, the ant lunged forward, snapping violently. Having two legs was definitely an advantage for me, since the ant's ability to move quickly from side to side on its six was limited. As the creature made a second spring at me I stepped around it and brought the bat down solidly on one of its legs, sending it off balance. Then I stepped in closer and slammed the barrel of my weapon into its head. The ant stumbled left and appeared to be crumpling before its back legs splayed out for balance. My mind screamed to attack again, but my body was as rooted as a sycamore tree as I watched the scene playing out like some old sci-fi movie. The sense of unreality was so great in those vital few seconds that I almost laughed. Luckily a long glob of slime trickled down my temple and I remembered that even the most unlikely scenarios in my life were real enough to get me injured or killed.

Before the ant could get fully righted, I stepped in once more and finished the job, bashing its thin neck until its head was cleaved off. One down, only a few dozen more to go.… The rest of the ants maintained their line formation and came at me one after the other, scuttling forward, some rising up on their back legs to spray acid, others attempting to catch me in their front pincers. I bashed away like an all-star centre fielder, dancing away from swipes and stabs. At one point I moved too slowly and got splashed with a fine trickle of hot liquid that seared through my T-shirt and left a golf ball–sized hole. Instinctively I wiped slime on the burning wound underneath, which cooled my raw skin.

As I fought I slowly began to realize that my arms were growing heavy and that the interval between swings was becoming danger-ously long. If I didn't catch the insects where their segments joined, the steel would bounce off their hard exoskeletons and do little more than stun them. As the next ant veered around the pile of carcasses at my feet, another went over top. I stepped on one, then the other, and with a desperate lunge managed to just grab the hanging strings of the basketball net. I dropped the bat and struggled to get hold of the straining fabric as fountains of hot acid spurted my way. Using my body for momentum, I swung back and forth precariously until I gained enough height to make a frantic grab at the steel hoop. The thin metal cut into my fingers as I fought for a hold. Making the situation worse was the river of slime now pumping freely from my pores.

Pools of black spread out around my dangling legs as the ants broke formation and gathered below, jawing aggressively and rising up to snap at my running shoes. As quickly as possible, I took one hand off the basketball rim and dried it against my jeans, then did the other before using the last ounce of strength in my aching arms to pull myself up. I threw one elbow, then another, over the top of the rim and managed to struggle up into a seated position. I slumped against the glass backboard, breathing hard, and looked forward to the day when I could collapse in a large, comfortable bed for maybe a week and a half. I'd never bemoan my life again. Every morning when I got up, even if I was going to the most boring class in the world, I would look around and be thankful. I glanced down at the floor full of predators.

"Nice try!" I taunted. "Not much you can do now!"

The remaining dozen ants had stopped and were weaving around inspecting the ground for my scent. The huge muscles in their heads contracted as their pincers moved though the air. For a few seconds I savoured victory, hoping they'd lose interest and disappear—at least until the rim jerked and began to bend precariously under my weight. I scrambled to get hold of the backboard for stability. One of the ants balanced on its two rear legs and appeared to stare.

"I thought ants didn't have eyes?" I gulped.

Apparently some of the heartier varieties do. I also forgot that ants' legs are designed to help them easily climb walls. As the group began its single-line advance upward—leaving two guards directly below me spraying acid to prevent any escape—I tried to focus and come up with either an adequate defence or a new plan to get away. The bat had been good, but a flamethrower would certainly be better, which was advantageous since I was now suddenly holding one in my hands. The petrol tank was strapped to my back and the nozzle was aimed at the line approaching from below. I smiled and pulled the trigger.

And nothing happened.

The whole device seemed to droop in my hands and slowly turn into a puddle of colour without definition. I focused on the flamethrower, but it continued to dissolve. I thought of a machine gun, but ended up with chewing gum. I thought of an axe and ended up holding a toothpick. Evidently my brain was short-circuiting under the pressure. Only a few feet away the lead ant was extending a pipelike foot from the wall onto the steel bars that kept the apparatus in place; luckily though, it didn't get a good hold and plunged to the floor. A second ant climbed higher and tried to drop itself onto the bar. It too fell.

I tried to think of who could save me. Nate2, Gus, and Delores wouldn't be much use. Rex would scarcely be better. And besides, they were all probably dealing with their own horrors. I wanted to imagine my parents here, but Dad wasn't much of a fighter—equations were his area of expertise—and though Mom was good with a pesticide bottle, I couldn't bear to put them in harm's way. Given the nature of my dilemma, there was perhaps one person who could explain this situation and get me out alive. I pictured his face from www.loveofturnips.sci and attempted to mentally pull him into my reality.

"Anton Kavordnic!" I screamed.

The ants continued to climb up to where the wall met the ceiling. The new leader tried to walk upside down over me, but lost its grip and fell. The next one released and turned in mid-air, grasping the piping above me. I screamed as its legs scrambled to get a hold. Then, from somewhere outside the white room, the faint strains of piano came wafting in.

"Anton Kavordnic!" I yelled again.

Echoing footsteps compelled every creature in the room to pause. A doorknob to my left turned slowly and a head appeared, looking confused and curious. *If* this was indeed the world's greatest genius and the man who'd come up with inter-dimensional theory, he wasn't what I expected. I could only assume that the photo on his Web site was a publicity shot taken a few decades ago. The man at the door was in his seventies at least, with long mottled flesh that hung like thin pizza dough from his thin arms and chin. He was tall and gangly and looked like a heavy smoker. There was something about the pallor of his skin, the depths of the wrinkles on his face, and the sunken eyes that gave the overwhelming sensation of sadness. He had a thin moustache not unlike Ridpath's, though a touch fuller, and his hair stuck out in dull blond spirals beneath a crooked tweed Mack hat. Slowly the door opened farther and he stepped inside, taking in the situation. He didn't seem particularly distressed by the ants, even as several peeled off the walls and made in his direction. He glanced around at the white room, noting the score clock and the bleachers. He raised his eyebrows at the pile of carcasses in the corner.

"Having a good day?" he asked. "I hope you weren't in the middle of a picnic when these dear creatures arrived."

When the ants reared back and flexed their pincers, Kavordnic finally seemed to notice their attack. He waved his hand and they became old, hunched women with stooped backs. Almost to a person they wore long floral skirts and knitted shawls. The one above me lost her grip on the backboard and flopped to the ground, where she moaned pitifully and didn't get up. The women gathered around Kavordnic, making a fuss. Their voices were loud and extremely high-pitched and their clothing and posture made them look like shuffling teapots.

"Anton, let us get you a cup of tea," one said, ironically.

"I'm fine, thank you very much, Gladys."

"Oh come on, one cup and a pinch of cake."

"My how you've grown," another said. "Seems like just yesterday …"

"Have you heard about the Hendersons?" a third murmured. "I think you went to school with their eldest. He got married to that Thatcher girl—lovely, if not a bit dull. But there you go."

Kavordnic watched me climb down, dropping the eight feet onto the hard tiles. A shot of pain came up from my feet into my knees and every new bruise screamed. My hands ached and had identical lengthwise cuts across the palms. But at least I was safe. The scientist waved his arms to indicate the swarming mass of women.

"My aunts," he explained. "They were the first things that came to mind. Families were bigger when I was young, though scarcely less annoying, as you can see."

One of the women paused. "I take offence to that."

"You would," Kavordnic answered. "But you don't really exist, except as a portion of my memory, so I can't pretend to care. And besides, I never liked you. You were a tyrant."

"Still …"

"No," another cut in. "He has a point, Gladys. You don't really exist and you are moody. Always was a smart one, our Anton. I thought he should have gone into medicine. He would have made a fine doctor. Or a veterinarian."

"Real men work with their hands," another woman said. "Like my Harry, God rest his soul. Worked in the mines for thirty-seven years and never complained once, even when his lungs fell out. Being a scientist is no way for a man to live life. It's not reliable."

"It *is* reliable," Kavordnic replied, slightly peeved. "I invented the greatest theory known to humanity. It calculates time's effects on three-dimensional space and binds with Einstein's theory of relativity. Not that it's any of your concern."

"Needs a good woman this one," the woman said haughtily. "Always too proud for a wife. That's a sad life, being alone. I suppose you're still living in that one-room flat in Marylebone?"

"No, I live in a bucket in Nantucket."

The woman looked confused. "Must be difficult getting all your furniture in there."

Kavordnic rolled his eyes. "I think it's time for you all to disappear."

He waved his hand again and they dissolved into a dozen tiny black ants on the floor, scattering in all directions. He raised his foot as if to stomp, then paused and thought better of it. Apparently it was true that no matter how old you got, your family always treated you like a child. Kavordnic looked at me, seemed to formulate a thought in his brain, nodded silently, and then turned to shuffle wearily to the door. He waved vaguely toward the white walls.

"You have a true heart," he said. "I'll give you that. I hope for your sake that you inherited some of your father's brains. Better yet, all of your father's brains and some of your mother's as well. You can never have enough smarts in this universe. Though it'll still never get you anywhere. Might as well have been a plumber …"

"Wait!"

I ran after him, circling around to get in front before he left. Grudgingly he stopped and stood still like a statue. For a second I thought perhaps I'd accidentally frozen him, but then his eyes shifted and I realized he was waiting for me to speak. His eyebrows ascended wearily.

"Can you help me get my parents away from DIMCO?" I asked. "They've been captured by Ridpath and I need to know where they're being held."

He put up a hand. "I know, but there's nothing I can do. Whatever happens is already done. I'm too old to go back into proper time, and besides, all I ever seem to do is make the universe's situation worse."

"Can you give me ideas? What can I do?"

He frowned. "If I were you, I'd buy a piano. It helps pass the time."

I made to follow him but he shook his head. "You'll only get vaporized if you come through this door. It would be like walking into a paper shredder. On the positive side, your life energy would get recycled. The universe hates to lose energy."

"Can I go through any of these exits?"

"I'm afraid not," he said wearily. "You'd be a cow walking into an abattoir. Have you ever seen one of those places? Awful. The things human beings do to make a living."

I stomped my foot. "Will you at least tell me how to get out of here?"

"If that's the least I have to do, absolutely. Close your mouth for a few seconds and listen. And don't worry about that gunk on your skin. I was worried the first time I mutated in a reality distortion. The body is an amazing vehicle, but it takes some time to reverse the process. Think of your snail qualities as toilet paper stuck on your shoe."

And with that, Anton Kavordnic closed the door and shut me in, alone in my perfectly white room with no logical way out and a brain that had lost its power to create weapons. If he was the father of inter-dimensional theory, we were all doomed. He wasn't even friendly! I was coming to the conclusion that there wasn't anyone in the world you could count on. I sat cross-legged on the tiles and put my head in my hands.

And that's how Gus found me.

CHAPTER 14

FIRST CAME THE POUNDING, and then the monotone voice touched with the slightest hint of urgency. I looked up at the toilet bowl, which my forehead had apparently collided with on the way down. There was blood on the rim.

"Come on, Johnny boy," Gus said. "A man gets thirsty after six bags of pretzels, and when he drinks two cans of ginger ale there's a price that has to be paid. I hope you're not lancing your boils in there."

I wasn't sure if I'd slipped into a porthole in the space–time continuum or simply passed out from pain and conked my coconut on the toilet seat. Either way I had a bad headache, was shaken, and was glad to see Gus shifting from foot to foot in the aisle. He jammed past me and closed the door. When he re-emerged we gathered the others and I explained my story. No one else had noticed anything unusual, other than that I'd taken an outrageously long time in the toilet.

"I assumed you were constipated," Nate2 said. "You don't eat enough vegetables."

"Well maybe I was sent into a partial reality distortion or something. Kavordnic was there. And I heard Ridpath's voice. Maybe DIMCO is involved and this is some sort of trap. We got through that porthole way too easily."

"That was skill," Rex replied. "And it sounds like you're hallucinating. I've never heard anything about partial distortions or residual energy."

"What did Ridpath say?" Delores asked.

"He said 'There's only one way out.' It was definitely his voice, though I didn't see him. I think he was threatening me with death."

Ridpath2 in the back waved an arm, sending the odour of cat food wafting toward us. Delores tucked her nose into her arm and turned away. The old drunk was cackling as he swigged more high-octane cider.

"What do you want?" Rex snapped. "If you don't settle down we'll tie you up again. This time even tighter."

"I'm the one!" the drunk laughed.

"You're the messiah?" Gus asked.

"Ignore him," Rex muttered.

Ridpath2 continued to laugh to himself. "The boy was scream-ing *I want out,* the little bastard. People don't teach these kids to be tough no more! Needs a good walloping! Too many women raising men these days. Makes them soft."

"You're the ideal person to write a parenting manual," Gus said. "Watch yourself. You just spilled some of that XXX cider on your sleeve."

Ridpath2 looked down and sucked the wet patch of his shirt. He looked up and smiled crookedly, kind of like a dimwitted dog, and then began to shake again with silent laughter.

"I told him there's only one way out. Then he started shouting *door,* like a fool. Knew he was wrong in the head, then. Women should have nothing to do with raising boys. They'll start yelling *door* instead of knowing how to fight. It's a fact."

Rex nodded to Gus, who shrugged wearily, and together they got the duct tape. Underneath my slippery slime my skull pounded in pain. If the voice I'd heard *had* come from just outside the toilet door, then maybe I'd just blacked out and had a stupid dream. Everyone probably thought I was an idiot. I clenched my fists and wanted to punch Ridpath2, or the nearest seat, or something.

I sat alone for the rest of the trip, nursing my injuries and wondering about my sanity. My body still ached from colliding with the gymnasium wall, but I supposed I might have bounced off the sink and walls of the toilet when I fainted. Still, images of Kavordnic, the searing white, and the smell of formic acid were all so clear in my mind. I tried to remember some words of wisdom that Kavordnic had passed on that might prove he really had been with me, but the only advice that stuck in my head was to buy a piano. That could have been code for some greater strategy, but somehow I doubted it. I made my way to the front where Rex was speaking with Nate2.

"I don't suppose *piano* is a code for a covert operation?" I asked.

"No," Nate2 replied. "It's a musical instrument that you play while sitting down. I'm fonder of the mouth organ, myself."

"You would be," Rex said.

"You don't like the harmonica?"

"Um, back to my question," I interrupted.

"No clue," Rex said in a doubtful tone. "But you might want to get seated, because we're beginning our descent. I wouldn't like to see you faint in the aisle as we made our approach."

I still couldn't believe we'd made it through the porthole undetected, but we landed without any complications. I'd been looking forward to seeing Heathrow again, but we landed at a regional airstrip manned by a single obese security guard who was slouched in a computer chair watching the soccer game. He looked us over briefly, scanned our passports, and waved us through while munching on a meat pie.

"He's not usually that thorough," Rex said as we got into a car. "We've got him on the payroll, but I've never fully trusted him."

"Too ambitious?" Nate2 asked.

Rex, nate2, gus, delores, and i made a very long journey into London, moving through suburbs that expanded outward like layers of an onion. A fine rain began to fall, spitting on the windows of the small hatchback. I'd forgotten how different from home the city looked. The buildings were shoulder to shoulder and lawns were practically non-existent. The architecture was old, majestic, and made me feel like there was a lot in the world I didn't know. The people looked slightly different, too. There were more track suits, more formal blue suits, and a lot of guys had a really short, almost shaved style of hair.

The closer we got to central London, the more aggressive the driving became, with people accelerating, weaving in and out of lanes, leaning on their horns, and braking at the last second. I felt like I was in the Grand Prix, except with traffic lights. We'd go from zero to sixty in about five seconds, then brake, swerve, give someone a rude gesture, and start again. Finally Rex pulled over in front of a subway station and jammed the car into neutral. He handed me a piece of paper as we all got out.

"Yet another safe house," he said. "This time in Greenwich. If that's been compromised—heaven forbid—then take everyone to the Calypso Hotel. You do remember that fine establishment, I assume?"

"How could I forget," I groaned. "I'm still taking penicillin."

"Trust me, it's the ideal cover. I haven't seen a single DIMCO agent go past the front step yet."

Probably because that particular so-called student hotel *had* no front step. The first two had crumbled, and so a person had to jump to the third step in order to get to the door. Once inside, the place deteriorated even more. I had mistakenly tried to sleep there after arriving in London the first time, but bedbugs, cross-dressing guests, and a mattress that snagged me like a Venus flytrap made that impossible.

"Where are you going?" I asked.

"I have to gather information about your parents' whereabouts and get up to speed with my network. I feel like I've been away for years. Also, I wouldn't mind seeing my girlfriend. I told her I was popping out for the paper and a pint down at our local. She's probably living with someone else by now."

"Shouldn't we be going with you?" Nate2 persisted.

"No. You'll only slow me down."

Rex reached across the passenger's seat and pulled the door shut, jammed the car into gear, and cut into traffic in front of a delivery van that barely slammed on its brakes in time. Rex motioned with two forked fingers and drove straight across three lanes to make a left.

"I can see why you don't own a car," Gus murmured to Nate2. "It's like playing Russian roulette with a gas pedal. Still, I suppose in some ways it's better than public transportation. At least the only foot odour you have to suffer is your own."

Nate2 looked startled. "That reminds me, I do have to change these socks."

He began to walk away from the subway entrance toward a long row of black cabs that looked like big hunchbacked beetles.

"You think my money will work here?" Gus asked as we wandered behind.

"That guy on the back of the fifty-pound note is still smiling," I replied. "I'd have to say no."

"But we're in that dimension now," he said. "This really is their money."

"Oh yeah. I guess you're rich."

Somehow, in all the chaos of our escape from Toronto and my white-room experience, I'd forgotten that Gus and I would once again be vulnerable to distortion waves and dimensional fade. Delores would continue to suffer, because nobody seemed to know where she belonged. The only person who could be relieved to be back home was the tall, wild-haired eccentric loping ahead of us. He opened the door to a black cab and we piled in. The driver looked at us through the mirror and put down his tattered copy of *Today's Golfer*. "Where we off to then?" he asked.

"Greenwich," I said.

"Islington," Nate2 announced. "Call it a pit stop. I've got to pick up a few items and change the tape in my VCR. The old one will have run out by now and I'll be missing *Prime Suspect*."

Twenty minutes later we headed around the side of a huge double-storey house that had once belonged to my paternal family. Nate2's decrepit house was around the back, past the piles of broken plaster and torn-out beams. It was basically a cottage, with two small windows, a red door, and a single stovepipe jutting up out of the low roof. The door was over-hung with creepers and vines, the walls were dirty and murky yellow, and piles of decaying books blocked any view inside. Nate2 threw up his arms in joy.

"Home! I never thought I'd see my palatial residence again!"

As he let himself in Gus and Delores hesitated on the path.

"Is it safe?" Delores asked. "It looks like DIMCO has been here and really roughed the place up. That roof could cave in at any second."

"This is how it always looked," I murmured.

Nate2 returned to the doorway of the granny flat and waved us in. "Come on, come on. I've already put the kettle on."

We ducked inside, moved as many books as we could from the couch, and sat awkwardly beneath a pile of wavering Penguin titles. The entire room was like a hundred-year-old library and the dust was outrageous. Gus couldn't stop sneezing for at least a minute. Delores moved away from me incrementally. I self-consciously tried to mop up my ever-present thin layer of slime. Without thinking, I put a hand to one of the bumps on my forehead.

"They're getting worse," she said.

"Soak them in warm salt water," Nate2 offered. "Like I said, that will kill the infection and help bring up the pus sac. And you should drink lots of water. Anyone want biscuits with their tea?"

"I'm peachy," Delores replied stiffly.

"And they're not pus sacs," I said. "Kavordnic said my body would take some time to recover from my snail mutation. It's a lot to cope with physically."

From the way the others avoided my glance and stayed silent I could tell they still didn't believe my story.

"How do you live here?" Delores said, changing the subject.

Nate2 tugged his goatee. "I have no idea," he murmured. "It does explain some things, doesn't it? I have to admit I remember it as being much bigger."

"You've been away for, like, a month," I said.

"True. I must say I've got quite used to sharing your family home in Toronto. If I had any money, prospects, or hope, I'd buy a house myself."

"Why don't you start by getting a job?" I said.

Nate2 fidgeted with the kettle, pouring hot water into chipped cups. "I'd *like* to apply my mental aptitude to become fabulously wealthy, but unfortunately the working world is so *functional*. My talents aren't as valued as the manual dexterity of a short-haired, tattooed, toothless, uneducated, recently-released-from-prison electrician's assistant named Steve from New Cross. Which reminds me, I've got to send him a cheque for fixing my space heater."

"Uh, right," I said. "I know how proud you are of your brain. But if you can't get a job with your current *talents*, why don't you go back to university?"

"I'm too old. I wouldn't get invited to any good parties."

"But you might find your place in the world, and people who are like you. Well, in some ways similar to you. It's better than sitting around this granny flat all day reading paperbacks."

Nate2 sighed wistfully. "I understand your logic, but the fruitful season of my life has passed. I have been continually constipated by bad luck and I can't foresee that changing now." He looked up from the kettle. "Of course I don't mean that I've been physically constipated. Like I said before, regular bowel movements come down to eating enough vegetables."

"I don't even want the tea now," Delores said under her breath.

I straightened a leaning pile of books above my head. "All I know is that you're capable of more than you think. My father wouldn't settle for a lifetime of unhappiness."

"No, I don't suppose he would," Nate2 replied, barely above a whisper. "But then your mother wouldn't let him. Lucky sod."

CHAPTER 15

AS WE DRANK our tea and watched Nate2 eat a solitary mouldy cookie, he explained the circumstances surrounding the granny flat. Apparently, following the death of my grandparents, the family home could be sold only if the flat was leased rent-free for two generations. Not that Nate2 had wanted to sell the big home, but his father's finances were a muddle of poor investments and the upkeep was expensive. If he hadn't taken the option the bank would have stepped in and evicted him, leaving him with nowhere to live.

"No wonder you're a mess," Gus remarked. "We should get you into therapy."

"Doesn't work," Nate2 said. "Shock treatments were fun for a while, but the thrill wears off when you lose sensation in your fingertips and start dropping steaming hot cups of tea onto your lap. Nothing helped." He slurped his drink and sat up. "But we shouldn't be worrying about my circumstances. We have bigger problems at the moment."

We discussed the current situation and decided our best course of action was to go to the Greenwich safe house and wait for Rex to return with news about my parents. If we knew where DIMCO had them we could make plans with local members of the resistance. Rex had mentioned that there were a lot of people in the London organization who would help us if they could. My stomach ached with dread as a thousand scenarios filtered through my thoughts, most prominently my dad being tortured for his knowledge and my mom being kept in a cold prison cell. I hated DIMCO with a force that surprised me. Every rational thought about peacefulness and negotiations I'd ever had disappeared. I'd do anything to get my parents to safety—*anything*.

"All right," Nate2 said. "I'll pack an overnight bag and enough socks for the week, and then we can go fight evil people."

"Can we eat first?" Gus asked. "I'm getting really spacey with hunger."

"Hard to tell the difference," Delores said.

"You can have a biscuit," Nate2 said, offering the box.

"They're mouldy!" Delores replied. "You're going to die eating stuff like that."

Nate2 patted his belly. "Iron stomach. I can even eat spoiled meat, which has come in handy on more than one occasion when my disability cheque has been late. Did you know that the spices in Indian food were originally used to cover up the flavour and odour of bad meat?"

"Count me out for a curry," Gus said. "How about Chinese?"

As we trudged out of the granny flat I wondered why Nate2 would be drawing a disability pension. He seemed perfectly normal in a physical sense, and though weird, wasn't what I would classify as mentally unstable. Okay, so maybe he had gone through some therapy, but lots of people needed help and advice. As I thought about his situation I remembered that when he was arrested in Scotland a month earlier he'd been released and given a card stating he was "Certifiably Mental," but to the best of my knowledge that was a direct result of assaulting an undercover agent and telling the authorities that all his friends were seven feet tall and invisible. He'd been lying to protect us. I wanted to ask him more, but the topic was probably sensitive and best left to another time when we were alone. We made our way to a small shop tucked into a side street and followed Nate2 inside to what he described as the best Chinese joint in all of London.

"Of course I haven't tried many others," he said. "Call me a creature of habit. I haven't actually gone to a restaurant outside my area in eleven years. I think that once you find an establishment you can tolerate you should never deviate. You'll only be disappointed."

"Is the food here as tasty as the dim sum place in Toronto?" Gus asked.

"Oh goodness no. Not even close."

We sat at a big round table and I told the waitress that we had to be fast. The others responded by ordering appetizers. Delores asked for no MSG but Nate2 dismissed her, saying she was too young to worry about her blood pressure. The waitress returned a few minutes later and distributed dessert bowls full of what appeared to be creamy orange Thousand Island dressing. Inside the goop were the pale white corpses of several limp shrimps.

"What is this?" I asked.

"Prawn cocktail," Nate2 said, licking dressing from his fingers. "Famous British–Chinese cuisine. Goes very nicely with Shanghai chicken and chips as a main. Sweet and sour pork in a Yorkshire pudding is also excellent—well, at least typically edible. You can't beat minute, fatty pieces of pork coated in batter and drowned in bright orange glaze."

I pushed the dish away. "Shrimp cocktail is supposed to be healthy looking and served with a tomato and horseradish dip, not drowned in oily dressing."

"Think of it as a new cultural experience."

"Spoken by a man who'd never left England before he went to Scotland a month ago."

"Yes, but look at me now. I'm a walking advertisement for Lonely Planet." He extracted a limp shrimp corpse from his dish and popped it into his mouth, dripping dressing onto his goatee and shirt in the process. "Be a good sport and dig in."

"I can't," I said. "This is a bowl of fat."

"Have you looked at the menu?" Gus said, slurping a shrimp. "Everything is a bowl of fat."

"Well yes," Nate2 conceded. "That's elementally true. This place isn't exactly in the health food market. But the whole point of any take-away is to load up your body with lard. It helps get one ready for the long, damp winter months when an extra layer of padding protects one from the chill, especially if one doesn't have a girlfriend. I know it's summer, but we're insulating in advance. Now eat up before your dressing gets ruddy orange on top from exposure to the air."

Delores wasn't arguing, but she also wasn't eating her appetizer. She ordered a vegetable chop suey—easy on the oil—and white rice and didn't say much through the meal. No doubt her fatigue was bringing her down and she just wanted to go home. She offered around some of her meal, which was pretty bland without the MSG. I reached for the saltshaker and accidentally knocked it over, spilling white granules across the paper tablecloth.

"Quick," Nate2 said. "Throw some over your left shoulder or you'll have bad luck for all eternity."

"That'd be a change," I replied.

I reached for a pinch of salt, and then recoiled as a burning sensation ripped through my fingertips. It was as though I'd placed a lit match right against my skin. I waved my hand to ease the pain, but the sensation didn't go away until I plunged my fingers into Gus's glass. Several people around us stared and whispered.

"Thank you," Gus said. "Yes, I'm done with my water. Maybe you'd like to stick your elbow in my braised beef with oyster sauce. What's the special flavour in this dish, by the way?"

"Charcoal," Nate2 said. "They have a difficult time with beef for some reason and often burn it. Just be thankful you didn't order the Szechwan duck with crispy skin. Their bird plucker hasn't worked right in years."

"Why don't they get a new one?" Gus asked.

"Because he's a very nice man. He doesn't speak a word of English, at least not to me. He's one of two brothers who own the business. I think these family-owned companies are a beautiful thing."

I examined my fingertips and saw that the skin was raw and raised. More slime than ever was flowing onto the wound, covering it like a soothing balm. My forehead burst into pain as if I'd been hit with a lightning bolt and I stumbled from the table toward the bathroom sign. The waitress watched me warily and raced to the kitchen, no doubt to report that one of the customers appeared to have food poisoning. It had to be a regular occurrence at this place.

I staggered through the thin plywood door and locked myself in, trying not to think of the old adage that you can tell the cleanliness of a restaurant's kitchen by the cleanliness of its bathroom. I used some toilet paper to clean the mirror and then winced in pain. I couldn't resist squeezing the bumps, thinking that if they were boils, they were definitely near their breaking point. I pressed hard and fully expected two hot jet streams of putrid pus to blast out onto the wall. Sure enough the forehead skin gave way, but instead of runny liquid, two solid lumps popped out and stayed connected to my skin. I squeezed again. Blood and slime ran down into my eyes, but barely anything sprayed.

"Oh come on …"

I rubbed the mirror harder, but the reflection wasn't the problem. I looked up hopefully at the bulb above and then dropped my head in defeat. I touched the grey lumps protruding from my brow and admired their soft, silky texture. I didn't know how I was going to explain this to anyone who saw me on the street, but I appeared to have grown two enormous snail antennae on my forehead.

CHAPTER 16

EVEN WITH THE NEW PHYSICAL EVIDENCE the others were hesitant to believe my Kavordnic story. Gus suggested that maybe the slow-recovery theory could have come from my subconscious mind. Nate2 took a long look at my bumps, made a few *hmm* sounds, and said he might have an idea. We high-tailed it from the restaurant immediately.

I couldn't conceive of Nate2's doing any strenuous physical activity, especially tennis, but apparently my own love of the game was implanted somewhere deep down in my genes. We returned to his hovel and waited while he rooted around an old trunk, finally pulling out an ancient wooden racquet missing some strings, several deflated balls, and a cream-coloured tennis outfit that once might have been white.

"Aha!" he said. "I knew I'd still have this gear stashed away. They're probably collectors' items by now."

He handed me a mildewed elastic headband still encrusted in stains. I'd seen them worn mostly in pictures of old matches from the 1970s when no one on the planet had any fashion sense. It was white, thick, and woolly. I widened the item slowly and grimaced. Seeing my pain, Nate2 scrubbed off the lingering salty sweat residue in his sink using dish detergent and wrung it out. With my pride already decimated by high school dances, Burger Hut, and moving between dimensions, I figured wearing the band couldn't do much more harm. Gus leaned in close.

"It's as if everything you do is designed to drive Delores farther away. We have to have a serious talk about ways to attract the opposite sex."

"This isn't funny."

Nate2 was cackling in the corner, and even Delores couldn't contain a smirk. I found a mirror and felt my shoulders slump on sight. My reflection belonged in an exhibition on tennis history in some museum. At least the headband covered my lumps.

"So," Gus asked Nate2, "were you good?"

"I looked stunning on court."

"But how about your skills?" I asked. "I bet with your height, you'd have a great serve and lots of reach around the net."

Nate2 scratched his chin. "My coach said I had the best overhead smash of anyone in the nation. My forehand was above par and my serve was equal to that of the great John Newcombe."

"Get out," I said, seriously impressed.

"Have I ever lied to you?"

Gus picked at his nails, looked away, and whistled pointedly. Delores scanned the yard from the one window that wasn't bricked up or completely blocked by old paperbacks. I drummed my fingers on a pile of yellowing magazines and didn't drop my gaze. Nate2 frowned.

"Have I ever lied to you ... *directly*?"

"Why didn't you turn pro?" I asked.

"Well that's a complex question, one that involves such factors as desire, practice, financial resources, and stamina, though basically the problem was that I have no lateral movement. I can't move from side to side. It's some sort of hereditary disposition on my mother's side, as if I might be missing the vital *crab gene* embedded in the first human microbe that crawled from the primordial sea. I was excellent when the ball was hit directly at me, though. Absolutely stellar."

To get to Greenwich we travelled the Picadilly Line to Leicester Square, then walked down to Charing Cross and took a train headed east. The River Thames skirted out of view as we passed old brick buildings and gleaming new office low rises and moved away from central London. The train was crowded and filled with a heavy cloud of B.O. as we accelerated along the track. Two guys in Manchester United shirts were looking my way, smirking.

"All right, Bjorn?" one finally asked.

"Six–love in the first set," the other said, pretending to speak through a PA system. They killed themselves with guffaws and continued to crack themselves up by asking if I was ready for Wimbledon and if I'd just flown in from Sweden. I'd like to say my fellow travellers looked down upon such rude mocking of a defenceless tourist, but with all the muffled cackles in the compartment it could have been closing time at the Comedy Club. The second guy was wheezing so hard I hoped he might asphyxiate. Finally I turned my back to everyone and faced the door. Delores squeezed in next to me, so close that I could feel the heat coming off her body. The hairs on my skin stood up—at least the ones not weighed down by slime.

"Ignore them," she said. "You look … fine-ish."

"Think what they'd say if you took the headband off," Gus murmured.

"And you certainly don't look Swedish," Nate2 added. "They have very distinct facial features. And you're not even blond."

Nate2 told us about Greenwich, which turned out to be a significant place in history. It was home to a large observatory, a maritime museum, and the Royal Naval College. Several kings and queens had been born in Greenwich, and the London Marathon started there every year.

"The observatory," I interrupted. "I wonder if that's why we have a safe house in the area. I'm sure we'd have a few astronomers on our side. They must be mapping more portholes."

"Greenwich is also the point of zero longitude," Nate2 continued. "Every time zone in the world follows from its radius. I suppose you could say time begins and ends exactly where we'll be staying."

I looked over the map and saw that Greenwich was close to Blackheath. The name sparked something in my memory, but I couldn't remember what. Maybe it had been in a movie. Delores was gazing blankly out the window, lost in thought. It was strange to be this close to her and weird to be able to really look at her face. I could see the texture of her skin, the lines of her makeup, the length of her black eyelashes. I could even see her pores, those tiny craters of skin. I resisted a weird urge to touch her hair and run my finger down her neck. I swallowed hard as she turned and looked directly at me. But she didn't explode in annoyance and ask what the hell I was staring at, as she normally would. Instead, she smiled gently and touched my elbow.

"How are you coping?" she asked.

"I'm not used to crowded trains."

"Yeah, me neither. Where I come from everyone has a car."

"How are you?" I asked. "With the situation and your energy and all that stuff?"

She exhaled. "I'm not going to complain, especially to you. I don't know how you're managing to stay so calm given your parents. I'd be more worried than a goat roper at a hoedown—a total basket case—even though my folks are anal, middle class, and scary conservative."

"I try not to think too much," I said. "Sometimes a person has to accept what they can't change. I'll get upset when I know something bad has really happened. Until then, I'm going to be ready to break my parents out."

Delores nodded. "I know Ridpath is crazy and there's a lot at stake with inter-dimensional travel technology, but this country is still a democracy, so he can't do much more than hold them under arrest and question them. We'll find a way to get them back."

I admired Delores's faith in the system, but I had no reason to believe Ridpath was acting within the law. Rex had said before that DIMCO was highly secretive, with most of their covert actions hidden from even the prime minister. I was determined to compartmentalize the situation, tucking fear way in the back broom closet of my mind, behind hope, bravery, and resolve. My dad was the smartest person I knew, rivalled closely by my mother, and they'd both do everything in their power to protect each other. They were a team, solid and unbreakable.

"We're here," Nate2 moaned. "Squeeze out. Don't be afraid to use your elbows."

"Good luck in the finals!" someone shouted behind me.

"Say hi to Maria Sharapova!"

The latest safe house wasn't far from the station—down a winding street next to a large, mostly treeless park. The place was number 82, a brown townhouse that didn't strike me as fully secure, mainly because the key was tucked ingeniously under the front doormat. We crept through the entrance slowly, but the stale air suggested the place had been tenant-free for months. The front room was fully furnished with moderately good couches, a small TV, and paintings and photos of what I recognized to be Greenwich at various times through the ages. There was a shot of bomb damage from the Second World War and a more recent colour photo of a wooden sailing ship, the *Cutty Sark*.

"Wonder who used to live here," I said.

Delores collapsed into a chair, causing a small mushroom cloud of dust to rise up. "As long as they owned a bed—well, several—I don't care. I'm plumb worn out. I've never been so exhausted in my life. Does anyone's brain still work well enough to figure out how long it's been since we slept?"

"At least a day," I said.

"Should we all bunk down in the same room so that we can stay together in case of a distortion wave?" Gus asked.

I hadn't thought about that. The idea of having to share sleeping space with anyone else was unpleasant. All I wanted was a soft mattress, a pillow that would swallow half my head, and dark silence. I still had the sunglasses in my pocket, which would mean one of us could rest securely, but Gus had a point about safety.

"For comfort's sake," Delores said, "why don't we split into pairs? If a wave hits, hopefully it won't be a strong one since we've just arrived in this dimension again. Maybe we should fight through them in twos. It'll mean only half the number of predicaments to overcome: two people face two problems."

"But they'll have half the help to resolve the issues," I said. "We've always come up with solutions together."

"But we might be able to get out quicker. I don't know."

"But there's the old cliché about safety in numbers," I replied.

"Better the devil you know," Gus added.

"A bird in hand is worth two in the bush," Nate2 chimed in eagerly. "A stitch in time saves nine. Never feed a cat unless you know where it's come from."

Gus raised his chin. "I've never heard that one."

"It's one of mine," Nate2 said proudly.

Delores hunched her shoulders and appeared ready to scream. Instead she spoke softly. "If y'all want to keep gabbing, please wait until I'm gone to bed."

Together, we all trudged upstairs, the question of who would pair off with whom clearly at the back of everyone's mind.

Delores went into the first bedroom off the hall and Gus, Nate2, and I all jammed together in the door frame as we made to follow.

"Well I'm not sleeping with him!" Gus said, pointing to Nate2. "He's enormous and would probably roll over in the night and crush me. Besides, he's your father ... kind of ... in this weird inter-dimensional way. You share blood."

"Moot point, m'boy," Nate2 said. "I don't share beds with teenage boys. It starts rumours I don't need in my life. You saw what happened to Michael Jackson."

"You're not sleeping with me," Delores said. "Sorry, but you're old and it's creepy."

Nate2 looked at her blankly. "Fair enough. At least you're honest. You have wounded my nearly non-existent ego, but there you go. Lads, why don't you flip a coin to see who'll get to spend the night with the maiden fair."

Delores grabbed me by the arm, yanked my body inside, and slammed the door. Apparently there were times for debate and team decisions and other times when a person just wanted to go to sleep. She peeled off her heavy leather jacket and poked the large bed with her hand. It seemed wide enough that we could comfortably sleep without ever coming into contact with each other. As for me, I hadn't moved from my spot by the door and couldn't think of anything that would calm my racing brain. I wondered if I could kiss her. I supposed it would be easy to make the first move if we were lying next to each other, maybe face to face. We could talk for a while and then lock eyes and then all I'd have to do would be to nudge my lips forward an inch or two. I wondered if she wanted me to hold her. As I ran possible scenarios through my head my extremities began to get cold and numb. Swallowing became difficult and my sweater felt several sizes too small. And then, without so much as a word, Delores jumped sideways onto the mattress and bounced several times.

"Firm," she mumbled. "This'll do nicely."

She overcame the intimacy of the situation by turning over, tucking the blanket over her shoulder, and almost immediately beginning to snore. I flipped off my shoes, nearly gagged at the rampant odour, and crept into the cold far edge of the bed.

So much for romance.

CHAPTER 17

I WOKE UP as if out of a coma. My mouth was flypaper sticky and my body was as heavy and immobile as soggy newspaper. The sunlight was streaming through the window, which in my experience was rare in London. I looked at the clock by the bed and saw that it was two in the afternoon; although, considering this dimension had only fifteen hours in a day, I hadn't slept an excessively long time. Gus was sitting on the edge of the bed as Delores rubbed a towel through her wet hair. Her face was pink and pale and soft and innocent looking. I bet she couldn't wait to fish out her black lipstick and get to work. Gus was speaking to her in a hushed tone. Neither of them noticed I was awake.

"I've been having this feeling," he was saying. "Like I might have a higher calling. All this turmoil has to have meaning in the grand scheme of life, like, when you think of existence in terms of spirituality and having a soul. Sometimes I feel like I might be a prophet."

"For what?" Delores asked skeptically.

"Well, I don't know exactly. I'm not into organized religion, so I suppose I might have to start a small cult. But my life has been full of signs of impending divinity. Like last year, I spent a summer in the rainforest around Cairns in Northern Queensland helping to build a friend's vacation home. We slept in the frame with only mosquito netting to separate us from nature. It was very Zen."

144

"Sounds like hell to me."

He shifted slightly closer to her. "Not at all. I was connecting with the natural world. I was one with my surroundings."

"I can't imagine you building a house. That would take effort."

"Yeah," Gus conceded. "I wasn't into that part of the project. I carried around some wood, but mostly I was in charge of making herbal tea and getting the vibe right. Anyway, I had this dream where a goddess came to me and showed me a bright wall of light. I could really feel her presence. And the next day, when I woke up, a python had shed its skin in my room."

"You're joking."

"No. The place was infested with rats. It was no surprise that a snake would come in."

"Rats *and* snakes. Nice."

"Well, if it's any consolation, we didn't have many rodents after that night, not that I stayed long. I thought the vibe was pretty good, so I caught a bus back to Brisbane. Still, looking back, I can see how *pivotal* the experience was for me. It's the reason I sold my car and went to Europe."

"I thought you said you wanted to meet Irish girls?"

Gus scratched his chin self-consciously. "Uh, yeah, that too. The Irish are a spiritual people."

Delores rolled her tongue around the inside of her cheek and looked generally disinterested. "That's really deep," she muttered.

"Thank you. I like that shade of nail polish. What is it?"

She looked down at her hand. "Black."

"That's what I'm talking about: *purity.*"

I felt betrayal seep over me like odour from a sewer vent. Not only had Gus wanted to abandon the team in Toronto, now he was hitting on Delores. I wasn't sure whether to feign sleep and let his tongue ruin his chances or sit up and confront him. I decided to wait and see where this conversation went. I didn't need to worry, I told myself, because Delores clearly liked me best and he didn't have a chance. I was the one she'd pulled into the bedroom, and even though nothing happened, she had made her preference clear.

"People don't understand you, do they?" Gus continued. "I bet you've never felt like you've been in the right dimension."

Delores thought about this for a few seconds and then launched forth with a surprising passion. "I don't feel like I even come from my own planet. It's like everything I value—honesty, conversation, leather—isn't respected by society. All people want is money and giant houses. I'm into so much more."

Gus moved closer once again. "You're intense and passionate. You shouldn't feel ashamed of that."

"I don't. That's why I have trouble fitting in to society. But there's no way public opinion is going to break me. I'm worth more than that."

I didn't like the way this conversation was going. Delores was sounding engaged, so I let out a loud yawn, stretched my arms, and sat bolt upright in the bed. Gus got up slowly.

"Wow," I said. "How long was I zonked out?"

"Not quite long enough," Gus replied.

"About ten hours," Delores said. "You flail around in your sleep. You elbowed me in the head twice. I figured you were having nightmares, so I didn't smother you with a pillow."

A vague imprint of memory flipped across my conscious mind. I remembered a dream about my parents—that I'd found them and had to fight Ridpath in hand-to-hand combat—but I couldn't remember how it ended. We'd been in a grey room, and there'd been laughter.

Delores explained that Rex still hadn't shown up, so the others had spent the morning milling around and eating tinned foods from the cupboards. Nate2 had found a tool kit and was currently attempting to fix the display on the tracking device that he'd fished out of the toilet in Toronto. Then she left the room to apply a no-doubt thick layer of makeup, leaving Gus and I to linger in the bedroom. He turned to me, shaking his head slowly, like my father did when he was disappointed.

"Mate," he said. "You're a difficult man to fathom. If you're not going to make a move on D, step aside. I've been biding my time as your straight man, but your window of opportunity is up."

"What does that mean?"

"I've been working for you since we met. I've laughed at your jokes in front of the girl, guided you toward cunning plans, and let you be the star. But you've consistently let opportunity slip by. Now I want a crack at that mouth. There's something about her black lipstick that's got me hypnotized. So be a mate and step aside. It's the code of conduct."

"Really? I wasn't aware there was a rule book."

"Maybe it's a Brisbane thing. Still, don't be lame. I want to make out with her and you're not having much success."

"I'm letting things happen slowly," I said. "Besides, I feel weird trying to date her when we're on the run. It's all about priorities. I like her, but now is not a good time to make some dumb fumbling move to kiss her. And besides, she's from another world."

"See, you're talking your way out of taking action already. I'm a believer in going with the flow, pursuing the spiritual side of two human beings making a connection. All the rest can work itself out."

"But she's going to disappear into another universe."

"No long-term hang-ups. Perfect."

"But—"

"I don't care about the consequences," he blurted. "I just want to make out!"

At this point Delores appeared at the doorway looking utterly confused. She looked from Gus to me and back again with her eyebrows raised. I wanted to explain that Gus didn't want to make out with *me,* but then I'd have to get into our attraction for her and that would be a real mess. Instead, I turned to Gus and bit my lip.

"I just don't feel that way about you," I said.

I got up, took Delores by the arm, and together we went downstairs. She asked what all that was about, but I changed the subject to what was around to eat, and we made our way to the kitchen where Nate2 had electronic scraps spread out across the dark oak table. He was scratching his head vigorously, looking over various pieces, screwing the mechanism back together.

"How are the antennae?" he asked.

I touched my forehead lightly. "Yeah. Good, I guess. What are you doing?"

"I replaced a circuit," he said. "Should work fine now. Must have shorted out because of that toilet water. Oh, and I found some bread in the back of the icebox and made us all tinned beef sandwiches."

"Not hungry," Delores replied.

My stomach was aching, so I hoped that the big guy had scrubbed his hands thoroughly and dug in. Gus wandered downstairs in slow, stiff steps and lounged silently at the end of the table as Nate2 continued to systematically piece together the tracking device, showing a hitherto unseen level of skill and concentration. As he worked he told us how the Earl of Sandwich had invented the sandwich because he was so addicted to poker that he hated to leave a game to eat a meal. He asked his servants to find a way he could eat meat, cheese, and bread conveniently, and voilà!

"I can't imagine a guy named Earl being smart enough to invent anything," Gus murmured.

"That was his title," Nate2 said, "not his name."

"Old eccentrics invented a lot of things in this country, didn't they?" I remarked.

Nate2 sighed. "I suppose. You'd be surprised how many good ideas raving loonies come up with when they've got time on their hands. I've invented a few contraptions myself. I've even got patents. For a time, I really thought the Animal Health Distributors' Association might finance my cat shaving kit, at least until I received the restraining order. My design was painless and could have prevented a lot of unnecessary allergic reactions."

"I've got an idea of my own," I said.

"A kettle that makes gravy?" Nate2 asked.

"Uh, no … I'm tired of being unprepared for reality distortions. You know, never knowing what we're about to face. I realize that we don't have much control over our brains, but it makes sense to take some precautions. Like with tennis, or any sport or hobby, you only get better with practise. Training your muscles to do what you want through constant repetition. It makes sense that our brains would work the same way."

"Haven't we done that before?" Delores asked. "We manipulated the distortion wave on the plane over here."

"Yes, but that was a controlled wave. We never have enough time when real ones hit. I know it sounds strange, but if we train ourselves to think of a very specific, well-developed, highly positive memory or idea as an automatic reflex, we might be able to create safer, easier reality distortions."

Delores ran the tip of her tongue over her crooked bottom tooth. "I'm not sure that's exactly how people's brains work—like a light switch—but what do I know. If mind-over-matter can allow people in India to walk barefoot over hot coals, I suppose we might be able to engineer a few pleasant memory reflexes."

Nate2 took a break from his reconstruction work and we gathered in the living room in a line. We closed our eyes to maximize concentration and tried to clear our minds of their cluttered thoughts. At irregular intervals I would yell "Wave," then we'd lock arms and focus silently on one positive thought, each time trying to make it clearer and more defined in our mind's eye. I thought of playing tennis, building the fantasy to increase my power and skill, so that by the twentieth time I yelled "Wave" I was winning Wimbledon in a romp. I was completely in charge and every shot went exactly where I wanted. No one could even hope to beat me. As the task progressed, I envisioned what I was wearing—pure white shorts and a collared shirt—and the crowd came into view. They were all smiling and were firmly on my side. I had no enemies.

We honed our mental skills further by envisioning things that caused fear, like being stranded alone, sharks, heights, and falling. At the key second we would sweep away these bad thoughts and instantly replace them with our good ones. I was really happy with our progress and within an hour was exhausted but ready.

Nate2 went back to the tracking device as Gus rested and Delores and I went through the cupboards to see exactly how much food we had. The answer: enough for a day. We decided that we'd have to go out and shop. I was itching to get fresh air and was trying not to think about Rex's extended absence. He should have made contact with us by now. I needed to get moving to feel that I was being productive.

"Eureka!" Nate2 enthused, holding up the device. "I really do amaze myself with my untapped potential. I'm surprised the BBC hasn't approached me about starring in my own reality TV series. Of course, I can't abide those types of shows, but it would be nice to be asked."

He adjusted the knobs and levels as the instrument attempted to connect to a satellite. Within seconds maps of London began to filter onto the screen, the program coming to rest on our area. I could see that Greenwich was separated from Blackheath by the large park outside our door. Again, I tried to remember why Blackheath seemed so familiar, wondering if my father or Rex might have mentioned it as an important area for DIMCO. I knew the connotations were negative.

"Anyone know where DIMCO's headquarters are?" I asked.

"Allegedly under the former power station that now houses the Tate Modern art gallery," Nate2 replied. "At least that's what most of the chat-room traffickers seem to believe. But then most of them are outrageous geeks."

I nodded slowly. We huddled around the tracking device and scanned east toward the city from the four red dots representing our location. There were two dots—one blue, one red—in Earls Court, location of the Calypso Hotel, perhaps the worst accommodation choice in the developed world. And sure enough in Bankside, across the Thames from St. Paul's Cathedral, inside the Tate Modern, three red dots were clustered together.

"We should assume two of those are your parents," Nate2 said glumly.

"The two in Earls Court are likely the pilot and Ridpath's twin," Delores said. "I think that's where Rex said they were going, which means Rex must be …"

"Inside DIMCO," I finished for her. "Let's hope he's doing reconnaissance and hasn't been arrested. Though you'd think he would have checked in by now."

We exchanged worried glances, but no one expanded on the thought. Instead, we scanned through more and more districts—Kensington, Covent Garden, Wimbledon City, Hounslow—gradually moving west and then north.

"Wait," Delores said. "What was that yellow dot in St. Pancreas?"

Nate2 turned. "St. *Pancras*. The founding fathers and city administrators would never be so ridiculous as to name a borough after an internal organ. An appendage maybe … The area was named after a fourteen-year-old Roman orphan boy who was decapitated two thousand years ago."

"What did a kid do to become a saint?" Gus asked.

"Not much other than die," Nate2 replied. "I suppose he must have refused to worship pagan gods, like Zeus and Hermes and that one on the tuna cans."

"Skippy," Gus offered.

"Neptune," Delores mumbled.

"I thought a person needed three miracles to become a saint," I said.

Nate2 did an agitated spasm. "I don't know! I'm not even Catholic. Perhaps the Church hit a dry spell and decided to play fast and loose with the rules to aid their PR. It has been known to happen."

Within seconds the yellow dot disappeared and didn't return despite Nate2's skilled attempts to retune the tracking device by pounding it with his open palm. I had no idea what the different colours represented. We decided that Rex's situation demanded action and voted to trek to the Calypso Hotel in Earls Court to find the mysterious pilot, Hank, who'd flown us into this dimension. Maybe he'd have information and technology that could help us break into DIMCO.

As we walked out the front door I looked at the park that separated us from Blackheath. The word *black* stuck in my brain. I wanted to pair the word with another one. I was close—the relevance of the place was right on the tip of my thoughts, needing only a gentle nudge for me to remember why this place was so remarkable.

Nate2 looked up at the blue sky. "Well, it's a lovely day: slightly hazy, touch of humidity. We might be on the cusp of a heat wave."

"Why is there never a cold wave?" Delores asked. "Or a heat snap?"

"Hey, Nate," I said.

"Hay is for horses, m'boy."

"Right. I've been trying to remember why Blackheath is signif-icant. Do you know much about the place?"

Before he could answer, I felt the first ripple pulse through the air, running across my slimy skin and into my spine and stomach. The initial burst was followed by a powerful blast that spun me off my feet and onto the sidewalk. This distortion wave was a wallop—far too strong for the amount of time we'd spent in the dimension. I jammed one hand into my pocket, grasping for the missing sunglasses, and with my other attempted to reach Delores's outstretched hand. Her face was twisted into an anguished scowl and she was grunting loudly while clutching her stomach. As the final crash of invisible pressure overwhelmed us, I managed to grab the fringe of her jacket.

Suddenly, the bustling city full of car horns and voices and grinding engines all went eerily silent.

CHAPTER 18

I DIDN'T EVEN WANT to get up off the sidewalk. I wanted to lie there and refuse to move until the universe apologized for excessive torment and for jumping my brain at its weakest moments. Nate2, Gus, and Delores were all scanning the still street, waiting for our minds' first projections to appear.

"Everyone automatically think their happy thought?" Delores asked.

This was met with noncommittal moans. Gus ventured to the corner, looked up the side street, peered into the park, and came back to the group. He spread his arms wide.

"I think my brain worked," he said. "Surprise, surprise. I wasn't sure I had it in me, not traditionally being what a person might call disciplined. But the world seems to be completely void of human life, so my positive thought was bonza."

"A world without people makes you happy?" I said.

"From a strategy point of view, I think it's ingenious," he replied. "No crazy tour guides or homicidal Scotsmen to torment us. An empty world isn't my ultimate dream, of course. Ideally, if I were the CEO of Earth, I'd like to pick and choose people for the planet. You know, keep Kylie Minogue, get rid of Dannii; allow Guy Ritchie to stay and make movies; accidentally knock Madonna off the list unless she promises to stop with the acting and children's books."

"Wasn't Madonna that one-hit wonder from the eighties?" Nate2 asked. "She sang the song 'Vacation.'"

"It was called 'Holiday,'" Delores said. "And she's huge in my dimension."

"Oh, she's enormous here, too," Nate2 replied. "She tried a comeback in the nineties and must have weighed at least three hundred pounds."

Gus meanwhile was smiling smugly at the brilliance of his idea, doing a little shuffling dance like an arthritic eighty-year-old. He made to hug Delores in celebration, but she batted his arm away and shoved him back. She was looking up and down the road with a frown. I was looking keenly too, but also listening for any suspicious noises.

"What were you thinking?" Delores asked me.

I shivered slightly as a breeze cut through. "The wave caught me off guard. I was thinking about the weather."

"I suppose that's not too bad."

"I can see already that the clouds are moving in," Nate2 said. "Oh well, three consecutive hours of sun is a record for this time of year."

"It's summer," I pointed out.

"Exactly."

This was tolerable enough—a slight change in the weather and a world devoid of people. Except the planet wasn't empty. I jumped, startled, as a woman with blazing pink makeup, a perfectly managed short coiffure, and a leather handbag came striding around the corner with her nose held in the air. She waved a hand full of long pink nails our way and cooed Delores's name.

"Mom!" Delores shouted in return and ran off to meet her.

Nate2 whistled through pursed lips. "If the apple doesn't fall far from the tree, her father must be Dracula." He nudged me. "They say you can tell what your wife will look like when she's older by observing her mother. That's your future, boy."

"She's not my girlfriend, and there's no way we'll ever get married, because she doesn't even come from my dimension. Are you two deaf?"

Nate2 tapped his head. "Partially in one ear—middle school rowboat accident—got hit with an oar. Never make a snide remark about a female's paddling technique, no matter what the age."

"So, big fella," Gus interrupted. "What was running through that stuffed cranium of yours when the wave hit? No more living statues in the park, I hope."

Nate2 cleared his throat and looked positively upbeat, his voice rattling at a slightly higher pitch than usual. "Oh goodness no! I managed to focus all my mental energy on the good of the group. Team player am I! Not for one second did I allow even the smallest potentially lethal idea to squeeze into my conscious state. I've always had a great control over my mental world."

Gus slapped his forehead. "You blew it, didn't you?"

"I couldn't help it!" Nate2 pleaded. "I was perfectly ready to think of being in the world's largest library when John planted the seeds of Blackheath's morbid history in my mind. And then the way you fumbled around for my shirt collar, I thought I might have it turned inside out. I didn't realize we were being assaulted by a distortion wave until I felt breakfast insinuating that it wanted to come back up my esophagus. Isn't someone supposed to shout out a warning?"

"I was in too much pain," I said.

From the park a loud groan that didn't sound fully human echoed through the barren plain. This was followed by several more. Nate2 bit his nails and then clenched his teeth. Delores stopped talking to her mother and turned our way. Nate2 pointed to Gus, who'd turned in the direction of the growing cacophony. And then my memory finally clicked.

"The black plague!" I said. "That's how Blackheath got its name, because tens of thousands of people were buried under the park!"

"Bit of an urban legend," Nate2 replied, holding up his hand. "The name existed long before the plague, but it *was* a site for burying a swath of the diseased population. That's why they have no tube running underground here—too many burial pits."

"So what exactly were you thinking?" Delores asked.

Nate2 smiled politely and tried to pat her head. "There can't be more than a few thousand plague victims strolling our way. Anyone else chilly?"

The wind had indeed geared the temperature down a notch. The thin layer of slime on my arms and forehead was chilly to the touch and the sun had retreated completely beneath dark clouds. The tone of the light gave the street a shadowy feel—all colour bled into grey. Across the empty park several black outlines appeared to be moving in our direction.

"Anyone have any ideas?" I asked.

"Why don't we go for a lovely lunch?" Delores's mother said. "My treat. I'm Esther by the way. I haven't heard anything about you people, but Delores can be quite secretive about her friends. It's a phase she's going through. The same can be said with all this black clothing. Her father and I have decided to let her get it out of her system before college. I'm all for individuality in people between the ages of sixteen and nineteen."

"It's not a phase," Delores replied. "We don't have the same beliefs. This is who I am."

Her mother tittered. "Say what you will, young lady, but this ain't my first rodeo. I know how the world works. You'll grow to see the things different when you want to buy a house and have children of your own."

"I'm never having kids," Delores said.

"Of course, dear. But I've kept my old cookie jar *just in case*. I'm ready to make my grandchildren gingerbreads, like the ones you loved."

She patted Delores on the head, which provoked a tight scowl. Delores looked at me with an air of embarrassment. Her mom dug a compact out of her handbag and fixed her heavy pastel makeup in the tiny mirror. They had one thing in common.

"Okay," Gus began. "I think we can safely overcome Delores's part of the reality distortion by feeding her mom to these zombies."

"HEY!" Delores shouted.

"Well, she's not real," Gus said matter-of-factly. "Are you, Mrs. Watson?"

Delores's mother paused and looked up. "Oh, I'm not sure … I'd have to check with my husband."

"He doesn't own you," Delores spat. "I'm never getting married either."

"I've kept my wedding dress in case."

Nate2 was eyeing Esther from her high heels to her coiffure, raising his eyebrows at the parts he apparently liked.

Gus continued talking to Delores's mom. "Why do you think your daughter spends so much time in her room alone?"

"Because she's sad and thinks people don't like her," Esther responded happily.

"That's so not true!" Delores screeched.

"Honey, you think people hate you and that boys find you uglier than flies on a cow's rear end. You feel a lot of anger and often cry into your pillow. But Mommy loves you."

Delores hauled off and belted Gus solidly in the stomach, doubling him over. Her face was raging red and her teeth reminded me of those machines in junkyards used to crush cars.

"She has a lot of overwhelming emotions," Esther said quietly. "But she's a nice girl underneath it all."

"We know," I said. "And Gus is going to lay off."

Gus nodded eagerly, still struggling to breathe.

"We're not feeding my mother to zombies," Delores said. "Real or not, that would scar me for life. She lays enough guilt trips—and tells enough exaggerated tall tales about me and pillows—without me having to deal with the image of sending her to her death."

"Speaking of which," Nate2 interrupted.

The zombies were now halfway across the plain, close enough for us to see the tattered remains of old wool shawls and draped nightgowns. Some had most of their flesh, while others had arms hanging on by only a few tendons. They were all moaning and calling for what sounded like—

"Ears?" Gus said.

"Yes," Nate2 said. "I suppose it's from that movie *Dawn of the Dead,* when all the zombies went on a murderous rampage looking for human ears."

"That was brains."

"I beg to differ. I distinctly remember the scene in the grave-yard when the cheerleader zombie was chewing on the football player's earlobe. Or was that a teen frat movie?" He scratched his head. "Or maybe it was just a dream."

Regardless, the dead now running our way had an insatiable appetite for ears. I covered mine and pulled Delores toward the safe house. The others scrambled close behind. I fumbled for the key under the welcome mat and could barely control my shaking hands as I jammed it into the lock. We rushed inside and bolted in different directions.

At that moment the kitchen window smashed and a grey, half-rotted arm groped for the lock. Delores grabbed her mother's handbag and beat the appendage savagely, sending fingers flying across the counter before the arm snapped at the elbow and fell into the sink, where it squeezed a sponge several times before falling still. An icy wind came blowing through the shattered glass, whistling through the empty left eye socket of the small head looking in.

"How did that thing get here so quickly?" Gus shouted.

"I used to be an errand boy," the head said. "I did a lot of running about."

"It can talk!" Delores cried in shock.

"Of course I can talk," the zombie replied. "I'm not a dog. I might be a commoner, but I do speak. Now give us your ears."

"Die!" Delores screamed.

"I'm already dead. Give us one ear, and I'll be on my way. It's only fair. I've been stuck under the sod for three hundred years. I'm peckish."

Gus used the broom handle to push the head away, jamming the handle into the empty eye socket. The boy's remaining hand came up to fend off the assault, and he fell backward into the yard, taking the whole broom. Nate2 was shifting a small wooden cabinet toward the kitchen to block the window.

"You've got a very disturbed mind," Delores said.

"I'm a lateral thinker," Nate2 said. "It's both a blessing and a curse."

Together they lifted the cabinet into place, wedging it securely between the frame and the sink basin. I pleaded with Mrs. Watson to help me lift one of the couches and block the large picture window looking onto the park, but she mumbled something about man's work and sat down on the loveseat instead. Across the street a wall of decaying zombies was streaming from the grass onto the sidewalk.

Gus rushed back to lift the sagging end of the couch, which we propelled toward—and unfortunately *through*—the front window. Glass shattered and fell around the base of the house as the furniture toppled eight feet onto the sidewalk and bounced into a BMW, leaving a substantial dent in the driver's door. At least this gave the zombies pause. Several stopped and craned their semi-functional necks up toward us. To my surprise, at least half burst into hearty laughter and tried to clap. The ones missing or having only partial arms stomped their feet. I waved, and then we both grabbed the other couch and pushed it toward the open gap. Upstairs, a tinkling of glass echoed. Gus patted my shoulder and raced off to stem the tide.

"There's no way we can block all the windows," Delores said.

"I've got an idea," Nate2 interrupted.

"Maybe we should make a break for it out the back," I said. "There are only five or six zombies in the yard. We could catch the train back into central London. That might overcome the distortion."

"I have an idea," Nate2 repeated.

Delores shook her head. "If there are no people in the world, there won't be anyone to run the trains. And besides, if you think my mother is going to run anywhere, you're nuts."

"My idea is this," Nate2 butted in. "We need to be tricky but practical. These people are deceased, morbid, pushing up daisies, and come from a time when people were superstitious and uneducated. Why don't we get them on our side by convincing them that this is Heaven? I'll play God and you can all be my angels. We'll show them such miracles as a blender, running hot water, and the television. That will sedate the lot of them, especially if there's a cooking show on."

Gus bounded down the stairs with a skull suctioned onto a toilet plunger. He tossed it into a hall closet, slammed the door, and stood in the circle wiping his hands together. He motioned upstairs and gave a thumbs-up. The cabinet in the sink rattled, but didn't become upended. Before we could comment, Nate2 strode to the front door and threw it open dramatically, thrusting out his large chest. Several lecherous-looking women eyed his lobes greedily, creeping slowly toward the stairs.

"Listen all of you that have ears to hear!" Nate2 bellowed.

"We don't now, do we?" a zombie shouted. "That's why we're here."

"I am your wrathful god!"

"No you're not," another zombie yelled. "You're an English fellow with an odd haircut. You'll go to hell if you keep that blasphemy up. That's a mortal sin."

Nate2 paused and glanced down, annoyed. "How do you know I'm not God?"

"Beard's all wrong. And God's skinnier and has iron spikes through his hands."

"That's *the son* of God. I'm God the father. The big cheese, *numero uno,* created the world in six days. I spoke to Moses as a burning bush, destroyed Pompeii, invented Velcro … Oh come on, people, work with me!"

"I'm an atheist," an Irish zombie said. "I don't care one way or the other. All I know is you got them plump lobes that go all fleshy at the ends. Them could feed me whole family for the winter."

Nate2's hand flew to his ears. He whimpered loudly and retreated into the hallway, slamming the door as the first assailant crested the top step. The room echoed with fists and bones on the door as we slid all the locks into place and pushed the loveseat Delores's mom was resting on across the entrance. The top corner of the door began to splinter.

"So Esther," Gus said. "What kind of men does Delores really like?"

"This isn't the time," I interrupted.

Esther smoothed her skirt over her legs. "She likes men who know their manners, drive trucks, and respect their kinfolk. I think she's also partial to boys looking to join the military."

"That's so not true!" Delores screamed from the living room.

"You need a husband with a sound income," her mother replied. "So that you can take care of the babies. And we have to support our loyal armed forces. They keep the Devil from the door."

I grabbed Gus by the collar. "Not now," I hissed.

"Okay, okay," he said. "Don't get touchy. I realize that bit about the army wasn't what either of us wanted to hear, but it's nice to know the truth. As for our rotting friends outside, I've got a Plan B. What about a talisman to ward off evil spirits? The pagans used to enchant stones and crystals to protect themselves."

Nate2 rolled his eyes. "Really, you can't believe in that palaver."

"God has spoken," Delores muttered.

Gus swept his arms to indicate the scene outside. "Zombies from the black plague are lining up in the street looking for a way to gnaw off our ears. I can see where you're coming from, but for now, you might be willing to suspend your disbelief."

"Fair point. Please go on …"

"High priests used to charge rocks and stones with energy by placing them in their right hands and saying a chant, like a spell. Maybe we can channel some of our positive mental energy and use it for protection."

Delores rubbed her temple. "I can't believe I'm saying this, but okay. Gus's got as much chance of being right in this stupid world as anyone, I guess."

"That's the nicest thing you've ever said to me," Gus replied. "I think our relationship has turned a corner."

As they raced around the room looking for useful items to enchant, I retrieved our tracking device from the kitchen to see if anything on screen had changed. Ever since the Queen's Park statue incident, I'd been curious about where we were physically when we got caught in a wave. Being in a separate reality meant that we should be the only dots on the map, but there were still three dots at the Tate Modern and two at the Calypso Hotel. This implied that we were still in contact with Earth 5. A plan began to form in my brain. We were enclosed in a physical field built from the universe's energy and the power of our neural nets. If I ramped enough power through the tracking device, I might be able to blow my own porthole out of this bizarre reality distortion. I had no way of knowing whether my theory would work, but I figured science had a greater chance of overcoming our situation than voodoo.

I returned in time to see Delores, Nate2, and Gus all standing in a circle with their right hands extended asking the Earth to charge their talismans with protective powers. Gus was holding a spatula; Nate2 a small mortar and pestle for grinding herbs; and Delores a heavy glass paperweight, inside of which was a miniature model of Buckingham Palace. As she turned it over in her hand, sparkles began to scatter through the water. I pried the lid off the tracking device to access the wires as the top corner of the front door burst. A face filled the gap and smiled, revealing two muddy teeth. The full-out assault of the dead had begun.

CHAPTER 19

WE MADE A BREAK for the kitchen, pulling away the microwave cupboard that had been propped against the back door. Nate2 went out first, kicking a zombie off the steps and holding his spatula out like a crucifix warding off vampires. Delores and Gus fanned out behind him, both holding out their talismans. The zombies backed off in fear—to my great amazement—at least until they figured out that they weren't about to get beaten to pieces by real weapons. One stepped toward Nate2 and snapped the spatula away so hard that the hand tore off at the wrist and landed in Gus's top pocket. The wind was definitely cold now, winter-like, with a fine haze of frost floating through the air.

As the other zombies made to attack, Delores threw her glass paperweight in a perfect strike at a grandmother's midsection, bursting her apart. Meanwhile Gus pestled the errand boy until his second arm fell off. The kid then tried to bite him. I picked up a large plastic garbage bin and bowled over the remaining two zombie kids and then raced to catch up with the others who were bolting into the back alley. The only person not running—and wholly unconcerned with the situation—was Delores's mother, who was applying a new layer of pink makeup. Delores stopped to go back, but I grabbed her arm and pulled. There was nothing she could do as the dead swarmed the protesting Mrs. Watson, who faded away in front of our eyes.

"She wasn't real," I said. "Come on."

Up ahead, Gus had already jimmied the door of a three-wheeled delivery van parked on the curb. He ripped off the plastic panel beneath the steering wheel and yanked down a handful of wires.

"Don't disconnect the radio," Nate2 said. "I'd like to find a classical station to calm my nerves. I also wouldn't be averse to stopping at a pharmacy for some muscle relaxants. I haven't been this agitated since David Caruso left *NYPD Blue*."

"Why are we hotwiring this piece of crap?" Delores asked. "There's a BMW over there."

"Hmm," Gus murmured. "What would have better security features, a crappy truck that looks like it was designed by a seven-year-old or a state-of-the-art, highly expensive sedan?"

He crossed two wires, shook his head at how easy it was, and put the truck into gear. The engine moaned in annoyance as a wave of bodies in front of us ran toward the van. Gus hit the accelerator and smiled.

"You can't," Delores said.

He could, and did, running straight through the flailing torsos, sending some of them flying and disintegrating the older zombies into chalky dust and clothing fragments. A cloud came puffing in from the air vents, causing us all to choke for several long seconds until we got the windows down. Gus had his foot to the floor, but the van couldn't push beyond forty kilometres an hour. We made a sharp turn north onto a winding street and fought to crest a hill onto a main road. To my surprise, packs of zombies were moving in all directions.

"All the burial pits in the city must have opened up," Nate2 murmured. "That's odd. I could have sworn I was thinking only about Blackheath. But live and learn."

The frost had begun to turn into larger flakes of powdery snow that were killing our traction on corners. Luckily, the zombies didn't have the best reaction times, probably due to the fact that they'd been buried beneath the earth for a few hundred years. Unfortunately, they seemed smart enough to set traps. Blocking our way to the centre of Greenwich were several cars that had been pushed out onto the high street to create a barrier. There was no way our wimpy little van could even nudge them out of the way. Gus shifted gears and backed up. Hands reached through the windows, clawing at Delores's earrings. We tore through a narrow, winding side street and then around the park until we reached the Thames, where, logically enough, the road ended. In front of us was the large wooden sailing ship, the *Cutty Sark*.

Gus tried to turn around, but Delores grabbed his arm.

"Wait! Why don't we get on the ship and sail it down the Thames to the Tate Modern? I doubt the zombies can swim."

"The ship's been in dry dock for decades," Nate2 said. "It's a museum. You've got a better chance of sailing this van to Bournemouth."

He squealed as a young zombie with a missing jawbone and no eyes collided with his door. Nate2 reached down and jammed the van into gear for Gus, who drove through an abandoned patio back toward the park. As we revved ahead, a Jaguar came rolling across right in front of our van. The collision didn't kill us, but it did bend the single front wheel and collapse the left side of the van. We scrambled through the doors, kicked the legs out from under two zombies (literally), and ran into a fish and chip shop, past the smoking deep fryers and into a large walk-in fridge, slamming the door behind us.

"You'd think we'd be good at fleeing by now," Gus said. "Instead we've ended up in a very cold room with two thousand slabs of cod and some french fries. Who led us in here?"

"I followed Delores," Nate2 said.

"I followed John," Delores replied.

"I followed you," I said.

Gus looked at us blankly. "Was I in the lead there?"

"You're not very good at running away," I snapped. "Despite how often you try."

"I didn't want to get in the way!" Gus said. "I wasn't quitting on the team back in Toronto. I thought I was doing a good thing. I *knew* you were holding a grudge."

"Let's not play the blame game," Delores said, swallowing hard. "We can't stay here. Maybe no one saw us come in. Even a zombie wouldn't think we'd be stupid enough to run ourselves into a freezer."

"True enough," Nate2 said. "But before we make yet another break for it, why don't we come up with a plan. That might save a bit of anguish. We could hotwire another car. I thought that was quite exciting."

"Didn't seem to help get us out of the reality distortion," I pointed out. "And the way the temperature outside is dropping, I'd say we'd better get moving. Time is of the essence."

I explained my aborted plan to rip open a seam of the distortion wave using the tracking device and an amplifier, pointing out that the concept was similar to Delores's channelling energy using her cell phone. Nate2 remembered that an amateur radio studio had been set up in the Ranger's House on the prime meridian to broadcast at the millennium. Apparently the house was on a hill in the middle of the park. Surely a transmitter capable of reaching outside London was sufficient to blow us out of this distortion. By the end of Nate2's explanation, and with frostbite becoming a concern, we were all ready to move.

Unfortunately, as we opened the freezer door, the temperature didn't change. If anything, the air outside was colder, not to mention filled with wicked sheets of thick, driving snow. A full-on Canadian-style blizzard was pounding London, leaving no more than a ten-foot visibility. We found some aprons, tied them around us for protection, then pushed into the street, stepping into snow that covered my ankles and came up to my knees in drift patches.

Lingering around our destroyed van was a group of zombies standing completely still. None of us saw until we were almost upon them, but luckily the dead appeared to have reverted to a passive state. Gus touched one with his foot and it fell to pieces.

"They're frozen," he said.

"Not much meat on those bones," Nate2 observed. "At least not any more. Getting old is such a frightening prospect. There's nothing to wait for but death. Speaking of which, I certainly hope they don't still carry the pestilence that killed them. Some viruses can lay dormant for centuries, and we did inhale quite a lot of those two individuals who came through the vents of the van."

"Let's worry about that later," I said. "I've got enough on my mind. Long-term health is something I'll think about tomorrow."

"I'm with Johnny," Gus added. "No use *crying in our pillows*. That's what your mom said you do, isn't it, D?"

Delores turned and caught him with a laser-like death glare.

Despite the urgency of the moment, the whole rest of the way through the park all I could think about was getting the plague. I'd hate to go through all this hassle just to take a four-hundred-year-old epidemic back to the real world. The Ranger's House was a huge manor on top of the crest, a brownstone with a white facade and an enormous black metal fence running around its periphery. By the time we reached it we were freezing.

"The gate's l-l-locked," Gus said. "Quite a high quality l-l-lock at that."

"Can you p-p-pick it?"

He fumbled for his ring of keys and tools, but seemed to have difficulty getting his fingers into his pockets. Our hands, feet, and toes were absolutely frigid. Finally, Gus yanked out the mass of steel and promptly dropped the key ring into the snow, which was coming down harder than ever and really accumulating. He dug around in a large drift for several seconds, and then had to pull away in pain.

"Put your hands under your armpits," I said. "It's one of the warmest places on your body."

He did.

"Now flap your arms," Nate2 said. "And do the twist about and turn yourself around."

At this point Gus stopped doing the chicken dance and kicked snow Nate2's way. We took turns prodding the drift until Delores came up with the keys. Gus tried again to pick the lock, but after dropping the keys twice more and nearly crying from the cold, he had to concede defeat.

"I come from a very w-w-warm country," he said. "I was actually excited about an hour ago, because I'd n-n-never seen snow in my life, except in movies, but I'm over it. Give me h-h-heatstroke any day."

In utter misery, we trekked the length of the fence looking for another opening. By the time we returned to the main gate, the snow was waist high. At least we hadn't seen any plague victims for a while.

"I don't understand," I said. "Even without my plan to blast us out, if the zombies are dead we should be out of the distortion. After all, D's mom has disappeared, and the weather and the planet without people are beyond our control. We've overcome our thoughts, so why all the snow?"

Delores shivered a reply. "Unless some of the zombies found shelter and are waiting out the storm. Or maybe we have to find a way to conquer the weather."

"I vote we f-f-fly to the t-t-tropics," Gus chattered.

I could no longer see the front door of the Ranger's House, but I had an idea for one last, desperate attempt at breaking in. I took off my apron padding and began to unbutton my shirt.

"The slime," I said.

Delores seemed to understand, and thankfully turned away. I flipped off my shoes, danced around as I took off my jeans, and winced. It was like I was standing on solid blocks of burning concrete. I got my shoes back on and pressed my thin, slick body between two bars. My chest edged forward—my mind fighting the panicked thought of getting stuck—before popping to the other side with a wet *splock*. My butt and thighs, however, didn't slide because of my underwear.

"Oh, lord, why does everything have to be so embarrassing?" I muttered.

I attempted to slide off the last piece of clothing protecting my modesty, but couldn't reach back far enough to get them off both cheeks. I motioned for Gus to help, but he put up his palms and pointed to Nate2. They pushed each other toward me several times before Nate2 finally reached out and yanked my underwear down around my ankles. I burst through to the inner court, landed flat out in the snow, screamed and bolted as fast as possible in the buff to the majestic front doors. This was streaking for survival—nudity for freedom.

Once inside, I was relieved to find that the British Heritage Council had at least had the foresight to install a temperature-controlled thermostat system. I tore an expensive-looking curtain off a window, wrapped myself up, and raced around looking for a radio transmitter.

Meanwhile, the storm grew worse. For a second I could see Delores, Gus, and Nate2 hunched against the gate, and then they disappeared in whiteout conditions. I started on the ground floor and worked my way up without success. If there was a radio station hidden in this mansion, they'd certainly done a good job of hiding it. It wasn't the sort of place I associated with tunes, giveaways, and the usual banter of radio. Portraits and landscapes hung on the walls and antique furniture was everywhere. I used a fire extinguisher to bash open a door that descended into a storage space chock full of wires, electronic panels, and microphones. I flipped switches and buttons, peeled spiders off the headset, and sat down, amazed that the long-neglected components were coming to life. I tore the back off the tracking device and wondered how I could hook the wires to transmit. Suddenly a thought occurred to me: even if I made this work, there was no way to know how large the tear in the distortion would be. We had to be together.

I scrambled back to the administration office and rifled through drawers until I found the custodial keys. Then I raced to the front door, tripping twice on the curtains dragging around my feet, and opened the door to a mini avalanche of white. I plunged onward toward the huddled black figures near the gate, noting that they weren't moving much. To my horror, not twenty feet away, a group of thinner figures was trudging up the crest of the hill, somehow hovering above the waist-high snow. I pushed hard as frigid, wet snow bit my legs and ankles.

"Behind you!" I yelled.

The zombies were moving forward, sure to get to my friends long before me. I could see now that they were more resourceful than I would have thought dead people could be: they'd torn rib cages from the shattered skeletons of frozen zombies and were using them as snowshoes. I wondered which of my friends might have the best coordination, decided none of them were exactly sporty, and made a random choice based on the biggest target.

"Nate!" I screamed.

He looked my way slowly, as if doped from the cold. I threw the keys into his chest. His hands went automatically to the sting and he nabbed the ring by his pinkie finger before it plunged into the snow. Within seconds he'd located the master key and was shoving his full weight to budge the gate through the drifts. Luckily, gates are mostly air, so there was enough give to squeeze through and jam the steel shut just as the first bony fingers reached for their lobes.

All three collapsed onto the warm floor of the Ranger's House. I swiped my clothes from Gus, but they were frozen stiff and impossible to put on. I was stuck wearing a curtain for a while longer. I led them to the mass of equipment.

"Doesn't look like Triple J to me," Gus said. "I bet this station doesn't even have a mascot."

"It *is* amateur radio," Nate2 replied. "They're lucky to have a broom closet. I was involved in community theatre once and we ended up staging 'the Scottish play' in the meeting room of our local library. The librarian kept coming in to *shush* us, which was very off-putting, especially for the witches."

"I didn't know there were witches in *Braveheart*," Gus said.

"We weren't staging *Braveheart*."

"You said the Scottish play."

"Yes, *Macbeth,* but to say it out loud is forbidden, because the name is cursed. Any actor who utters *Macbeth* puts himself and the cast in mortal danger. More people have died in suspicious *Macbeth*-related accidents than were killed in the Crusades. It's a fact. You can look it up at the British Museum."

A loud banging came from the front door.

"You see," Nate2 said. "Bad luck already."

The zombies must have gotten through the gates—an obvious advantage of having so little flesh on their bodies. I looked for a way to hook up the tracking device as Nate2 hung over my shoulder.

"IC-756PRO linear amplifier," he murmured. "Very nice. 28 MHz. That's more than enough power to blast us out of here, I should think."

I untangled about ten wires and felt my brain cramp in pain. I started to hook two together, but Nate2 made a subtle grunting noise and cleared his throat. I chose an outlet wire and was about to bend it onto our transformer when he began to cough loudly. I pushed the mess away and stood up, presenting him with my seat.

"You were about to short out the entire house," he said. "I respect your right to learn through doing, but perhaps we could practise with fewer corpses on the doorstep."

Within seconds he rewired the tracking device and instructed us all to hook arms. He whistled happily as the sound of a window shattering filled the house and the lights flickered and died.

CHAPTER 20

THE SECURITY GUARD who opened the door seemed more puzzled than alarmed by the sight of a Goth, a hippie, a naked teenager with slug antennae on his forehead, and an older English eccentric with a long multicoloured goatee who appeared to be patting himself on the back in congratulations. The guard stood munching his egg sandwich slowly, like a cow chewing cud. His face was round, pink, and topped with short ginger-coloured hair in a straight fringe.

"What's going on here?" he said.

"Publicity event," Delores replied. "We're friends of the DJ."

The guard took another bite, a piece of lettuce tumbling onto his blue shirt. "Licence ran out years ago," he said. "Station only broadcasted for sixty-one days over the millennium. Want to try again?"

"We're repossessing the equipment?" Nate2 said.

The man stared blankly.

"We've been locked in here since the year 2000?" Nate2 offered.

The guard unhooked the radio on his belt.

"Fine," Nate2 said. "There was a snow storm and several thousand zombies—"

"How do you feel about bribery?" Gus asked, pulling out his wad of bills. "My crazy uncle often wanders into museum storage areas. It's a compulsion. What would you say to a hundred pounds to pretend this never happened, and fifty to escort us quietly out a back door of the building?"

Another segment of sandwich disappeared into the large mouth. I wondered if this guy would speak without showing us ground-up, saliva-covered food. Maybe his vocal cords didn't work without egg. As for Gus, I'd given him a lot of trouble about collecting his bags of currency when we were escaping from this world the first time, but they certainly were coming in handy. The security guard nodded and stuck out a fat hand.

"They pay us six pound an hour," he mumbled. "Used to have a union, but government subcontracted the job out to a private agency. For an extra fifty, you can take any painting you fancy."

Gus began to peel off another bill, but Delores touched his hand and shook her head no. There was no need to be genuine fugitive art thieves. I lingered behind, waiting for the door to close so that I could slip my icy wet clothes back on in peace, but the guard lingered. He motioned toward my head.

"Might want to get them grey stumps looked at."

"Yeah, I will."

"Look hideous."

"Thanks. I had an infection."

"Kids'll think you're a monster. You're just asking for trouble. I knew a guy who got arrested near a primary school just 'cause he was wearing an overcoat and had a hunched back."

"I'll keep it in mind."

"'Course, he was also taking photos of kids playing."

"Would you mind … the door?"

He touched the side of his nose with one finger, winked knowingly, and left. I could barely pull the soggy denim over my raw legs, but eventually I managed and re-emerged, walking like the victim of an atomic wedgie. As we wandered across the park I considered the amazing advances my father had made against waves. If we could find a way to amplify the link between the real world and reality distortions without the use of a radio transmitter, we could protect all non-dimensionals. A large hand slapped against my chest interrupted my thoughts.

"Ow!" I yelped. "Be careful with the hitting. I'm still freezing and might even have frostbite."

A big black van was parked in front of our safe house. The front door was open and two armed guards lingered near the hallway. They must have picked up on the blast of energy we'd let loose from the hill. We decided to avoid public transportation and instead took a clandestine route down to the Thames, which we knew would take us back into the heart of the city and the Calypso Hotel. Yet even here I didn't feel truly safe. I thought of all the cameras in the metropolitan area—security cameras in banks, shops, on street corners, and over ATM machines. If DIMCO could convince the government to let them have free access to public surveillance equipment, it would be impossible for us to go anywhere. But I figured Ridpath's asking for that much power to ensure *protection of the environment* would raise too many eyebrows.

We collapsed on a set of empty stone stairs by the water to regroup and plan. Nate2 bought a newspaper to scan for any useful information. The cover story was about England's defeat by the powerhouse Northern Ireland squad in a soccer tournament. This was beside a picture of Cyndi, a scantily clad bank teller from Finsbury Park who enjoyed inline skating, treacle pudding, travelling overseas to Wales, and reading great works of art like Charles Dickens and *Hello!*

"Mmm," Nate2 murmured.

"I know, I know, I know!" Delores grunted. "You men are all the same. What are you going to say: she could check your balance any day; you'd love to open an account at her branch; oh, what you wouldn't do for some of her interest. What sexist remark were you going to make?"

Nate2's lips puckered like a dying fish. "I was going to say that reminds me I've got a utility bill to pay. I haven't been able to get to my local bank branch because I've been away. I don't want to have my water and power cut off. I wouldn't want to give my landlord, that smug Brahmar, any more ammunition to get me evicted."

Delores showed her tiny teeth in an embarrassed smile. "Oh. Sorry."

Nate2 nodded at the photo. "Besides, you should know that this young lady isn't my type at all. I can't stand the smell of treacle pudding and have absolutely no interest in Wales."

"Delores," Gus began. "You shouldn't feel threatened by pin-up girls. You're much better looking than Cyndi. She looks airbrushed. I bet in real life she's uglier than flies on a cow's rear end."

Delores massaged her studded wristband. "Gus, you ever been whipped to within an eyelash of your life?"

"Not yet, but I'm sure it's coming."

Tucked away on page thirty-two was a small DIMCO-related article outlining a request for a budget increase to monitor ozone degradation in Northern Scotland. The story gave details of the agency's great success in pioneering scientific research, a five-year greenhouse reduction plan, and continuing negotiations to gain a world pact on environmental control. Clearly Ridpath was advancing his plan for global power through legitimate channels. I felt like a little pebble being swept up in a giant wave.

"Looks like the colonel is a popular man," Delores said. "The public has given him a 90 percent approval rating for his work. They say he might take a run at becoming leader of the Conservative Party for the next election."

"He's done a lot of good things for the nation," Nate2 said absently. "On the surface, of course. After the second freak hurricane in York people were really becoming serious about environmental change. By the Great Amsterdam Flood most European governments were looking for a saviour. Who knows, if I hadn't been kidnapped, shot at, attacked by zombies, run down by a metal statue, gagged with socks, and soundly abused at every turn, I might even be a potential Ridpath voter. As it stands I'll once again be supporting the Official Monster Raving Loony Party."

"I can see it now," I said. "Ridpath will become prime minister and he'll engineer some environmental crisis to get people so petrified that they'll give up all their basic rights and freedoms. Once the government has total power, he'll be able to do whatever he wants, whether citizens support his measures or not. If you get someone as demented as Ridpath in charge, the opportunities for abuse are astounding. It'll be a total dictatorship. There'd be no way to fight back."

Gus got off the step and looked toward the towering skyscrapers of Canary Wharf. He shrugged and took a few steps down to the footpath, turned, and waited for us to follow.

"Or maybe things will work out all right," he said as he hailed a taxi. "Don't underestimate the universe and the power of good in people. Things might be dodgy now, but there's still time. I say we make tracks."

"No use burning the sun," Delores agreed.

We were small specks in a big universe—particles of dust that people in DIMCO wanted to brush away. We were targets simply because we knew about their ongoing program to steal from our dimension to benefit Earth 5. The world was by no means fair, but still, I wanted to believe that things would get better.

THAT FEELING WAS OBLITERATED as soon as I stepped out of the cab and caught sight of the Calypso Hotel, which looked exactly how I remembered: filthy, barely intact, an ideal breeding ground for bugs and cockroaches. As we entered the front desk clerk was separating pirated DVDs into two piles: those with black-and-white photocopied covers and those with badly printed covers. He eyed us suspiciously, glanced toward a steel bar lying next to a busted phone with no receiver, and cleared his throat.

"You come about the pantyhose?" he asked.

"I didn't," Nate2 replied, looking around at us. "Anyone else …?"

The clerk cocked an eye my way and then smiled. "Hey, you're the kid who paid for a night's stay and didn't even steal anything. Loved it so much you had to come again. That's exactly the kind of customer loyalty we've never had from anyone sane. Back on skid row?"

"That's a good way of putting it."

"What's the significance of the pantyhose?" Nate2 said. "Is that a code?"

"No, ladies wear them," the clerk whispered. "They fell off a truck. I've got eighty-two hundred pairs if you're interested."

"That's a big truck," Nate2 said.

"Okay, they fell off a container vessel at the docks. But they move them by truck eventually, so we just cut out the middleman. Why not buy a box of a hundred for your lovely missus?"

He pointed to Delores, who recoiled and appeared ready to spit. She could have and no one would have protested. There were already several large wads of phlegm on the carpet. Nate2 made to put his arm around her, but she kicked him hard in the shins.

"Ah, newlyweds," the clerk said. "Lovely. I'll put you down for two boxes, give you the members' rate, and even throw in a rooster as a wedding present. Ask me no questions, I'll tell you no lies."

"We're not interested in pantyhose or poultry," I said. "We need a bed each in one of the dorm rooms."

I thought the clerk was about to keel over. He shook his head, speechless, and wiped a tear from his eye as he reached to pull down a security cage over the desk. He came out the office door and gestured for us to follow him upstairs. I noticed that since my last visit he'd replaced a broken step with a busted section of ironing board. We lingered to admire his handiwork.

"One of the regulars shattered that board over her boyfriend's head when she caught him in bed with her sister," he explained. "Then she did his kneecaps with the iron itself, before finally trying to strangle him with the cord. Ingenious the ideas people can come up with in an assault situation using simple household items."

It occurred to me that I didn't know the clerk's name, so I asked. He stuck out a hand reeking of cheap cologne.

"Fred de Klerk," he said. "My great-grandfather was Dutch. He came to England from South Africa after working secretly for the British army during the Boer War. He sold them pressed camel meat stolen from local tribes."

"So you're de Klerk the clerk?" I said.

"No, I'm de Klerk the *hospitality management engineer*. But call me Fred, unless the cops are around. In that case, call me Bruce and ask how Sally's been since the operation. Then run."

He led onward to the second floor. The door to our dorm was tied shut with electrical wire that de Klerk slowly unwound while mentioning the security features of the room. I wandered down the musty-smelling hall, along the ultra-faded red carpet, glancing through cracked doors, broken doors, and gaping entrances that probably once had a door but were now open concept. A Chinese family sat in one room, playing cards and surrounded by buckets of shellfish. In another room were several caged roosters. Two rooms were empty except for an inch of dust and the buzzing of flies. The door at the end was closed and had recently been installed with an actual lock. I could hear movement inside, so it wasn't just a storage room for valuables.

Bingo.

Every closed door I encountered now filled me with dread and hope. You never knew what was on the other side. I hoped whoever was on the other side could help me find my mom and dad and wondered if I was a good son. The thought came suddenly, almost out of nowhere, but I knew it had been gnawing at my mind for a while, constantly pushed away by fear, fatigue, and trying to stay alive. I thought of times when I'd snapped at my mom or taken my dad for granted. I was a typical kid, taking and never giving back. Now I might not ever see them again and would never get the chance to buy them dinner or pay for their rooms in an old age home.

But at the worst points in life, there's nothing else to do but go on.

I rapped firmly three times and listened intently. There was some shuffling, and then the tanned, smooth face of a guy in his late twenties appeared in the half-opened door. He had sandy brown hair, a square jaw, and shoulders that appeared to start at his ears before spreading into thick bulges of muscle. He appraised me silently, scanning up and down. He sucked his tooth like he might have a wad of gum stuck between his molars and opened the door farther.

"You room service?" he asked in an American accent.

"Are you joking?" I replied.

"I s'pose so. I ordered a burger and fries yesterday, but I have a feeling the guy at the front desk was joking when he said they'd be right up. Should have known when he called me *monsieur*. I'm still not used to the English sense of humour."

"How did you call downstairs?" I asked. "The front desk phone doesn't have a receiver."

"I shouted down the stairwell."

He seemed to catch himself, glanced back into the room, and closed the door slightly. He coughed and looked at me with a more focused expression.

"Um, who are you?" he asked. "Don't mean to be rude, but I've already had a couple Chinese fellas try to sell me some funny sort of oysters, and a man dressed as a woman invited me to a party."

"I'm John Fitzgerald."

He smiled and clicked his fingers. "I flew you over. I'm Hammering Hank Greenwood, pilot extraordinaire and known heartbreaker. I met Rexxy boy in flight school in Boston years ago. We're like brothers."

"Nice to meet you, *Hammer*?"

"No, no, please don't call me that. It brings back bad memories of early rap music and parachute pants. I hate the nickname. Got it from a couple of teammates on my university squash team. They had a deep-seated inferiority complex about the sport and compensated by giving one another overly masculine nicknames." He leaned in close. "Before I went to flight school, I studied psychology."

"You don't say."

He pulled me inside the room and slammed the door. Ridpath2—the chicken farmer from my world—was lying on the bed passed out, a line of drool running off his face, making a round mark on the tattered wool blanket. Several tins of extra-strong Polish beer lay empty on the floor.

"You're not supposed to be here," Hank said. "This place is only for emergencies and very, very unfortunate people. Tell me you didn't get raided."

"Sort of ... We had to blast our way out of a reality distortion and the energy pulse must have given away our location. We rigged my dad's tracking device to a radio transmitter."

"Anybody hurt?"

"No, we're all fine. The others are down the hall."

"Is Rex with you?"

"We're pretty sure he's in the DIMCO building."

Hank thought about this for a few long minutes, pacing the floor. He looked out the window and drummed his fingers on the dirty sill. I wondered if he'd forgotten I was even there.

"I don't like this at all," he murmured.

"Yeah, the place is a dump. I tried to sleep here once, but the bedbugs prevented any real rest."

"No. It's not like Rex to go barrelling into a dangerous situation. Actually, scratch that. It *is* like Rex to barge ahead recklessly, but not without the latest technological gadgets and a backup plan. At the very least, he keeps us informed so that we can bail him out if things go wrong."

If Rex had been picked up by surprise, there was little doubt that someone in the organization was passing information. There'd been too many coincidences to believe DIMCO were simply lucky. I trusted my friends a hundred percent, so it couldn't be anyone I knew.

Ridpath2 grumbled, snorted, rubbed his face vigorously, and sat bolt upright shouting gibberish.

"Oh, shut up, ya mongrel," Hank said. "He does that every hour on the hour, like he's a retarded cuckoo clock. And he's even worse when he's awake. It's like he's doing everything in his power to annoy me."

"You did kidnap him."

"Yeah, but … I'm not really responsible, so he shouldn't be cursing me. He keeps calling me *a squirrel-faced fart,* whatever that means. I threatened to tie a cloth sack around his head and that shut him up for a while. I didn't really want to do it, but we've been together in this tiny filthy room for a couple days now and it's enough to send everyone a bit loco. Had a nice break when he grabbed his stomach and disappeared into a reality distortion for an hour. I didn't see him snap off the inhibitor we'd attached to his ankle. I was a bit worried, but he showed up a while later covered in whipped cream and looking fine. I didn't ask."

"What have you been doing in here?"

"Well, I tried to get reception on that there TV."

He pointed to a black square in the corner.

"That's a space heater," I said.

"Yeah, I came to the same conclusion. I like the U.K. It's like going back in time twenty years. Look at the sink. The hot and cold water come out of separate taps and we're not supposed to drink it because of lead. I know the place has history and is quaint, but there's something to be said for elevators and air conditioning."

"I'm sure the Calypso isn't typical of the entire hospitality industry. I'm pretty certain most places have normal running water and stuff."

"Yeah, I've probably just been inside too long. I did four hundred push-ups and sit-ups yesterday and must have inhaled two thousand dust mites. There was half a tooth on the floor and a hypodermic needle under the bed."

He grimaced and put his cowboy boot–clad foot onto a black chair that might once have been a much lighter colour. Suddenly, fists hammering on the door interrupted our discussion. Hank motioned for me to move to the corner and pulled up the back of his shirt to reveal a large hunting knife tucked discreetly out of view. He opened the door slowly and was knocked backward hard as an enormous body hurtled into the room.

Within seconds, Nate2 had been flipped facedown onto the seedy carpet with one arm cranked behind his back and the tip of the hunting knife against his neck, just below goatee level. Hank was about to speak, but paused and began to laugh instead. He hauled Nate2 up and slapped him hard on the back, jolting the big guy forward like a rag doll. Although they were approximately the same height, Hank had at least forty pounds of muscle on Nate2.

"Fitzy Boy!" Hank said. "I was beginning to think we'd never see you alive again. But you've always been a resourceful cuss, even if I've only known you for the last year and technically only saw you that one time when I dropped off those documents after flying through the porthole. You got spunk. Or at least that's what people say. I suppose I don't rightly know for sure. But it's good to see you."

"I've got rug in my teeth," Nate2 replied. "And it doesn't taste like chicken."

"That's not my dad," I said. "He's this dimension's version of my father—a slightly defective model."

"Ah," Hank mumbled. He shifted his eyes self-consciously. "Didn't mean what I said about not seeing your dad alive again. I meant all the other stuff, though. Say, anyone hungry? We've been eating this tinned seafood chowder for the past couple days and it's disgusting but edible."

He held up a can, but Nate2 scoffed and waved his hand. "Never touch processed foods. It's a bad American habit, like country music. Besides, I've just bought two buckets of cockles. The Orientals are stewing them as we speak."

Gus and Delores appeared at the door then and I introduced everyone. We discussed the situation and Hank agreed that the time had come to plan our own foray into the nether regions of the Tate Modern. He told us about how Rex and the organization had been trying to convince some unnamed government officials to go public with the news of inter-dimensional contact. But there was fierce debate within the highest echelons of several ministries and the prime minister's office as to how to proceed. Since DIMCO was an independent wing of the government, they were reluctant to share information about their technologies and how much they knew about our world. Everything they passed along showed non-dimensionals as a dangerous threat to national security.

"DIMCO is like an independent state within the British government structure," Hank said. "The U.S. has an agency set up to look into the science of inter-dimensional travel, but we're way behind this country, and DIMCO isn't sharing information with us either. A couple of their scientists have sought immunity in Colorado, but Congress and the CIA are skeptical to say the least. Most of our lobbyists have been treated as nuts, given campaign signs, and asked to leave. You have to understand that contact between our worlds first occurred only a couple years back and people are slow to care about what they don't understand. It took years before people took the Internet seriously."

"Same with Robbie Williams," Gus said.

"Who?"

Gus scratched his eyebrow. "Oh yeah, I forgot that his career didn't really surge in this dimension after Take That."

"You Australian?" Hank asked. "I sure do like that Nicole Kidman. I was heartbroken when she married Lyle Lovett."

"What about Tom Cruise?" Gus asked.

"I think he was only engaged to Lyle Lovett. But he's a good actor. I loved him in *Gladiator*."

Gus's eyes blinked like a malfunctioning traffic light. "What happened to Russell Crowe?"

"The boxer?" Hank said. "I think he retired after knocking out Mike Tyson for the third time. Anyway, I'm actually glad you're all here. A contact is supposed to be sending me schematics for the DIMCO offices—a floor plan that might help us find its weakest points. I can also try to organize a backup team from within the resistance for when we go in."

"I'd rather we did this on our own," I said.

I explained my suspicions about a spy in the ranks, and Hank reluctantly agreed. He hauled a large suitcase from under the bed, tossed out all his clothes, and opened up a secret compartment where a laptop and several other gadgets were hidden. He said he'd have to go down the road to a coffee shop to check his e-mail because he didn't want to send out a signal from the Calypso. He asked if we'd mind watching Ridpath2, who was scratching his head vigorously. No doubt a couple days in this place and a guy would have to shave his head to get rid of the lice.

After Hank left, Delores and Gus amused themselves by throwing various items at the cockroaches on the walls and in the corners. It was one point for a direct hit, five for a kill. Nate2 looked at me silently with utter disappointment.

"I don't like this one bit," he said.

"Yeah, but if you don't kill the cockroaches, they just breed."

"No, I mean …" He leaned in closer and hissed. "An *American*! Once they get involved in any endeavour you can kiss control goodbye. Britain was well on her way to being the first country into space, but then a handful of Yanks heard about the idea and next thing you know Neil Armstrong is hopping around like a fool hitting golf balls into the Sea of Tranquility. Edmond Wallace would never have done that."

"Who's he?"

"The first British person *not* to go to space."

Delores came over, stood beside Nate2, and cleared her throat pointedly.

"Dust getting to you too?" Nate2 said. "We should go to a chemist and buy some antihistamine."

"Your comments about my homeland are about as welcome as a skunk at a lawn party," Delores said. "You might want to close that lip of yours before any more stupid comments fall out."

Nate2 thought about this for a moment, made a silent *ah,* and winked in understanding. "I see what you're saying. I'm not against everyone in your country, just one cross-section—the fanatical control freaks, like those who instigated the Boston Tea Party."

Delores looked around the room. "Anyone got a stapler?"

Nate2 squeaked and stepped gingerly to the far side of Hank's steamer trunk at the edge of the bed.

"Hank seems like a pretty smart, reliable guy," I said. "He's got loads of good ideas and knows tons about DIMCO. And he knows how to handle himself when attacked by surprise."

Nate2's eyes darkened slightly. He mumbled to himself and scratched a patch of oily discharge that had come off the floor and soaked into his sweater. Finally, he leaned forward again.

"Okay, forget his origins. But I'm not sure I trust the man."

"Why?" Delores asked. "Are his shoulders too broad?"

"Well, yes, that, and he seems shifty."

"Again, can I ask why *specifically*?"

Nate2 shook in agitation, searching for an answer, like a kettle getting ready to boil. "I don't know! I don't need a reason to disapprove of him. It's instinct, like how a baby knows not to touch a hot stove, or a Native child can tell which berries are poisonous, or a starling knows to flap its wings when its mother tenderly tosses it from the nest into open air."

"You have no reason to dislike Hank," Delores snapped. "You're just being paranoid."

Nate2 conceded the point. "It wouldn't be the first time."

Gus put up his hand. "You know, everyone, maybe we should think about the situation carefully. Hank *is* pretty eager to share information. He didn't even see us on the plane, so why hasn't he checked our identification? Not that I have any. But that's beside the point. A competent spy would be wary of giving us vital information, but he's been pretty talkative while all the time encouraging us to march into DIMCO headquarters."

"I smell something rotten," Nate2 chimed in. "And I don't just mean this hotel's repulsive stench."

"You guys are crazy," I replied. "Hank's on our side and I plan to listen to his ideas. Besides, we don't have much choice."

"Maybe we'll have two missions into DIMCO," Nate2 said.

"Oh, that's bright. Why risk one intrusion when you can have two? I thought you didn't even want to take action. Isn't there a cop show on?"

Nate2 thought about this and then began scanning around for a TV. Not seeing one, he got off his chair and wandered toward the open suitcase on the bed. Ridpath2 eyed him with a scowl. He'd just broken out a fresh tin of Polish beer and was sucking on it greedily.

In some ways I could understand what Gus was saying about being cautious—we'd walked into more than one trap lately—but my sixth sense told me that Hank was reliable. He'd flown us here, knew about the Calypso, and was the only person who seemed determined to help get my parents out of harm. I needed him. Nate2 picked up various items and began to activate switches.

"Interesting …" he mumbled. "Fascinating …"

Hank came back into the room and watched Nate2 rummage through his things. Ridpath2 mumbled something that sounded like *cheese-shaped mullet* and spat on the floor. Nate2 held a small black device up to the light and ran a finger across its silver foil surface.

"Fascinating technology."

"That's my electric razor," Hank said.

Nate2 tossed the item into the suitcase, flipped the lid closed, and sat down on the bed with his legs casually crossed. He yanked his goatee, uncrossed one leg, and crossed the other.

"It doesn't work with the electrical sockets here," Hank continued. "Luckily I brought razors. I believe a man with a shaven face is taken more seriously by society. It's a principle I've always been keen on."

Nate2 stopped pulling his goatee and frowned. Hank put his laptop on the small corner table, rebooted the system, and pulled a cordless mouse from his pocket. After a minute he touched the top of the mouse and an electronic voice welcomed him back by name.

"Aren't you afraid all this vital information could fall into DIMCO's hands if your laptop were to get stolen or left behind in a raid?" Nate2 said. "Or if you went to a roadhouse in America and got shot by a street gang?"

Hank took a deep breath. "The computer is programmed so that Rex and I are the only ones who can use it. The mouse is equipped with an infrared light that scans our hands and matches what's basically an X-ray outline of our vein blueprint to the authorized patterns in its system. You've got to love Fujitsu technology. The laptop itself is made from biodegradable plastic engineered from vegetable starch. If I bury it in the ground, within weeks microbes will naturally begin to break down the components into nitrogen and water. I can destroy the evidence easily enough."

"The Japanese probably stole that from England," Nate2 said.

Hank glanced over at me briefly. "Classic compensation complex."

Together we studied the DIMCO schematics that Hank had procured from the government architect who designed the lower structure of the Tate Modern. He wasn't supposed to keep a copy of the floor plan for security reasons, but was so proud of his accomplishments that he'd stashed a file away in his home safe. After all, it wasn't every day that a person designed a secure, clandestine government agency underground. Gus was right: the weakest link in any security setup was always human beings.

Seeing the layout gave me the confidence to bring up an idea I had for fighting Ridpath. "We've been trying to train ourselves to automatically flip our minds to a specific positive thought when we feel a wave starting," I began. "It didn't work perfectly in Greenwich, but certain parts of the reality distortion were easier to overcome. I thought we could use the same theory in a different way for when we meet Ridpath. If we can induce a wave and all be thinking of ways to exploit his greatest weakness, we might be able to immobilize him."

Hank looked pained. "Inducing a wave is difficult unless the environment is strictly controlled, usually in a small space like a hermetically sealed room or a fully pressurized plane. We can't induce artificial wave realities in open spaces. The energy just won't focus properly. It's a good thought, though."

"A great idea," Nate2 said. "I'm sure in six months someone will have a working version and you won't see a penny of the royalties. That's what happened with the Frisbee—invented by a flying saucer enthusiast in Swansea, but stolen by the Swedes."

"What if we can lure Ridpath into a closed room?" I asked Hank.

"Well, then we could just bash him on the head and save ourselves the trouble of fighting him in a distortion. But there's no harm in practising offensive skirmishing thoughts in case you're in a bad situation when a natural wave hits."

As Hank spent the next hour examining the DIMCO plans, I led the others back to our dorm to practise our defensive and attack thinking. I noticed that the polyester sheet on my bunk bed looked to have been swapped with the one on the bed above. There was a stain across mine that looked disturbingly like blood. Still, I supposed last in the room gets last pick. We reinforced our positive thoughts first, prodding Nate2 to clearly define the luxurious and fully stocked library in his mind so as to avoid unnecessary screw-ups involving the *un-dead*. I concentrated harder than ever to see myself winning at Wimbledon. Then it came time for our combative exercise.

"Okay," I began. "What do you think Ridpath's greatest weakness might be?"

"His knees," Nate2 said. "Trust me, when a person gets to a certain age, the first thing that goes is either the knees or the back. I've been lucky, but from time to time on damp winter mornings even my cartilage aches."

"We have to think in more specific terms," Delores said.

"Why?" Gus replied. "If his knees buckle, he'll go down like a load of stone. I think the big guy has a point. Sometimes the simplest answer is the best."

"What if he has a gun?" Delores asked.

"Then he'd probably shoot us from the floor," Gus replied. "Okay, I get your point. I bet he doesn't like spiders. We could imagine a swarm of giant poisonous tarantulas falling from the sky."

"Probably not smart," I said. "There's a good chance some of those spiders will come for us. We need an attack plan that will affect only Ridpath."

We made a list of fears, including enclosed spaces, heights, and the dark, but I didn't see how we could control these or use them to our advantage. We needed to unsettle the colonel. He was a tough guy and wouldn't be fazed by the usual weaknesses of others.

"We need him to act stupidly," I said.

"Let's imagine a karaoke machine," Gus replied.

"Can we be serious?"

Gus sat up on his bunk. "I see where you're going with this. You want Ridpath to focus all his anger and hatred in a way that will boomerang back on his own forces. Note the cultural allusion to my homeland. But I reckon Ridpath would be pretty lethal with his anger. He seems to have had a bit of practice. We don't want to give him any extra power."

"But we need him to lose his cool," Delores interrupted. "What John's saying is we need him to make a mistake, and the only way he's going to act rashly is if we find his vulnerability and knock him off stride. Seeing as he's got an ego bigger than a football field we should be attacking that."

"We all know what pride comes before," I said.

"Prejudice," Gus murmured. "We had to read it in school."

I hoped that Hank had a second, better plan brewing.

CHAPTER 21

"I LOOKED AT OUR OPTIONS," Hank said. "On the north side of the building there's an abandoned subway line that runs within ten feet of the bunker. There are dozens throughout the city, apparently, all teeming with rats."

"Don't worry," Nate2 said. "We've learned to co-exist in relative harmony. They don't bother us and we don't burrow into their extensive underground kingdoms."

Delores ran a finger along the abandoned subway on the map. "So can we tunnel into DIMCO that way?"

"Not exactly," Hank replied. "We'd need tunnelling equipment that can bore through dirt, rock, ten feet of concrete, and solid steel walls. And I'm sure they have motion detectors and all sorts of sensors. Don't suppose you know anyone in mining who can help us out with an ultra-quiet, diamond-toothed grinder?"

"Or dynamite," Gus said.

"Yes," Hank said. "That's also a great way to *sneak* into a top-secret building. The only ways in would appear to be the actual entrance, which is located somewhere within the Tate Modern, or through one of these air ducts that run to the surface. But they're full of turbines and fans that can only be stopped using an internal control panel. There might be other ways in, but they're not marked on these pages."

Ridpath2 was flapping his arms at us. I supposed he could have some idea about how to infiltrate the place, considering he was genetically identical to Ridpath and probably shared some of his deviance and cunning. Hank pretended not to notice the gesticulating chicken farmer for several long seconds, at least until Ridpath2 picked up an empty tin of beer and chucked it our way.

"What?" Hank hissed.

"You're a donkey's ankle!" Ridpath2 said, then immediately passed out.

"That man is an utter mess. I don't know how a human being can let himself go that badly. You'd think everyone in the world would have *some* pride."

"I pride myself on my pride," Gus said. "But I have to admit I'm beginning to get a soft spot for our toxic alcoholic friend. At least he's got personality. It goes a long way. He reminds me of my uncle Cliff."

"He can't speak in complete sentences," Delores said.

"Neither can Uncle Cliff."

We debated various options for breaking into the DIMCO building, most of them quickly voted down as obvious, impossible, or suicidal. Nate2's ideas seemed to come from cop shows and involved Delores dressing up as a runaway street kid desperate for money. The lack of entrances was a problem, as was the likelihood of intense surveillance from both DIMCO and museum security cameras. Hank had learned that DIMCO also used retinal scanners as well as the usual picture ID and digital passkeys.

Hank went back to his suitcase of gadgets. "We just need to get past the main entrance. I've got a handheld hack pad that we can use on the doors once we're inside, as long as no one's around to see us place a large electronic interface against every scanner."

Delores snapped her fingers suddenly. "Why don't we use this room to set off a controlled reality distortion and all imagine we're inside DIMCO, like we did in Scotland to transport ourselves to Heathrow Airport?"

This was brilliant and so obvious that I couldn't believe none of us had come up with it before. For two very brief and wonderful seconds my hope surged to nuclear levels, at least until Hank began to shake his head.

"They've got a protective field around the building. There are ways to get through that sort of barrier, but we'd need more power and technology than what's in my bag."

For the next twenty minutes we continued to brainstorm. Delores suggested bribing the guards. Gus suggested making contact with one guard and begging for help. Nate2 came up with several ideas, including making a run at the front door with Tasers; posing as delivery men; and baking me in the middle of a giant birthday cake. The longer we talked, the more impossible the situation seemed. We were inexperienced at secret attacks, whereas the security forces had been combating enemies for years.

"We could contact Ben Wizard," Gus said. "He probably has some ideas."

"I'm afraid that's impossible," Hank said. "He's moved into exile overseas for security reasons. We're a hunted and endangered species. They want him more than anyone."

In the corner Ridpath2 belched himself awake. When he saw our faces he gave us the finger with one hand and picked his nose with the other. He obviously hadn't shaved in weeks—his face was covered in white and grey hairs—and his skin looked brown and leathery, like he'd been left out in the sun too long or had been baked like a loaf of bread. His gut was definitely bigger than the colonel's and his back was bent from either a lifetime of physical work or too much time slouched over a bar.

"What about Anton Kavordnic?" I said.

Hank laughed. "You mean Big Foot? I don't know anyone aside from your father who says they've ever met him. Personally, I think his writings were put together by a whole panel of scientists, none of whom wanted to be identified. We might as well go to Loch Ness and look for the monster."

"Nessie," Gus murmured. "If you go, look up a local guide named Herman. He gives a nice tour. Don't pay for lunch, because he might buy a spider web and a spatula. We had a bad experience."

"Uh … right …"

I didn't tell Hank that I'd met Kavordnic, because I still wasn't sure that I actually had. The incident in the airplane bathroom continued to confuse me. We'd established that it wasn't a wave, and yet I didn't feel as though I'd dreamed the entire sequence of events either. I'd begun to wonder if there were mini waves or fissures in the space–time continuum. DIMCO and our scientists had been tearing all sorts of holes in it lately. Maybe that was why I had so much residual energy stuck to me. I twitched antennae as a thought sprung in my brain. I excused myself from the room and retreated to the front desk where de Klerk was polishing a box of expensive silverware.

"Those fall off a truck?" I asked.

He jerked the box closer to his chest. "Not that it's any of your concern, mate, but this fine silver cutlery comes from our kitchen. Remember, guests get free jellied eel from 3:00 to 5:00 A.M."

"I thought it was five to seven."

"Management decided to change the hours due to an overflow of patrons."

"Someone actually went down for eel?"

"You'd be surprised what goes on around this place. You want to buy a dozen silver-plated spoons?"

"I thought those were from the kitchen."

De Klerk smiled. "I was taking the piss—you know, having a laugh at your expense. They fell out of a house in Kensington last night along with two Persian rugs, an antique desk, and a very impressive selection of towels. If you're going to be living here, you should probably get in on the action. We can always use a kid with small fingers."

I hid my hands in my pockets and stepped aside as a completely tattooed man walked by dragging a cat on a leash. The clerk said hello to "Norbert," but the man didn't reply, so I assumed that had to be the cat. I couldn't believe the Calypso actually had regular guests. I got permission to use the kitchen, as long as I promised not to touch the tinned seafood, and made my way downstairs to a room so damp and saturated by leaks from the upstairs toilets that the floor was spongy and green. It was like walking on moss. The table was warped and the cupboards wouldn't close. I could have sworn something growled at me from the shadows. Still, this was as far away from the hotel's patrons as I could get to contact Anton Kavordnic, the father of inter-dimensional theory and one heck of a piano player.

I tried to remember what I'd been doing and feeling when I'd entered the white space while on the plane. I looked at my reflection in some bent aluminum that propped up the taps and tried to relax every muscle. I imagined the white walls and closed my eyes, then very calmly yelled.

"Anton Kavordnic!"

I waited a few seconds, looked around to find nothing changed, and tried again.

"Anton Kavordnic!"

This time there was a faint echo, a distant voice calling to reach me.

"Anton! Kavordnic!" I screamed.

And then the other voice became clear.

"Marilyn Monroe!"

This was followed by another, lonelier sounding refrain.

"Sam! Why did you leave me Sam?" and,

"Mother, did you ever really love us?"

Seconds later, the entire hotel seemed to have come alive, pining for people they missed, had lost, or thought they were. A cascade of thundering footsteps came down the stairs and the flimsy door swung open. Fred de Klerk looked bewildered.

"Never stimulate the hotel's long-term residents before seven o'clock!" he said. "That's when most take their medication— prescription or otherwise. Now this dump is going to be like Transylvania under a full moon for the whole rest of the night." He turned to go, wiping sweat from his greasy brow, then paused momentarily. "By the way, there's an old guy upstairs to see you."

I raced up the stairs two at a time, at least until my foot splintered the second-last step. A rusty nail cut through my shoe, drawing blood, and I knew a tetanus shot was probably a good thing to look into, but I was too excited to stop. I rushed around the corner fully expecting to see Kavordnic's sad eyes and crinkled skin, but instead found Nate2 skulking by the main door. He reached for my arm to draw me closer.

"Ah, I see you're having second thoughts about Hank too. Good, that's what I've come to speak to you about. I've got a new plan, one that doesn't involve arrogance, a strong chin, or a muscular upper torso."

"Why don't you like him?" I said wearily.

"Because …" He drummed his fingers on the dirty railing nearby. "This adventure was much more fun with just our little gang. Remember all the laughs we had in that snowstorm?"

"We nearly died."

"Ah, yes, but we didn't. We've always been able to find the mental fortitude to succeed, or at least not be utterly destroyed. I must admit I enjoyed being the respected elder. I'd never been in the position before."

"You're not very good with change, are you?"

"I've lived alone in a decrepit granny flat for twenty years, so, no, probably not." He took me by the arm and pulled me even closer. The smell of Old Spice was sweet and overwhelming. "But please pause and listen as I quickly and succinctly outline my extraordinary initiative in a concise and proficient manner, so as not to appear lugubrious."

"Huh?"

He rolled his eyes. "Listen to my wonderful new strategy. Honestly, the education system these days is so disappointing. Like I was saying—"

Nate2 paused as de Klerk leaned closer, craning to hear. We both turned and met the clerk's gaze, waiting for him to take the hint and retreat behind his counter. Instead he straightened up and insinuated himself into our conversation.

"Well go ahead," he said. "I'm listening. I don't have all day you know. I've got bedsheets and pillow cases to launder."

"Really?" I said. "You do that in this place?"

"Okay, no. I've got money to launder, which is twice as difficult. If people want stain-free linen they can go the Ritz, steal it, and bring it back. Now come on, big boy. Give us your gossip."

Nate2, to his credit, placed his large palm across de Klerk's semi-bald head like a giant spider and guided him away gently. We decided to get some air and went outside, walking along the dark street to a corner shop. Nate2 talked and I listened, thinking vaguely that, with his odd theories and the number of social faux pas he made, it was easy to forget he was actually a smart guy. His plan made sense, or at least was more feasible than anything else we'd come up with. And let's face a fact: by this point, we were pretty desperate.

When we returned to the Calypso de Klerk was haggling with a tall albino in leather pants and a black T-shirt. The man's partner was a four-foot-tall, completely round woman with half her head shaved and a vast assortment of piercings sticking out of her eyebrow, nose, ears, scalp, lip, and tongue.

"Hey, weird kid!" de Klerk barked.

He tossed an envelope in my direction. The handwriting was precise and looping and looked like it might have been done with an old-fashioned quill pen. There were blotches of ink and thick strokes. I lifted out a sheet of manila parchment and read what appeared to be marketing material.

Maria's Interface Promise

An enthralling tale of lust, entrapment, betrayal, and quark particle amnesia by Susie-Anne Watzenburger, author of the *Techno-Warp* series

Available in discerning bookstores in Wisconsin or online at www.mariaspromise.org.com.oops (ISBN 13-12/1-17/44-9/182-5/33-8/1-2)

The book cover photo featured a woman with flowing blond hair laying a hand across the hairless, perfectly constructed chest of a cyborg. Where his nipples should have been were switches and an anti-virus icon. The two figures appeared to be on a wind-swept beach.

"I don't get it," I mumbled.

"Junk mail," Nate2 said, tucking it in his pocket but glancing at me in a way that suggested the letter was important. "Everyone always wants you to buy something these days. The publishing industry must be getting really desperate if they've started sending random letters to teenagers in seedy hotels."

De Klerk wagged a finger. "I don't usually pass on letters or parcels when they're delivered, but the old guy who dropped it off slipped me a salami sandwich on rye. Said I looked like a man with an iron deficiency. My own father never said anything that sentimental to me. I was touched."

"Sounds like you're turning over a positive leaf," Nate2 said. "Becoming a new, kinder, more sensitive sort of man."

"Yeah, maybe ..." de Klerk mumbled, turning back to the albino. "Are you still here, snowflake? I told you the honeymoon suite don't come with a mattress, because it leads to problems. If you want a refund, you can chat to my partner, Tony. Unfortunately, he's currently away on business for four to six months."

"In prison?" Nate2 said.

"No, he fell off the back of a truck. He's in traction."

We went back upstairs and pored over the note once more. Nate2 had referred to it as junk mail only to avoid attention. Apparently Susie-Anne Watzenburger was the pen name Anton Kavordnik used for his science-fiction romance novels. Still, I didn't see how a little light reading would help us. I trekked down to the local coffee shop with Hank and his laptop to check out the Web site, but it was mostly filled with links to scathing reviews, a couple excerpts, and a sample chapter of the sequel, *How Maria Got Her Re-boot Sequence Back*. We found a late-night bookstore that was still open, but they didn't have any Watzenburger books and the store employee had to search hard to find them on their database.

"We've got one in our warehouse in Birmingham," she said.

"Isn't there a copy anywhere in London?" Hank asked.

"Um, no. The copy listed here appears to be the only one in the entire country. I can put in a special rush order if you're desperate for a fix of *interstellar lust told through the eyes of an innocent farmer's daughter*."

"Tell me you're reading that off the screen," Hank said.

"Very insightful," the girl said. "Oddly enough, I haven't memorized the plot of this stunning title."

We placed our order and returned to the hotel, which was still moaning from time to time with wistful calls to long-lost companions. The honeymoon suite situation was as yet unresolved, as the albino and his wife were sprawled on the lobby couch making out with loud, saliva-tinged moans of pleasure.

CHAPTER 22

WE HADN'T NEEDED to order *Maria's Interface Promise* after all; when we got back to our dorm a dog-eared copy was sitting on a side table next to a very smug looking Nate2. I knew that he'd read several of Kavordnic's books, but hadn't thought to ask if this particular title was buried in the mounds that filled his granny flat. Being a packrat did have its advantages.

"Not his best work by far," Nate2 said. "That would be *The Air Hostess from Earth 7*. Now there's a planet that went decadent in a very short time. I'm still not sure how I feel about robots in hot tubs."

I leafed through the novel. "What do we do with it now?"

"I suppose we read the whole thing and look for a clue," Delores said. "I'm not doing it, but one of you guys can. Are you sure it was Kavordnic who left that notice, and that it's not some sort of trick?"

"I'm never sure of anything in this dimension," I replied.

I looked at the order slip from the bookshop and was about to crumple it up when a discrepancy caught my eye. I took Kavordnic's note from its envelope and compared the ISBN numbers.

The receipt: 0-14-305198-9

The note: 13-12/1-17/44-9/182-5/33-8/1-2

"He's left us a code," I said. "The sequences are different. The note has a series of numbers divided into blocks by slashes and dashes. Those numbers must correspond to pages and sentences."

We flipped open the book and methodically broke down 13-12/1-17/44-9/182-5/33-8/1-2 into page 13, line 12; page 1, line 17; and so on, and came up with the following enigmatic message:

Her brother called himself a chip salesman, but his knowledge of circuitry was poor. / Maria pulled her chiffon scarf tight around her heaving bosom. / She twists and turns, tying the cables together with inferior polymer rope. / Lord Stargazer and Lady Stumpy invited the gentlemen to drink heartily at the well of Zatron. / "Get out, you space scoundrel," she said with the anger of a cutworm. / Space is cold, especially without the love of a good woman.

We stood staring at the message blankly, looking for any hint of sense. Delores had a good eye for patterns, but even she was frustrated by both the chaos of the selection and the poor writing. We decided to decode the ISBN assuming that the numbers referred to lines and word placement in the sentences, and came up with the following:

You can lips together try name.

Delores stared at the page. "Maybe we're supposed to all say Kavordnic's name together? Lips together, try name?"

We did this twice, but the renewed howling from the hotel guests and the overwhelming feeling of stupidity curtailed a third attempt. I tossed the book across the room and collapsed into a wooden chair, which creaked, threatened to shatter, but remained intact. I felt my eyes welling up and fought back the frustration. I knew I had to be strong, because as my dad always told me, negativity and defeatism are contagious and unproductive.

I bet he wished he had a more useful and resourceful son than me right now.

The others experimented with various strategies to rearrange and decode, none of which came up with an even remotely sensible message. The closest they got was *I forgot a glistening kitten Maria.*

"There used to be a glistening kitten in my neighbourhood," Nate2 said. "It belonged to an area baker who would let local cats lick out his empty butter containers. Their being industrial size, the animals would crawl inside and get completely saturated."

Hank got up slowly, his eyes and hulking shoulders equally heavy. He excused himself to get some air and check for any new messages from our agents. Delores quickly got up and followed him into the hallway, a strangely eager expression on her face. I remembered her ex-boyfriend Larry and her interest in older men and felt a twinge in my stomach. I wondered if Gus was right about my lack of initiative. Maybe I had blown my chance to be with her. Her enthusiasm to spend time chatting with Hank clearly had less to do with research and more to do with his large biceps and confidence. He was a rogue pilot, flying dangerous missions across dimensions and making dramatic landings on highways in Toronto; I worked at Burger Hut and had acne, not to mention two snail antennae that I hoped would begin to disappear soon. At least the slime had stopped flowing from my skin.

Gus tried to initiate a game of cockroach and shoe rodeo, but I wasn't in the mood. Nate2 was gravely contemplating a snoring Ridpath2. He flicked a cockroach and a half-dozen bedbugs from the chicken farmer's skin, then lifted a half-full tin of beer from the man's grasp.

"If my plan is going to be convincing, we'll have to get him at least partially sober. And he'll need much better clothing than those overalls. On our way to Tate Modern tomorrow, I suggest we stop in the theatre district and see about hiring costumes from one of their shops. The attire is quite authentic. I've used them before on Guy Fawkes Day."

"Friend of yours?" Gus asked.

"No," Nate2 replied. "Guy Fawkes tried to blow up Parliament in 1605, using thirty-six barrels of gunpowder. Fortunately he failed miserably. Now we use the anniversary of his torture and execution as an excuse to dress up and have a splendid party every year. We even burn him in effigy, which is nice because November can be brisk."

"Someday I'll get my fifteen minutes of fame," Gus murmured. "If they catch us trying to blow up DIMCO, maybe generations to come will have a Gus Surrey Day where kids will bash a giant piñata of my image until my head splits, spilling lollies."

"We're not going to fail," I said. "We can't. My parents and our entire world are depending on us."

Gus forced a smile and shrugged. A faint white streak ran along the part in his hair, making him look a little skunk-like. I was shocked that I hadn't noticed this clear evidence of dimensional fade. I'd been so consumed with my own health and welfare, and with my parents', that I hadn't taken much time to see how the group was holding up. I wanted to put a hand on Gus's shoulder but figured it would look stupid, especially since I'd given him such a hard time lately.

"I'm glad you stayed with us," I said. "I shouldn't have been mad that you wanted to go home. I don't blame you. But this team is the only thing keeping me sane in this stupid, nuts world."

Gus mock-punched my arm. "Ah Johnny, you're a sentimental guy. Sorry about momentarily surrendering to my survival instinct. I'm happy to be helping out. And I'll even back off with Delores. I've grown bored of the cat and mouse game."

"Sorry gents," Nate2 said. "Enough chatter. I could spend all day listening to your teenage angst, but it's time to set my plan into motion and rescue the glorious Helen and your father."

With that Nate2 got up and wandered to the bed. He took the comatose Ridpath2 by the shirt collar and dragged him slowly out of the room, whistling jauntily. Gus and I went to the doorway and watched as Nate2 and the chicken farmer disappeared into one of the communal bathrooms. The sound of water spitting out of a weakly pressurized tap echoed up the hall, followed by a phlegm-ravaged scream and several loud shouts of protest.

"That'll sober him up," I said. "And hopefully cut the alcohol and cat food smell."

At that moment Delores came rushing up the stairs, her heavy boots threatening to bring the entire structure down. She was waving Kavordnic's letter and breathing hard, sweating and turning a bright shade of red (visible even under her layer of white foundation).

"It was a Web site," she said.

We waited for her to catch her breath. Hank came up the stairs after her, smiled in triumph, and helped Nate2 drag a drenched Ridpath2 back under the water after he bolted into the hall. Delores slumped to the carpet and could barely speak. I'd forgotten that she'd been suffering distortion fade for weeks now, she so rarely complained. She took a few seconds to recharge by dialling information for the current time and pressing her cell phone against her forehead.

"The numbers corresponded to a Web address," she said. "They redirected us away from the book page. There was only a single sentence. *Nate2 has been electronically bugged.* They must have planted a tracking device on him when they had him tied up in that hotel room in Toronto. That's how they found out about our safe house in Greenwich, and probably the nail place, too. Hank figures the bug must have been damaged a bit during the trip into this dimension because DIMCO obviously aren't getting a strong enough signal to locate us quickly."

As happy as I was that we'd cracked the code and that no one was a spy, I didn't understand why Kavordnic couldn't be more helpful or at least make decoding his stupid messages easier. He was supposed to be on our side—a friend and researcher like my father. And really, he was the root cause of all our problems, because he was the one who came up with the inter-dimensional theory that had allowed DIMCO to infiltrate our world in the first place. He should have been actively helping instead of playing piano and sending opaque messages.

With Ridpath2 moderately clean and thoroughly angry, we retreated back to our room, gagged the chicken farmer with electrical tape to silence the swearing, and waited while Hank thoroughly searched Nate2 for bugs. The inspection turned up a small steel cylinder no larger than a pin under the skin of the big guy's elbow. With a firm pinch, Hank extracted the bug and took it to the window as Nate2 danced a jig around the room holding his arm and whimpering loudly. After a painstaking examination, Hank concluded that the tracking device had indeed shorted out. Now we could proceed with Nate2's plan. Everyone agreed it was our best option.

Nate2 left off whining about the pain in his arm and looked moved by our confidence in him. "This is how the mathematicians at Bletchley Park must have felt when they broke the Nazi Enigma code and stopped submarines from torpedoing convoys. Tomorrow morning we'll go to the theatre district and then straight to Bankside, and together we'll free John's wonderfully engaging mother."

"You're not going," Hank said. Before Nate2 could protest, Hank held up his hand. "I know you want to be part of this operation, but quite frankly, you don't blend in well. There's going to be tons of cameras and security and your size alone is a dead giveaway, not to mention that you look identical to one of the people we're trying to rescue."

"I'm much leaner than John's father," Nate2 protested.

"Besides which," Hank continued diplomatically, "you'd be better help to the operation if we fixed this little homing device and had you lead DIMCO on a wild goose chase through London. We'd have an improved chance of slipping into Tate Modern unnoticed if half of DIMCO's agents were away tracking you."

Nate2 considered this, stroking his goatee. "It's a good strategy. Though in my mind, you're carrying the homing device and running around the city while I lead the kids to DIMCO's secret lair and rescue the girl."

"You know London so much better than me," Hank went on. "And you're sneakier. Your expertise in navigating the various alleyways and neighbourhoods would be a real advantage."

Nate2's chin rose slightly as he considered the compliment. "True," he murmured. "I could cause some grand perplexity in my routing and see some areas I've neglected during my years of bitter isolation. Of course, it would mean a great deal of walking. But I suppose everyone must make sacrifices in these trying times."

Within an hour the plan had been honed and refined and Nate2 slipped out the back door of the hotel with three familiar-looking figures: two teenage males and a female Goth in a heavy leather jacket and Doc Martens. They caught a bus going north and took a very circular route back to Islington and Nate's house for the night. Delores wasn't particularly happy about swapping her clothes with an elderly Chinese woman—none of us were—but the decoys were a nice touch, and cheap for only a fifty-pound note from Gus. Our final, desperate scheme was in motion. Whether or not we could pull it off was anyone's guess.

CHAPTER 23

THE TATE MODERN BUILDING was a large, factory-sized structure with a high rectangular chimneystack towering from its middle facade. Gus, Hank, and I made our way across the river from Saint Paul's Cathedral and the Old Bailey courts along the Millennium Bridge, which reminded me of a steel caterpillar. As this thought entered my brain I braced myself, fully expecting the universe to whack us with a distortion wave. But thankfully, for once, nothing happened. The bridge walkway was narrow, gleaming metal with spindly railings and three long, thick cables securing each side. The water of the Thames below was brown and sluggish and smelled vaguely of oil. I hoped Delores and Nate2 were doing well with their parts of the plan elsewhere. I hated to be split up, but it was the only way.

The entrance hall was a long, cavernous space that reminded me more of a train station than a museum. The ceiling was high and drew my eyes upward into empty space filled by only a solitary gigantic metal spider and several rows of mirrors. There was a security desk manned by a gentleman in a white uniform, but he didn't pay us much attention. Even though it was only ten o'clock the place was already swimming with tourists toting cameras, guidebooks, and slightly confused expressions.

"The place is massive," Hank murmured. "I guess this used to be the turbine room of the old electric station. The Brits sure don't like to tear anything down. Quite the renovation job."

Gus looked at his watch. "Well, it's now officially a record. This is the longest I've ever been in a museum in Europe without seeing the Virgin Mary. Usually there are at least a dozen religious paintings near the front door, and maybe a sculpture or two. I thought it was mandatory."

"*Donkey's teeth backstabber,*" Ridpath2 said.

Gus smiled and chuckled. "Yep, just the sort of comment Uncle Cliff would make. He isn't an art buff either."

Hank pressed a button on his sleeve and Ridpath2 jumped slightly and rubbed his chest where two electrodes had been rigged as a shock-treatment device. I promised myself that once my parents and Rex were safe, I'd make Gus buy the chicken farmer several cases of his favourite liquor for the trip back to our dimension. He'd already been promised two thousand dollars as compensation, but the extra bonus wouldn't hurt. Ridpath2 definitely looked more impressive than usual in his blue military uniform with his hair combed and the forest of greying stubble shaved off his face. He wasn't a dead ringer for the DIMCO leader—years of hard drinking had left him with far too many broken blood vessels in his cheeks—but he'd fool anyone standing more than two feet away. Of course, the truly frightening thing was that he didn't act or talk any differently now that he was sober.

Hank stood examining a pamphlet. "Says here there's a Retrospective on the Urinal. Does that mean the art is about toilets, or do we have to go into the bathroom to see what's *on* the urinal?"

"Modern art isn't my thing," Gus replied. "Too many soup cans and bright colours. I have a slight stigmatism. Though I do like the fact that this place is filled with a disproportionate number of girls wearing cute glasses."

He waved to a group of females our age who smirked self-consciously and wandered into a gallery. They looked brainy and sophisticated, with cloth handbags over their shoulders and funky clothes. Hank shoved Ridpath2 forward. The chicken farmer grunted, but walked farther into the dim expanses of the hall.

"Where do you figure the entrance to the underground lair might be?" Gus asked. "There's got to be ten levels in this mammoth. It'll take hours just to walk the whole place and get our bearings."

Hank nodded. "I say we walk around until someone recognizes Chicken Little and comes to speak to us. They can take us to the door. There's always someone looking to suck up to the boss."

Sure enough, by the time we reached the third-floor galleries a security guard in blue came striding alongside Ridpath2 and whispered softly in his ear. The guard was young—probably in his mid-twenties—and had a military-style haircut that didn't suit his flush, buoyant cheeks. The chicken farmer, to his credit, grunted and pointed toward us.

"'Bout friggin' time," he said in a mock English accent. "These crappy pig-swill drinkers are guests. Take care of them inside the bunker. I'm gonna get drunk."

With that, he turned on his heel and marched in the direction of an elevator. Apparently the bar and restaurant were on the seventh level. I saw Hank fiddle momentarily with the electric stun button in his pocket before grinding his jaw and turning back to the DIMCO representative. I had the feeling we wouldn't see Ridpath2 again for quite some time, if ever, and hoped our plan would still work. The security guard seemed as surprised by the blunt departure as we were, but forced a polite all-teeth grin and asked where we needed to go. My mouth went as dry as sandpaper. Clearly we were fumbling to keep this scheme moving.

"We can wait in his office," Hank said. "Or better yet, a lounge where we can relax and stay out of the way. We showed up early for our … um, meeting. I think we caught the colonel off guard."

The security official frowned and looked back to the elevator. "He knows I'm not supposed to check anyone in without his physical presence. But I suppose I can let you wait in the guards' lounge. Might I ask what your meeting is about?"

"About an hour," Gus said. "But if we go over time we might need some catering. I'm fond of those cucumber sandwiches with the crusts cut off. Do you have a kitchen on site or do you mostly get take-away?"

"Can you give me an idea of what will be discussed?" the official asked pointedly.

"It's big," Hank said.

"Does it have to do with logistics, or a specific operation perhaps?"

"Definitely."

Hank slapped the official hard on the back before he could speak, wheeled him around, and pushed him forward. Oddly enough, this seemed to reassure the guard, because he began to stride stiffly toward a roped-off section of gallery. I was glad we'd rented naval uniforms, both to enhance our disguise and because the worn grey cotton outfits of the Chinese cockle fishermen had itched like crazy. The guard led us to a heavily panelled service elevator, where he swiped a square device across a scanner and then placed his hand across the screen. A red line flashed across the surface and we began to descend into the earth.

We got off in a dimly lit, featureless grey corridor and moved through an eight-foot-tall metal detector, which I set off—a possibility we had fully expected. I went through again with the same result and was scanned and searched by hand. I recounted my well-rehearsed story of how I'd busted my ankle playing tennis and had a steel screw in the joint. They examined the new, long red scar and oddly discoloured patch of skin at the base of my foot and seemed satisfied enough. I breathed a sigh of relief.

We were led into a small guards' room, empty except for a microwave, stove, and small table and chairs. And then the door was locked. The far wall was bare except for a large mirror.

"What do we do now?" I asked.

"We wait," Hank replied. "Give them enough time to forget about us."

Gus opened the fridge and pulled out a sandwich, which he unwrapped and began to eat. I looked around for cameras or some sign that we were in a nefarious underground lair. But the place seemed like my dad's office at the university—poorly lit, stuffy, and lacking even one window. As Gus crammed French bread into his overflowing mouth the door opened and an amused, familiar voice filled the room.

"The cavalry has arrived," Ridpath said.

I could tell he was this dimension's version, because he wore a normal grey dress shirt, didn't walk with a pronounced sway, and his eyes could focus. Behind him two men stood with submachine guns. Ridpath's eyes squinted in dark amusement, reminding me of the metal spider in the museum foyer. I rubbed a foot unconsciously against the skin patch on my leg, and then made myself stop and stay still. Just seeing the man provoked an overwhelmingly strong picture in my mind of my hands squeezing his thin neck.

"We picked you up coming over the bridge," Ridpath said with a mocking laugh. "I could not in my wildest imagination have anticipated such a useless and obvious rescue mission. I'm impressed you had the foresight to bring along my double, but surely it must have occurred to you that I'd be in my office?"

"We thought you might be out torturing kittens," Gus said.

"Ah, Australian wit. You know, young man, in this light you look quite feline, especially around the whiskers, so you might want to address me with more respect. I'd hate to see you get spayed."

"Females get spayed," Gus said. "Males get neutered."

"Thank you, boy. Another word and I'll rip out your spleen and serve it back to you as pâté."

"That's made from liver, not spl—"

Ridpath reared back and belted Gus squarely in the jaw, knocking him off his chair. The remaining half a sandwich went spinning under the microwave cupboard. Without another word, a squad of heavyset men came into the room and took Gus and Hank roughly, tying their hands behind their backs with plastic loops of wire. I expected to be roped next, but Ridpath blocked a guard with the flat of his hand.

"Leave this one."

He motioned for me to follow him down the hall and into a large conference room filled with a giant projection screen and an enormous table that could sit at least thirty people. He offered me a chair and sat nearby in the leather-bound recliner at the head of the table. He put his hands together, his fingertips touching, and watched me silently for close to a minute. Finally, he leaned forward.

"I honestly thought you were more intelligent than this, John. The ease of your capture makes me wonder if this is some sort of deception. I've been admiring your resourcefulness for many weeks now. This seems strangely out of character."

"I don't care about being clever," I replied. "I'm sick of distortions and DIMCO and dead people trying to eat my ears. All I want is to get my parents back and free my friends. Trust me, once this is over, you'll never see me again."

Ridpath considered this silently. "Your friends ... I had believed that the rabble you've consorted with represented a relationship of convenience. Tell me, did you honestly think you could walk into my territory unarmed with only that disgusting chicken farmer to get you past security?"

"We had to do something. You did kidnap my parents. And you're probably torturing them right now. We didn't have the time or resources to come up with a better plan. You've got us. You win."

I felt my face grow hot and my eyes burn, which amused the old man to no end. He pursed his lips and clapped his hands gently. My parents had told me growing up that good will always triumph over evil if given enough time, but looking at the sallow, pinched face and smug expression of the man in front of me, I doubted it. The truth of life was that we're all small, insignificant beings. Evil was well organized, whereas we were always scrambling to make plans and escape. I thought of Anton Kavordnic and his stupid piano again. He was the real quitter in this mess. But maybe he was right. Maybe all anyone could do was live in isolation, forget the world, and take care of themselves.

"I forgot that you're still a child," Ridpath said, his tone changing slightly. "An oversight on my part. But that's good, because there's still a chance for you to learn. Your father, who is in excellent health and has been torture-free, isn't as open to reason. He has a flawed perspective on this whole dimensional situation, one that is ultimately counterproductive for us all. I'm not going to talk down to you, John. You know that our organization has been taking minute quantities of ozone, polar ice, and cool ocean water from your dimension in order to stabilize our climate and offset the natural effects of an industrialized world. This has upset your weather patterns slightly—caused a more rapid warming effect than previously seen in the world—but I can't apologize."

I snorted. "There's a surprise. Did you really think my dad would help you re-open the portholes to kill our planet?"

Ridpath laughed. "Please. I'm not killing your planet. A half-dozen generations before you have already done that. I'm in the process of *saving* civilization. A reasonable man of science should consider the logic. You're going to help me, John."

"And why would I do that?"

"Because you're young and can accept that life involves innovation and change. Your father's generation grew up in a time of misguided liberal dreams when people wanted to believe that the world's ills could be solved through goodwill, which any student of history can tell you is unequivocally false. I'm just being honest. Do you know how many people live in China and India?"

"Is this a test?" I said. "If I pass do I get to go home?"

Ridpath smiled again, though not as jovially. "More than two-and-a-half billion. And like you and me, they want cars and big homes and consumer goods for their families, because they love them. But these items come with a price: exhaustion of resources, consumption of oil, pollution, and the destruction of the very planet we live upon. Do you think people will stop wanting to consume any time soon?"

"Maybe, if they see that the environment is being ruined."

"Please, the world's population has been told about the greenhouse effect for decades now, but it hasn't made them conserve. The melting ice caps, the rogue killer storms, and the expanding deserts haven't made people act differently. The human race is full of short-term thinkers, which is where I come in. I'm here to think about the long term, to help the strongest members of the race build a sustainable world of abundant communal wealth."

"You're here to destroy my planet."

He moved from his chair and walked across the front of the room, pacing with his head down and his arms motioning excitedly. "You're only seeing the small picture, John. Do you think when your Earth is dying that I'm going to allow the best, most intelligent people to disappear?"

"Yes."

"No! We at DIMCO see ourselves as the first step in the *evolution* of the human race. We can bring the finest specimens to live with us in harmony on a clean, healthy planet. You and your friends have nothing to fear from DIMCO and everything to gain. Oh sure, we'll leave the murderers, thieves, and evil people on your Earth to fight for the scraps. But that's what they deserve. If we do nothing, both our worlds will disappear. But I can save one. The planets are collapsing and DIMCO is building an ark. Don't you understand?"

"You can't justify killing people."

"*I'm* not killing anyone." He sighed impatiently. "Do you know who Charles Darwin was?"

"He was the biologist who discovered evolution, the idea that people came from apes."

"And he coined a maxim for all animals: *survival of the fittest.* He discovered that to live, the strongest and smartest members of every species adapt to harsh conditions and push onward as others perish. Life isn't always easy or fair. We've come to a cusp in history where difficult decisions have to be made. If we continue on the path we've chosen wars will be fought over fresh water, famines caused by rising temperatures, riots for fuel, and other horrible, horrible events. I don't want to see these things, John. I don't like human suffering any more than the next man. Together we can build Earth 5 into a utopia and create a place where peace-loving people can live with no fear of poverty, environmental disaster, or rampant crime. Poor countries will be regenerated. Deserts will be irrigated so that they can grow crops. You can live in a safe, clean city with your parents and know that you've helped millions. But only together can we fix this Earth."

"You're going to move people?"

"Once we get the technology to protect them from waves. You father has made some interesting advances."

What he was saying did make strange sense—moving all the good people of the worlds to a pristine planet—and yet I didn't want to believe him. My logic was fighting with a feeling in my gut, causing my head to ache. We'd studied the effects of global warming in school and had learned that the last twenty years had been the hottest in history and that the trend was continuing. Weather patterns were becoming abnormal and governments still weren't doing anything to cut pollution, because certain nations didn't want to risk hurting company profits. There were huge hurricanes, longer summers, and floods in all corners of the globe. Clearly, if people didn't change the way they lived we were all doomed. Everything Ridpath said seemed logical. I wondered if my father was wrong to be stubborn; and yet, when I thought about the proposal more bluntly, DIMCO was determined to leave millions of people on a planet without hope.

"Life is about difficult choices," Ridpath continued, leaning on the table with his palms flat. "Both large and small. I was raised with the knowledge. You see, I was breech when I was born, which means I was facing the wrong way in the birth canal and couldn't be delivered properly. My mother was bleeding internally, growing slowly weaker, much like our world. After several hours the doctors came to my father and told him that only one of us would survive. They asked my father to choose whether to save my mother or his unborn son or risk losing both. He didn't have an easy option."

My chest became tight, as if the air around me had become heavier or one of my lungs had stopped working. Sitting here with Ridpath, I realized that he was a real person and that this whole inter-dimensional business was more complicated than I wanted to believe. I couldn't find the words to argue. At that moment I felt like telling him that he could do whatever he wanted with the universe. What did I know about evolution and pollution and survival of the fittest? I was a teenager who worked at Burger Hut and lived with his parents. All I wanted was to go home.

"What do you want from me?" I asked.

"I need you to convince your father to hand over his research," Ridpath began. "That's all, nothing more. I promise we'll let you go back to your dimension without any complications."

"And if he doesn't agree?"

He looked resigned as he signalled to the guards outside to come get me. "No one will come here to look for him, or any of you for that matter. I can always find empty cells for long-term guests. Certain things are more important than individual liberties."

CHAPTER 24

Two thugs carrying black submachine guns thrust me through a thick steel door. I tumbled hard onto the floor, a wave of purple clouding my eyes as my wrists slid across the concrete and my forearms erupted with a pain that seeped deep into the bone. I heard movement from the far corner of the room. Chair legs scraped with a hysterical squeal.

"John!"

My parents didn't look exactly buoyant—their eyes were raw from exhaustion and the lights gave their skin a pale, unearthly hue—but at least they were together and appeared to have all their limbs. They swarmed me, squeezing the oxygen from my lungs and causing the fake plastic skin covering my left antenna to pop open. My mother stifled a scream, but calmed down enough that I could explain the lingering effects of my snail mutation.

"The antennae don't hurt," I said. "And I've been soaking them in warm water. Nate suggested it. He still seems to think they're boils."

"He might be right," my dad replied. "I've never seen evidence of residual effects from a reality distortion. It's probably stress-related."

"Maybe you don't know everything," I murmured, irked.

My dad paused, and then shifted the subject. "Tell me you all haven't been captured."

"Most of us."

223

His eyelids drooped as his gaze fell to the dusty floor. I wasn't used to seeing my father so still or without light in his eyes. Normally he'd be bouncing around detailing some recent news story or crazy scheme or enthusing about his latest breakthrough or my math grade. His hair had also gone white beneath the red at his temples. I hoped this was his natural colour coming through, not the result of recent torment or dimensional fade, and that all he needed was a touch-up with some dye. He hugged me again, so hard I almost passed out.

"Come on, Dad," I said, motioning toward the security camera. "They're probably watching and laughing their butts off. Don't be totally embarrassing."

"There's nothing wrong with public displays of affection."

Quietly, I told them about our escape from Toronto, the Calypso, and Kavordnic's clue. "He told us Nate was bugged, but other than that he's been useless. I don't actually believe he cares if we live or die. I thought I met him in a totally white gymnasium full of ants, but I might have bumped my head on a toilet."

On my mother's insistence I explained about the ants, though I made them sound a lot smaller and less dangerous than they'd actually been. She stroked my hair tenderly and looked close to tears.

My dad sat silently. "Anton is a torn man," he said finally. "He's made a decision to remove himself from all parts of this conflict, and we have to respect that choice."

"No, we don't," I blurted. "He caused this problem and now he wants to disappear while we get attacked by plague victims and get hunted down like criminals. He should be the one in this cell, not us."

"I know how you feel, John. But think of this from Anton's point of view: he devoted years of his life to inter-dimensional theory because he believed it could make our universes better. He saw a great potential for shared technology and pooled scientific research. He thought we could restore extinct species, share ideas, and promote peace. And now all that work is being used to destroy our planet. He feels he's done enough damage. The man is wracked with guilt."

"He's a coward."

My dad didn't continue, but walked to the heavy door and examined its bolts and hinges as he'd probably done a million times. I'm sure his mind had been racing over escape possibilities from the moment they arrived, but without any tools even he couldn't overcome DIMCO. My mom forced me to explain the plague victim comment, which I did, and this ended up with another smothering hug and some tears. For the first time in days I gave up my desire to be in control and simply let myself be taken care of by another person.

And then, still in my mom's hug, I reached down—blocked from the camera's view by the table—tore back the fake scarred skin that Hank had moulded around my ankle at the Calypso, pulled out the hidden micro-transmitter beneath, and got on with the rescue plan. We had fully expected to get caught in the Tate Modern, so Ridpath had been right to suspect a trick. Luckily, as we'd also expected, his overinflated ego had easily led him to dismiss us as just a bunch of dumb kids.

I motioned for my dad to come into the hug and the three of us stood with our heads together in a small huddle. Anyone watching would think we were wallowing in despair, but I'd slipped my father the smuggled micro-transmitter. I told him that Hank had shown me how it could be used to create a temporary distortion wave, as long as we were in a small, sealed space. Thank god for this prison cell and nano-technology.

"I can create a reality distortion that we can partially control," my dad whispered. "But it won't last long and we won't be able to get through the bunker's outer force field. I'm sure DIMCO will pick up the anomaly within a minute and start to break down our code to locate our position."

"Don't be a pessimist," I said. "We've got a plan."

"I'm just outlining the situation, John."

"Don't be hard on your father," my mother said softly. "He's been under a lot of stress and hasn't been able to come up with a plan of his own to get us out. He's very frustrated. He's usually very good at these things."

"I had ideas," my father said. "I just needed an energy source, seven feet of wire, and a screw driver."

I waved my hands frantically, then looked to the camera and sobbed as if I was having a total breakdown. "We only need a short reality distortion," I said. "I've got the satellite coordinates of our rendezvous point in my head, so one quick burst of distortion and we should get there. As long as the schematic drawings of the building's layout are correct we'll be fine. Gus and Hank will take care of the rest."

My dad looked at me blankly, then broke into a big smile and messed up my hair with a giant hand. "I'm so very impressed. My boy is growing up. Is this the sort of thing you were doing in Scotland?"

"Pretty much non-stop, yeah."

"I know I don't always tell you enough, John, but you're a good son. I've been noting your intelligence for years and knew that with a bit of application you could accomplish great things. I still think Father and Son Physicists Incorporated has a nice ring to it. We could freelance."

"Can we get into this another time?"

"*Carpe diem.*"

He walked over, picked up his chair, and slammed it several times against the camera in the corner. Being enormously tall definitely had its advantages when it came to vandalizing high-placed objects. Fragments of steel, plastic, and glass clattered to the floor and my dad tossed the chair into the corner. He used a small magnetic stick to set the meter fields on the micro-transmitter.

My mother gestured at the debris. "That's the third surveillance camera he's smashed since we've been here. They keep coming in and replacing them, but at some point the maintenance staff are going to get very annoyed."

"Wish we had some tea for this," my dad said as we locked arms. "I find it helps keep me calm when I'm screwing with reality. I especially like that chamomile peppermint we picked up at the health food store last spring."

We had to relax in order for this to work properly, and I had to focus completely on the coordinates. For that to happen, I needed my dad to stop droning. I put a hand over his mouth. His goatee was prickly in a familiar and oddly reassuring way. My mom held my other hand tightly and tried to regulate her breathing.

"The first time is always the hardest," I said.

"I know," my mother replied. "This is my second wave. You weren't with us when we were kidnapped and brought through the porthole to this dimension."

"*Bats,*" my father murmured.

Slowly I felt the air around me begin to pulse, pushing against my skin like warm water, easing gravity and simulating a floating sensation. My gaze dropped away like I was falling into sleep. Without warning, however, my meditative sleep was broken by the sound of shouting and a door being unlocked. I made to get up but couldn't move. The next thing I knew I was lying on a hard tile floor looking into fluorescent lights. Around us were boxes of office supplies and loose computer equipment. It seemed to be a maintenance room of some sort. A pair of large hands yanked me up from behind.

"It's about time you got here," Hank said as he whacked the dust off my arms and legs.

"I bet Nate wouldn't stop talking," a familiar voice said. I turned to see Rex slumped against a pile of boxes, half-supported by Gus, who was keeping a precarious grip on his loose jacket. Rex's face was bruised and his right eye was swollen shut. He seemed only half conscious. My dad shook Hank's hand and beamed.

"Thanks for coming," he said. "As I was telling John, I did have a plan—"

"Can we go?" Rex moaned. "I don't feel like being re-hung in those shackles again any time soon. I think both my shoulders might be dislocated."

Hank pointed to a large duct vent. The outer grate had been removed and the security panel on the side had been switched off. The opening was no more than two feet by two feet and would take us only in single file. Without another word, we climbed in one after the other, the thin aluminum walls echoing loudly as they bent under our weight. I led the way using a small flashlight that I'd bought off de Klerk for a pound. He said he had over ten thousand of them in a warehouse in Leeds.

"This is murder on the knees," Gus said behind me. "And they certainly don't dust these vents. We've been in here for less than a minute and my hay fever is really kicking in."

"If you want sore knees," Rex yelled from far behind, "try getting thrown down onto concrete repeatedly for two days by large, burly men in steel-toed boots. I suppose the beating I took with that pipe didn't help either. Should we go back and get the hippie some kneepads?"

"Forget I mentioned it," Gus muttered.

We moved along a series of channels, rising through grates at various intervals. From time to time we had to wait as a burst of air blasted our faces with dust and dirt particles. Finally the duct widened into a main intake area containing a series of steel turbines that looked like ship's propellers, each the size of a small car. They were fixed in place by square metal bolts and screws as big as baseball bats. Luckily Hank and Gus had managed to switch them off, at least temporarily. We waited for everyone to crawl from the vent before moving forward. Finally Hank appeared, dragging a prostrate Rex.

"Be careful going through those," Hank panted, indicating the turbines. "The edges don't look too sharp, but they'll spin and you could get a leg caught if you're not careful. And we don't know how long DIMCO will take to realize their air isn't circulating. If you hear one of those engines begin to grind, get out quick. From initiation, we have about less than a minute before they'll be going full speed."

"How many of these do we have to get by?" I asked.

"Two vertical and then two horizontal that we'll have to climb through going up. That should take us to ground level where Delores will have unlocked the grate."

The first two massive turbines were easy enough to navigate. We ducked between propellers and squeezed into a narrow crevice. Going up looked far more difficult. The bolt above was level with my head. I didn't see any way to climb without touching the blades. There were no ladders or even good finger holds.

Before I could say a word my dad and Hank grabbed my shirt and lifted me into the air. I put one knee onto the smooth steel and grabbed at the propeller shaft. Finding a foothold was nearly impossible and my running shoe kept sliding off the blade's edge, but finally I got a toe onto a flat area and gently put pressure down. The turbine began to drift on its well-greased axis, moving away from my reach until I had to step back onto the one coming in rotation behind. I couldn't seem to balance—moving from one blade to the next, the fan turned faster and faster running in place.

"Stop spinning them, John," Hank said.

"I can't help it!"

They tried to grab the blades to bring the turbine to a static position, but the momentum was too great. My fingers were beginning to burn on the sharp grooves of the shaft and my arms were numb from a loss of circulation. If I fell now there was a great chance of being struck hard by a passing blade. With all my remaining strength I attempted a chin-up. Grunting and feeling like my body was a sack of marbles, I somehow managed to get my face above the bar. I put my chin on the steel for temporary stability and lunged an elbow over. Finally I wrestled my way into a sitting position and took a few minutes to catch my breath and let my hands regain feeling.

I looked down to see that the turbine had stopped spinning and that Gus was being hoisted up next. He reached for the bar under my feet and stood up on the large metal blades without a problem.

He winked. "The key is to divide your weight evenly. Balance is important in all aspects of life. I'm Zen with the wheel of fortune." Then he wavered slightly and motioned toward the crest of light. "Don't suppose you'd care to keep this escape moving? I'm not usually crazy about schedules, but narrow tunnels in the middle of the Earth tend to freak me out."

I climbed upward, finally getting to a grate that opened into a courtyard near the foreshore of the Thames. I could smell fresh air and see people with knapsacks moving by on the sidewalk. Unfortunately, the exit was still firmly fixed in place. I briefly wondered why Delores and Nate2 hadn't been able to do their job, but put the unpleasant possibilities out of my mind. Precious seconds were being lost. Everyone else was trapped below between blades that would mulch us to pieces within a minute once DIMCO realized their air exchange system was off-line.

A wrench taken from the storage area was passed up and together with Gus I tried to undo the stubborn bolts, which had no doubt been firmly drilled into place with an industrial screwdriver. My hand slipped as my legs wavered below me and skin tore off my wrist like a piece of Scotch tape being removed from Christmas wrapping. Sweat and the last residual traces of slime trickled down my nose and into my eyes.

As I got the second of four bolts free, a pair of black military boots appeared on the steel slates above me. The smell of fresh shoe polish assaulted my nose, followed by an all-too-familiar scent.

"Old Spice!" I yelled.

The hairs of an overgrown multicoloured goatee trickled through the gaps. "Move away from the opening," Nate2 said. "I've procured an acetylene torch to cut the bolts."

Within seconds the last restraining fasteners dropped into the chasm below and Gus and I pushed our way into open space once again. From deep below a grinding roar shot up, followed by frantic shouting.

"The turbines!" Hank shouted.

I turned to help pull the next person up, or jam the blades, or do something to stop the potential disaster, but Nate2's fuzzy head blocked the way. I noted that he was wearing a policeman's uniform. Stretching his long arms and grunting loudly, he pulled my mom onto the grass then turned and yanked my father out behind her. For someone who sat around in a granny flat, read a lot, and didn't get much exercise, he had surprising power. I waited as both Nates reached into the opening and more shouting echoed upward. Finally, Hank emerged coated in black dust and gasping for air.

"I lost my grip on Rex," he coughed. "He fell before the blades really got going, but there's no way he can get up. He's trapped between the vertical and horizontal turbines. I have to find a way back in. I'll meet you at the river."

Hank turned to go back into the Tate Modern, but my dad grabbed his huge shoulder. "There's nothing you can do right now. If you stay, you'll both be captured."

"I don't care."

"That's exactly what he'd say, which is why he's got two dislocated shoulders. We'll find another way."

Hank resisted, but common sense seemed to prevail. There was no way he could get back into DIMCO. I wondered if security forces were scrambling up from the bowels of the earth right now.

"My dad's right," I said. "We need you. We can't lose two pilots. Someone has to fly us out of here."

Hank bit his lip hard and together we all moved quickly away from the brown factory-like building, past a smattering of trees, and into the courtyard leading back to the Millennium Bridge. Across the river, St. Paul's Cathedral sat watching us indifferently from behind a low line of buildings. We were one drama in a history of momentous events in this city. We wove through tourists snapping photos and buskers singing pop songs, then veered away from the path and down to the river's edge. My mom and dad were obviously confused as to why we were running toward the water, at least until Gus hopped the railing and crashed eight feet onto the river barge waiting below. I waved at the three Chinese women at the bow before my heart stopped and jolted painfully at the sight of Delores lying unconscious and pale as snow on a roll of thick canvas. Her hair was spread out and her arms were askew, a cell phone lying limply in one hand. Even from this distance I could see the blue of her veins through her skin.

"She was hit by a rather nasty distortion wave while you were inside," Nate2 said, reading my thoughts. "I suppose you lot were protected by their force field. She reappeared within a few minutes and immediately collapsed."

"We'll get some energy into her," my dad said. "But first, may I ask why we're making our escape from a well-funded, highly technologically advanced international security force in a slow-moving river barge?"

"This was supposed to be a speedboat," I replied.

"Best we could do on short notice," Nate2 said. "You'd be surprised how few boat rental agents there are in the city. I had to requisition this for official police business. It was all rather exciting."

We helped my mom down to the vessel as Hank jumped and landed solidly on the wooden base. He went over to Delores and felt her pulse, which gave me a bizarre pang of jealousy. I told myself this wasn't the time. Gus followed my glance and shrugged.

"I'm sure that's not affection," he said. "It's medical. But I did tell you to make a move sooner."

We pushed off into the river, the Chinese women using long wooden poles to propel us forward with the current, careful to keep us close to the high stone wall and out of sight of the Tate Modern above. From a distance I could hear shouting and the sound of hard leather soles hitting paving stones. Hopefully the security guards wouldn't come our way and instead scatter into the local neighbourhood. After all, the river edge was the most unlikely place for us to hide, except maybe for back inside the museum.

My stomach clenched. "We forgot Ridpath2," I said suddenly.

We'd left him in the bar. I wondered if he was still there following the distortion wave that had knocked out Delores. My dad turned and cocked his head. I hadn't mentioned that we'd kidnapped Ridpath's double and used him as a decoy, but after scanning my pained expression, he seemed to know.

"Tell me you didn't bring an innocent man into this dimension."

"Rex thought it was a good idea," I said.

"And if Rex jumped off a cliff, would you follow?"

"Probably," Gus said. "He's pretty capable and he's got us out of jams before."

"Fair point," my dad said, licking his lips. "But we can't leave the man here. It's morally unconscionable. I'll go back. Tell me where you've left him."

"It's too late," Hank said. "If I can't go back for Rex, that chicken farmer can fend for himself. Now, keep that giant hairdo of yours down."

My father stooped. "The situations aren't the same. Rex made the choice to put himself in danger. If we're responsible for an innocent man dying or being warped by reality distortions, we're no better than DIMCO. Their nastiness doesn't excuse our own injustices. We have to hold all human life as precious and noble."

"Fine, fine, fine," Hank muttered, waving him away. "He's in the museum bar getting plastered. But I'm surprised you'd put your life in danger for a worthless alcoholic who never stops swearing. Think of your family."

"No one's worthless," my father murmured, moving to the edge of the barge. The Chinese women manoeuvred us to a ladder leading back up to the bank. I made to follow, but my dad put his hand out. I swatted it away and slipped past, rapidly ascending slippery, slime-covered rungs that smelled like old fish guts.

"Plan B!" I shouted to Nate2.

My dad yelled for me to come back, but I was old enough to make my own decisions and responsible enough to accept my own mistakes. I climbed over the top edge and ran ahead through the crowded square. A small squad of security officers were attempting to corral people into lineups to check identification, but the mass of tourists either didn't speak much English or were refusing to comply. Near the main doors, I caught sight of a man in a military uniform sitting with a little group of homeless people on a large piece of cardboard. One guy in dirty jeans and ripped running shoes was strumming an out-of-tune guitar. Another had a bandana-wearing black dog lying near his feet. Several *Big Issue* magazines were stacked in a leaning pile. As for Ridpath2, he was passionately slurring a song about his long-lost woman and seemed oblivious to our presence. My eyes burned from cheap alcohol fumes as I bent close. Ridpath2 took a long, sloppy swig from a bucket of cider and then handed it to a woman with no teeth. My dad pulled up behind me, made a move to speak, then stopped in stunned silence. He examined Ridpath2 with a cocked eye.

"You've let yourself go, Augustus," he said.

"*Snot-faced lemon tart!*" came the reply.

My dad glanced my way. "This says a certain amount about our main enemy. I didn't think he had this sort of potential. Live and learn. I guess it all comes back to the nature versus nurture argument. Some people—"

"Grab an arm," I interrupted.

"Don't speak to your father in that tone," a homeless woman said. "You should show some respect. You're lucky to have such a fine gentleman as a parent."

"Thank you," my father replied.

"Can you spare us some change?"

"We're in a bit of a hurry," I snapped.

"Be polite, John," my father said. "You never know what might happen to you in the future." He turned to the woman. "I'm afraid all I've got is Canadian money."

She grimaced and waved him away disgustedly. "Keep it."

Together we hoisted the chicken farmer up by the jacket collar and my dad threw him over his left shoulder, spinning wildly back toward the Thames. Ridpath2's head whirled at me and I had to duck to avoid a collision. Acrid spit smeared against my cheek.

"Duck farmer slug tamer!" the foul mouth bellowed.

"I couldn't agree more," I said.

We ran to the water, but the barge was far away now, moving slowly toward the middle of the channel. My dad turned and we raced for the steel caterpillar bridge that led to St. Paul's Cathedral. I only hoped Nate2 had been able to use Hank's contacts to put the second part of the plan into action.

"This is amazing," my father said as our footfalls echoed on the bouncing steel below. "London has changed so much since I was here last. If you look back left you'll see the Globe Theatre where Shakespeare performed his plays. Of course that's a reproduction. Still, I'd love to visit some time."

I figured sightseeing could wait for another day, especially when I caught sight of the real Ridpath emerging from the Tate Modern. He saw us instantly. It was surprising how a giant with red, spiralling hair and a multicoloured goatee carrying a swearing drunk in a military uniform can stand out, even in a crowd. We hammered ahead, just reaching the halfway point on the bridge before police stepped into view on the other side. My dad put Ridpath2 down and scratched his head.

"Biting fish tails!"

I looked up river toward the barge and then down at the brown water, which was at least thirty feet below. My dad had never been a good swimmer. In fact, whenever we went to the local pool or to the beach he sank like a stone. Behind us, Ridpath and a group of security men had reached the walkway and were slowly coming our way. Several more troops in black uniforms with semi-automatic weapons had come out of the art museum and were looking on. This sent a general panic through the crowd, which began to disperse immediately. Ridpath smirked as he sauntered toward us as though he was out for a relaxing stroll. Finally we came within speaking range and stopped. Ridpath looked us over with a sad shake of his head.

"You were smart enough to leave Rex Armstrong in that vent," he said. "I wonder what on earth made you decide to come back for that piece of filth. I can see no strategic benefit in having a common vagrant in tow."

He motioned toward the chicken farmer, who'd stopped swearing and had sobered up enough to be perplexed at the sight of his second self. He shook his head and banged a palm against his ear, as if trying to adjust his tracking or get water out, then stepped toward Ridpath, squinting hard.

"Brother?" he asked.

"Get away from me," Ridpath grunted, moving back from the man's outstretched dirty hand as though it were a knife or a flame. "I'll deal with you later."

Ridpath2 also stepped back. He put a hand up and felt his rubbery face, and then slapped himself hard. He coughed and began to laugh, which made the DIMCO chief recoil in horror. For a second, Ridpath's eyes flickered with both a ghastly awareness and a flush of embarrassment. In a fit of manic laughter, the chicken farmer appeared to snap completely, whirling, singing, and bouncing from foot to foot in revelry.

"*When the cuckoo comes calling, all bets are off!*" Ridpath2 sang.

"Stop that," Ridpath managed.

"Now, now," my father said. "A little song never hurt anyone. And besides, that's your DNA on stage. Logically there's a part of you that wants to do the same."

"Don't make your situation worse, Fitzgerald."

"Give us a ditty, Augustus."

"*When the music stops playing, it's time to talk!*" the chicken farmer yodelled.

The colonel turned on him. "You will stop that *immediately!*"

To my surprise, Ridpath2 obeyed. He planted his feet shoulder length apart, facing the colonel and leaning forward with a bitter squint. "Papa wanted you dead!"

Ridpath regained his look of contempt. My dad and I took the opportunity to slip back a few more feet. The guards on both ends of the bridges remained about a hundred feet away, though several were creeping forward, no doubt confused by the scene being played out. I wondered if Ridpath2 had a sense of the situation or whether he was simply lost in some haze where he thought he was addressing himself.

"Shut up," Ridpath spat. "You are nothing like me. Where's your self-respect?"

"*Sock-drawer pony licker,*" the chicken farmer replied, beginning his dance again. "Papa hated us for killing mama. We're supposed to be dead. *Elf-bottom pond sucker.* He told the doctor to have you killed, snuff me out, but we fought back, *diddly diddly doo …*"

"It served him right," Ridpath replied. "No man should choose his wife's life over his unborn child. One of us took that spirit of survival and used it to acquire power in the world. You chose disgrace."

Ridpath bared his teeth, stepped forward, and took a swing. The chicken farmer ducked, laughed, then stopped dancing and extended his chin within range as if he were encouraging his twin. Suddenly, out of nowhere, a drone filled the air. From my right a flash of white came darting across the murky water. The wings tilted left and right as the water plane skidded toward the bridge. Before I could say a word my father hoisted me by the armpit and belt and sent me flying into open space. The fall seemed to last forever—a strange purgatory between air and land. I braced, straightened my legs, and cut into the water like a knife. Because of the height the water felt almost solid and a ripple of pain shot from my feet. I broke the surface and ended up with a mouthful of cold dank water. As I struggled for buoyancy a hand grabbed my collar and the taxiing plane dragged me away in a roar of engines.

Behind us the guards were running to the middle section of the bridge. Half were firing in our direction while the others were attempting to break up a fight in progress. I couldn't see who was grappling with Colonel Ridpath, but I sure hoped he smelled like cheap booze.

CHAPTER 25

THAT NIGHT we flew to an abandoned airfield near Exeter, a city severely bombed during the Second World War and apparently rebuilt by returning soldiers blinded by shrapnel. From there we switched to a larger plane and journeyed through the night to a lonely village in the Austrian Alps where we were to stay for a few days until we could get back to our own dimension. The air was cold, but the deep valleys and the horizon full of snowy mountains made me aware once again of the world's enormousness. Ben Wizard and his posse of scientists had set up a temporary base under an abandoned ski lodge, so we were able to rest and recuperate behind its strong anti-distortion-wave force field.

My dad, who'd managed to get off the Millennium Bridge seconds after throwing me, quickly disappeared into a lab full of computers and monitors, determined to lend a hand with research. As for Delores, she'd come out of her coma but was still weak and generally incoherent, recuperating in the chalet sickroom. I'd spoken to her only once, during which she apologized for not opening the grate at DIMCO. Then she called me Josh, waved to an invisible cat in the corner of the room, and passed out again. I hoped we'd get another chance to talk before we both returned to our own universes and away from each other.

Gus was glad to catch up on both his sleep and the slightly skewed entertainment news of this dimension. He was happy that Jim Carrey had done well, though surprised that he'd become the greatest Shakespearean actor of his generation. As in our world, rap and hip-hop were popular, but so too apparently was electric banjo music. U2 had started the trend and had even dabbled in polka on one of their less successful albums. As well as getting all the latest gossip, Gus focused on his spiritual side, staking out a section of mountain path where he could sit and meditate on his future career as a mystic. I'm not sure what the locals thought of the weird hippie wearing sunglasses and trotting along the steep alpine cliffs, whistling and twirling his white cane, but I'm sure there was talk in the local schnitzel haus. Gus felt his karma had to be good after giving the Chinese women ten thousand pounds in cold, hard currency. I hoped they also sold the barge for a profit.

Hank disappeared an hour after we landed, muttering vaguely about a new plan to rescue his good pal Rex. I hoped he'd pick up Ridpath2 as well—that is, if the chicken farmer hadn't been strangled by his double. Part of me wished we could stay and help, but my father said we had to leave as soon as possible, as the Wizard was once again set to close a rift in the space–time continuum to prevent DIMCO from accessing our world. If we didn't go within days we'd be stranded. Apparently Delores was going to stay behind until the Wizard could figure out how to get her back to her own dimension.

Thankfully, I was able to get rid of my antennae using Nate2's warm salt water cure and then Ben Wizard's much more effective electromagnetic wave therapy. On the second night my mom and I sat up, drank tea, and talked a lot. I asked about the deaths of my paternal grandparents and about my dad's feelings, and she told me what she knew. Nate2 found the subject fascinating and even took notes. Apparently he planned to write his autobiography while he lived in the mountains. He had a few possible titles: *Seeing Me for the First Time*; *Dead Handsome Times Two*; and

The Delicate Art of Saving a Bunch of People from Unsavoury Types.
I would miss him, but didn't want to think about goodbyes.

News filtered in from the Internet that the British government
was on shaky footing and that an election was likely. The opposi-
tion introduced a potential candidate who they felt would help
lead them to victory: Colonel Augustus Oliver Ridpath. As much
as I hated to admit the fact, part of me still wondered about his
theories of human evolution and the need to save one Earth. The
idea gnawed at me. I didn't say anything, because I trusted the
opinions of people around me, and clearly the colonel was our
enemy. Hopefully the Wizard could keep closing portholes until a
permanent solution was found.

On our final afternoon I was practising throwing a balled-up
sock with my right hand and catching it with my left—trying to
keep my mind off departure—when a horrific squealing noise
split the air. It sounded like a rusty pickup truck being dragged
across an enormous blackboard while a million deaf people
played out-of-tune violins in the background. I jerked upright
and was on my feet within a half-second, my brain white hot with
the thought that our hideout had been discovered and a full-on
invasion was taking place. Nate2 stuck his smiling head around
the corner.

"It's finally arrived," he said cheerfully.

"What are you talking about?" I said nervously.

My dad and Gus came pounding down the hallway, much to
Nate2's surprise. He looked at their flushed, panting faces and
raised his eyebrows before slipping inside my room with a series
of long black sticks in tow. They appeared to be attached to a plaid
carry bag. After a few seconds, I recognized the collection as a set
of bagpipes.

"Next time I go into battle, I plan to be prepared," Nate2 said.

"For what?" my dad asked. "Hogmanay?"

Nate2 and my father cackled so hard they doubled over, red-faced. Gus and I just looked at each other in silent confusion. Seeing the two Nates together was still disturbing. My dad had trimmed his goatee by an inch, but he continued to look like the victim of some kind of nefarious hair bomb. Nate2 wiped a tear from his eye.

"Hogmanay is a Scottish holiday," he explained before turning to my dad. "And no, chubby, I plan to be prepared for *war*. And since you're abandoning the underground resistance and me, I've been left to my own devices. As always, I've looked to history for guidance in these dangerous times. The bagpipes have long been a symbol of barbarism and tenacity, which is why our English ancestors outlawed them as a dangerous weapon following the battle of Culloden in 1745."

"You're kidding," I said.

"Not at all!" he replied. "Like Keith Richards of the Rolling Stones, this odd-looking contraption is capable of making music powerful enough to strike fear into a brave man's heart. When DIMCO comes, I shall play us onward into battle."

"But the Scots lost at Culloden," my dad said.

Nate2 scratched his chin. "Yes, but they were still *scary*."

He put the long black mouthpiece between his teeth and blew hard, producing a loud and horrible squeal that sounded like two seagulls having an angry fight. My eardrums popped and even Gus's usual placid calm was broken. He jammed his fingers into his ears and disappeared down the hallway. We watched as Nate2 followed, swinging his legs out in an awkward march, on his way to find a suitable place to practise.

"Incredible," my dad murmured. "I might have been a trifle odd when I met your mother, but I was never that delusional. He's a real specimen."

"Cut him some slack. He's been alone for a long time."

My dad bit his lip. "Must have been maddening. I can't imagine."

I expected my dad to turn and disappear back into his work-room, as he was making copies of important data for his home laboratory, but instead he wandered to the corner and collapsed onto my bed. His long legs hung off the edge by at least six inches and his hair completely covered my pillow. He blew a long stream of air from his lips and rubbed his eyes before turning my way.

"Rough day?" I asked.

"Mmm. Large black spots are appearing in my vision and I'm light-headed. There's nothing like a bit of hard work to get the blood flowing, but I'm afraid I'm overdoing it. I have a great fear you'll tell my future grandchildren your father was a workaholic."

"I'm not marrying Delores, if that's what you're hinting at."

His eyebrows perked up. "I *have* been working a lot. I didn't even know you were thinking about it. She's a nice girl—trifle frightening with all the black goop on her eyes—but she's defi-nitely pleasant underneath."

"I'm never going to see her again, am I?"

He scratched his temple awkwardly. "Ben Wizard will get her back to health soon enough, and no doubt get her home. My advice is to wait until you're thirty before you think of marriage."

"If I'm around that long."

We locked eyes before I dropped my gaze to the floor. I knew he was avoiding the subject of separating from our inter-dimensional friends, but I supposed there wasn't much he could say. I was old enough to deal with the situation alone. He sat up and winced. He refused to admit he was sore or that his time in DIMCO had been damaging, but as he slowly edged onto the side of the mattress, holding his lower back, I knew he wouldn't be running a marathon any time soon. I wondered what exactly had happened in that dismal bunker. He smiled.

"You might be surprised, John, but when we get through this experience there will be positives. Some of the best things in life have been invented or discovered because of hard situations. Penicillin and sterilization improved during the World Wars; women had to petition for years to get voting rights; and van Gogh sold a lot more paintings once he cut his ear off."

"What's your point?"

"A person can become stronger because of hard times. That sounds strange, I know, but struggling is a part of life. I went through a great period of tragedy when I was your age. My parents died and I felt so angry that I moved to a country where I didn't know anyone. But if I hadn't experienced that pain I never would have made the decisions that led me to your mother."

"I know. But hard times aren't always that great. They didn't exactly work out for the Earth 5 version of you."

"Nate made his own decisions. I'm sure he's learned certain lessons."

"He stayed in England because of a hamster."

My dad didn't have anything to say in reply to this revelation. He made a series of vague humming sounds and mumbled something about *the same person being very different*. He slowly got to his feet, holding the bedpost for stability and trying not to wince.

I had to broach the subject of Ridpath eventually, just for my own sense of clarity. And so, like a tap being turned on to full, I began to recount the colonel's theories about survival of the fittest and saving one planet so that both Earths wouldn't die.

"I don't know what to believe," I said finally. "I can't help but think some of what he told me is true. He said we could build an ark that could save the best people in both worlds."

"The best people ..." My dad took his time and collected his thoughts. "John, I don't have any empirical evidence—and you know I'm not exactly religious—but I can't help but think we're all on Earth for a reason. Every life is special, and strange, and often more confusing than a David Lynch film. On the surface, Ridpath's ideas *seem* to make sense, but good and bad are difficult judgments, and I don't think anyone has the right to decide if another human is worthy of life or not."

"But what about murderers and warlords?" I said. "They don't deserve the same treatment as good people."

"That's why we have prisons and an International Court."

"But what good are those going to do us if two planets die from environmental disaster?"

"Oh ye of little faith," my dad replied. "I'm not sure if you've noticed, but I've spent most of my life tinkering with science. I'd hate to think my ulcer and all this eyestrain has been for nothing. I admit we have global warming problems, but I'd like to think that, given a bit of time—and of course funding and public education—we'll come up with ways to reduce the effects of pollution and save both worlds. You'd be amazed at the good inventions eccentrics like me can come up with."

"Do you have patents?" I asked.

"Of course."

"Do any involve shaved cats?"

Again, I'd managed to stun him into silence. But as he stood there I thought about his work and the potential to find positive solutions for the world. Despite his reassurances that science would be our ultimate saviour, I couldn't help but feel uncertain. For the first time in my life I wondered if my father had all the answers. He was just human after all. He was smart, but no one could be a hundred percent sure that they understood the chaos of existence. After all, I knew from school that science had produced some great breakthroughs, like penicillin, computers, and bullet trains. But I also knew that inventors had come up with guns, nuclear weapons, and the machines that had caused our current pollution problems. Looking at my dad's puffy, hopeful face, I couldn't bring myself to take the conversation any farther. He was doing his best and had enough stress without my doubts.

"And you might see Delores again," he murmured. "Once DIMCO is exposed and made powerless and inter-dimensional travel is used for good. The time will come."

As I made to speak, I felt a stab of pain in my ears as a great guttural wailing and sharp squawking began to echo down the hall once again. Nate2's head popped around the corner.

"I think I'm getting the hang of it," he said. "And I've figured out how to empty my spit valve."

He put the instrument to his lips and pressed the air sac to produce another searing blast. Then he stuck out one long leg and marched onward to another part of the house.

"We have to find a way to stop him," I said. "Or Ben Wizard will never be able to concentrate."

My dad put up one finger, left the room, and returned with a small red bottle that he tossed my way. His stomach shook gently as I read the label. *Habaneros Suicide Hot Sauce: The World's Most Powerful Pepper! Beware: Extended exposure to this liquid can cause lip blisters and ulceration of the mouth.*

"We can't!" I said.

"Don't worry, I'll dilute it a little. Desperate times call for desperate measures."

I fell into a full belly laugh with my dad. My universe might have been upside down, but it was good to have my family back.